Blood Distraction

By

DL Atha

ISBN: 978-0692610886

Empress Publishing

This book is dedicated to my family. As always, Erich, you have supported me, both when I thought it couldn't be done and when I didn't care if it was done or not. How many hours have I given up chasing a dream that some say can't be reached? That's my only regret, the hours that I have lost with you guys. Those can never be regained. And to our three children, so different all three of them: Colton with his stamina, Sydney and her optimism, and Justin with his ability to always think outside the box.

A special thanks to Debbie Hewett. Her ability to read the same story time and again is amazing. And to Dr. Jennifer Burks, who is a tireless book pusher. And to my mother-in-law, who believes in me and has been a book/Facebook page pimp like no other.

And to the beta readers, who always smile when I push another partially edited book their way:

Christy Morrow

Margaret Clymer

Danielle Ritch

Kristy Brewer

Shera Bean

Carmie McChristian

Lana McLaughlin

Pamela Kenney Irvin

About the Author

DL Atha resides in Arkansas. She is a practicing internal medicine and wound care physician but otherwise lives a mundane life. She happily exists with her three children and husband on a farm, where she enjoys reading, writing, and raising flowers and herbs. She loves bicycling, late nights, chocolate, anything pumpkin, and mythological creatures. She despises early mornings and mean people. She also finds busybodies to be annoying. The greatest mystery on earth to her are people who find no joy in reading.

Other Books by DL Atha
For the Sake of Revenge

Blood Reaction Saga
Blood Reaction: A Vampire Novel
Blood Distraction

Short Stories
Only One Way Out

Blood Distraction

Chapter 1

M om eyed me warily across the square restaurant table, her eyes shifting restlessly from the menu back to somewhere in the center of my chest. My face was, apparently, a little too much for direct eye contact. I tried to smile, a simple, easy grin that would convince her I was the same daughter she'd visited a week earlier. It apparently had the same effect of a cat trying to beguile a mouse. She wasn't falling for it. Instead, Mom shrunk back as small as she could in her chair. I was equally nervous. The tablecloth frayed in my constantly moving fingers to the point that I was forced to use the sweat from my water glass to smooth the ends together. The water the waitress had brought looked inviting, and I swallowed hard before deciding again not to chance a sip.

Truth is, I was afraid to. What if I gagged? Or convulsed? Or who knew what? The vampire I'd spent nearly a week with had given me no instructions and virtually no insight. But to his credit, he'd had no plans to leave me alive.

The supernatural had crashed into my small, protected world and against all odds, I'd survived a home invasion by a vampire and beat him at his own game. What had seemed like certain doom had morphed into a brilliant display of good vs. evil. The underdog steals the show, that sort of thing.

The week prior had started innocently enough with me taking a two-week vacation from the emergency room where I work about sixty miles from my house. My daughter had been craving some time with her grandmother, so I'd finally agreed that she could spend a week away. I'd convinced the public school that she could easily catch up on her studies; Ellie is an A-student, after all. So Mom had driven down from Missouri to pick her up.

It seemed like an eternity, another lifetime ago, that I'd watched Mom pull away from the drive with Ellie. I'd had a little mommy guilt that comes with realizing you need some alone time, along with the excitement of a week to myself, but those emotions had given way to terror when I found I wasn't actually alone in my house later that evening.

And in less than the minutes that could be ticked off on my two hands, my world—the rational and normal one where I raised a child and went to work every day and then came home and helped with homework—dissolved into an ugly fight for survival with the supernatural.

Things that I'd never thought for a second existed—and would have prompted a psych consult if any of my patients had mentioned—became very real. A vampire, Asa, had invaded my home, threatened to kill me, but more importantly, my daughter and mother if I resisted him. And in an attempt to save them, I'd given in to his every demand—his every wish. I'd changed, underneath my captor's nose. He never saw it coming. At times, I didn't even recognize myself. Or maybe I hadn't wanted to. In the end, I'd killed him with a stake through the heart.

Not everyone got out alive, and no one got out untouched. I'd lost my dear German shepherd, Samuel. He'd died protecting me. And my neighbor, a sweet, elderly woman, had lost her life at Asa's hands. To make everything more complicated, I'd made a suspicious man of a local police detective. And, of course, there was the young man who'd died at my expense in the woods. Asa had wanted to show me how a true vampire lived, and I'd agreed to go. There was a point behind his request. He said he was considering changing me. Maybe I didn't have to die after all. He'd held out my survival like a carrot, and I'd swallowed it hook, line and sinker. To be fair, I would do it again if the situation were the same, which left me wondering, as I sat facing my mother, what kind of person I really was—at the core, I mean.

I'd willingly gone with Asa knowing he was going to kill this person, and I did nothing to stop him until he turned on me. With the dangers behind me, the truth wasn't as easily justified. *Survivor's guilt*, the less critical side of my internal conscience said. But I knew the truth: I'd do anything to protect my daughter— anything. Selling my soul still seemed a reasonable cost for her.

And finally, it had come down to me. I was his last casualty. My conversion was almost complete by the time I drove the stake through his heart and took the blood from his veins. Then in a final act of humanity, I died on the ground a few feet from his dried-up corpse. My heart beat out its last irregular beat, my guts emptied out the last of their human remains, and I'd taken my final mortal breath. But when that breath left my body and I was truly dead, I felt more alive than I had in a week, more hopeful than I thought was possible. I'd won, and the grand prize was my family.

The next evening, Mom had returned from Missouri unaware that her daughter had died the night before. We'd had no contact, a condition of Asa's that I was afraid to break, and I'd watched as the recognition overtook her features that something wasn't right about me. Her mind fought logic to accept both the truths she couldn't quite put her finger on and the changes that were so concrete they couldn't be overlooked— the feelings that were palpable and yet undefinable. Her movements were cautious and slow, and although I tried to pretend that I didn't notice, her fears couldn't be ignored.

We made small talk about the state of the house, and I told the truths that I could. There'd been a break-in, and yes, the police had been called. There were no suspects. "Of course, I'm okay. Nothing to worry about," I'd said. I could tell she didn't believe me. Not completely anyway. Why would a thief empty the peanut butter jars? And why would he drink all the milk? Why would I have taken the time to cut my waist length hair to a jagged mess but take no time to clean the kitchen sink? She'd asked. I shrugged and mumbled something about not disturbing a crime scene.

Feigning humanity and the need to get out of the house, I'd suggested we go into the nearest town to eat. That was perhaps the only lie I hadn't spoken. I *did* want to get out of my house. It'd been the scene of my own personal hell for the last week. The walls had been a prison, a holding cell, where I'd waited for the end to come.

Now, sitting across the table from Mom, I was doubting my judgement. I should have hung back and let her take Ellie to dinner alone or feigned an emergency shift at the hospital. It wasn't that I was afraid; Ellie and Mom weren't in any danger from me—at least not yet. I wasn't overly thirsty. The burn was there, but it was more like a low, slow ache and not a devastating need. The elephant in the room was that I just didn't *appear* human, and I didn't feel human. Across the table, my mom looked like a mouse on meth. Tiny, afraid and tweaking on fear.

"Nice haircut, Annalice," Lisa, my favorite waitress, said as she slipped around our table, laying silverware down in a well-rehearsed routine. I'd been paying so much attention to Mom that I'd ignored her altogether.

"I needed a change," I answered. My smile was forced; I could feel it stretched across my cheeks. I took a deep breath and tried to loosen up.

"She shouldn't have gone so drastic," Mom interrupted across from me. "Don't you agree?" She dared a glance in my direction.

"I said I needed a change." I looked at Mom, mentally wishing she'd drop it. She shifted her eyes as soon as I did, the hairs on her arms rising up like hackles. I dropped my head quickly. It stung to see this reaction to her only child.

"Well, it's certainly a change, but it looks really nice," Lisa answered back, walking the tightrope otherwise known as small white lies told for very good reasons. She didn't like my haircut and all of her vital signs pointed to a definite 'that is a *very* bad haircut.' I was my own personal lie detector. I couldn't blame her. I didn't like my hair either. My long tresses had fallen out while I was changing from human to vampire.

"I like it," Ellie piped up. "I think it makes her look cool. She doesn't look like a regular mom at all."

Where do kids get this stuff?

Mom raised her eyebrows and said nothing more.

I'd been preparing for these questions on the way to town as I'd fired the answers off in my head.

Yes, my hair was a lot shorter, but it would grow. I just needed a change. I'd developed a rare medical condition that made me allergic to the sun, even tiny amounts, so I couldn't get in the light at all. I'd say it was similar to Lupus and affected my connective tissues and blood vessels. It made my hands cold and my skin very pale. If people got suspicious, I'd blame it on a drug reaction and tell everyone I was in the middle of a lawsuit. Hadn't they seen the attorney commercial on TV?

The no sunlight thing would definitely be a game changer. I knew that. My career and family life would never be the same, but it was doable. That was my new catchphrase: *It's doable.* I could still practice medicine. The night shifts were always begging to be filled. As for aging, I wasn't too worried about that one yet. I was only in my mid-thirties, barely past twenty-nine. Plus those Goth people always looked so young—the added benefit of no sun.

As for what had happened while Mom was away, I'd blamed it on a break-in. She'd been skeptical, but after a few questions, she'd dropped it, and I had no intention of telling Mom about Ms. McElhaney's murder. At some point, I'd mention that she died and leave it at that. There was no reason to get into all the gory details. All in all, I was feeling pretty good with my prepared answers as we settled around the table at the restaurant.

Arrogance will get you every time.

"Want your usual?" Lisa waited with pen in hand. She didn't need to write it down, but the cooks insisted on a ticket.

Such a simple, routine question, and I'd thought of nothing to say. It threw me off, and for a few seconds, I stuttered and mumbled. I considered saying I wasn't hungry and I didn't want to waste food with all the starving people around the world. Then I thought about saying I had a stomach flu. I was dieting came to mind. Mom frowned at my hesitation, her forehead crinkling disapprovingly. I wasn't the kind of girl who lost her appetite. Finally, I just nodded, feeling guilty for all the starving people in the world and my wasted food.

Lisa moved on around the table. Ellie got the chicken nuggets, no big surprise there, and Mom got her typical salad. She didn't need the menu; she always got a salad, but she used the hard plastic menu like a shield to watch me covertly. I pretended not to notice, but I knew her mother-meter was a klaxon blaring in her head.

The ride into town had been much more than just uncomfortable. Mom had sat, leaning as far towards the passenger door as she could get, her neck twisted to keep her eyes on me at all times. The moments she did look away, she'd begin to hyperventilate. Ellie had sat in the back, thankfully oblivious to everything. If the ride into town was bad, dinner was promising to be much worse.

When I wasn't looking directly at Mom, she seemed to do okay. Otherwise, the hair stood up on her arms and her heart rate skyrocketed. Asa had mentioned that the ability to blend in came with time. Clearly, my abilities were lacking. For now, I avoided looking into her eyes or focusing all of my attention on her. So far, Ellie had been immune to my predator side. It didn't seem to matter how close I was to her, she hadn't noticed that side of me. My new hair and how pale I was, she'd recognized, of course. She'd asked if I'd had a facial and why I'd cut my hair as we'd waited for Mom to freshen up, but she'd acted completely normally. No hair standing on end. No screaming. No shivers.

Ellie appeared to be the only person completely oblivious though. The people seated around us all looked a little nervous. They fidgeted, looking over their shoulders. The smell of sweat permeated their clothes even though the temperature was in the fifties outside. No one was altogether at ease. Two of the five tables next to us had emptied out not more than fifteen minutes after we arrived—their plates partially uneaten. And these were southerners. They'd normally have cleaned them down to the last bit of fried potato. If you'd asked why they were leaving, I don't think they'd have named me as the reason. There was just a vague uneasiness they couldn't put their finger on that would have left them wondering what had been wrong once they were outside.

6

The Screamin' Eagle was your typical small-town dive. The building itself was situated on a large lot, a failed business on one side, and on the other, another death in process, and everyone in town trying to figure out why this business was the one that made it. Perhaps it was that the restaurant had history or the right collection of employees. Either way, this was mine and Ellie's favorite.

The building itself was old, at least for our neck of the woods. The two-story rock structure had originally been a general store sometime around the turn of the century. Since then, it had been a little bit of everything—a rumored brothel in the early 1900s, a post office, a pottery barn, and finally, a restaurant for the last twenty years.

The place was the eyes and the ears of the town, and tonight, they were all turned on me. I hadn't noticed it when I first walked in, but now, as we waited for our dinner, it had become very apparent. Luckily, Mom was too busy watching me to watch everyone else watching me as well.

Lisa noticed it though, I realized, when she brought our entrees about twenty minutes later. She was carrying all three plates on one arm, but even so, I saw her glance back over her shoulder at several customers who were making no apologies about openly pointing at our table.

"Be careful, Annalice, the fajitas are absolutely smoking tonight."

The jalapenos layered across the meat would have set anyone on fire—my favorite food, which I'd never eat again.

"Ms. Lovelace, I put the salad dressing on the side, and little Ms. Ellie, we were out of regular fries, so I brought you sweet potato instead. I know you like those almost as much."

Ellie had already begun dipping the orange fries into the syrupy sauce the Screamin' Eagle was famous for. The sugar content was appalling, but tonight, I simply had bigger fish to fry than worrying about Ellie's future diabetic status.

"Annalice, it's been a few days since you've been in. You been doing okay?" Lisa asked as she picked up a pitcher of iced tea and began refilling our glasses. Mine was still full of course, and I saw

7

her look at my untouched glass. "Did I bring you the wrong tea? Is it too sweet?" she asked.

"No, it's fine. I'm just not thirsty." If my answer was a Facebook status, I would've followed it by an LOL. The irony was just too much.

She nodded her head as she finished filling Mom's glass. She waited a minute as Mom picked the glass up and drank nearly half of it, and then she filled it again. "You must be really thirsty, Ms. Lovelace." Lisa motioned to Mom's tea glass.

"My throat's like cotton," Mom answered as she took another long drink. Her forehead was shiny with sweat, and her hands left prints on the glass topped table.

"Annalice, you got a minute? I want to run a medical question by you. It's kind of private." Lisa motioned with her head towards the door.

I knew it was a ruse, since Lisa had never asked me anything medical before. Besides, she was the healthiest person I knew. The 'I'm going to run a marathon this morning, process all of my home-grown food, then jog through the mountains to work to feed the rest of you people who go to eat the not so organically grown, over-processed food of the typical American restaurant' diet.

"Hey, Mom, be right back," I said. Mom just nodded and poured more ketchup on Ellie's plate. She hadn't paid attention to a word Lisa said. She was too focused on me. "Lisa wants to talk to me." I pointed towards the waitress, who was already halfway to the door.

I cringed at the sight of Lisa's back as I stood to follow. This was not going to go well. It would be just the two of us, and I still remembered the way I'd reacted the first time I felt Asa behind me. I waited for her to step across the threshold before I followed, hoping she'd turn to face me once outside.

"What's up?" I said, pushing the large oak doors open. She stood to the right, leaned against a column. Smiling my best 'I'm not going to hurt you' smile. I let the door close behind me and we were effectively shut off from the rest of the world.

"Is everything okay with you?" she asked pointedly, and not

wasting any time.

The Screamin' Eagle had placed benches along the front of the large porch that surrounded the old building. When Ellie and I had first moved there, you could still see the original hitching posts from a bygone era. Against everyone's advice, the owners had pulled them down and replaced them with a large wraparound porch. The non-rotting remains of the hitching posts had been incorporated into the benches. I ran my hands along the smoothly worn wood for a moment before I answered.

"I guess it depends on your definition of okay. My favorite neighbor, a good friend actually, is dead. I'm sure you've heard about it by now, and there's been a murder a few miles from my house."

She nodded. "Yeah, I heard about Ms. McElhaney a couple days back. I took over a chicken casserole yesterday, and her nephew asked about you at the funeral this morning. He was surprised that you didn't come. He said Ms. McElhaney was very fond of you and Ellie."

Mentally I cringed. I'd forgotten to make a casserole, and I had no good excuse that I could give to the family either. I'd completely forgotten about the funeral too. Not that it mattered; I couldn't have gone, but I should have sent flowers. I could hardly pull the 'I'm an undead vampire' card. My social mistake was going to look very strange considering how close Ms. McElhaney and I had been as neighbors. On the upside, Lisa hadn't run screaming back into the restaurant. She didn't seem to be afraid of me. Her heart rate was stable; her breathing easy.

"I haven't heard anything about another murder though," Lisa said.

"It's been all over the news," I answered, surprised she hadn't heard about it. "That hunter who died in the woods."

Lisa's eyes widened for a split second and then narrowed. "I thought that was a bear attack. Not a murder. Why would you say that?"

I realized my mistake then, but it was too late. "Well, that's what I meant. Death by animal, but it's still a murder. I'm going to have to watch Ellie so closely now and be more careful about the forest. We hike quite a bit, you know."

Lisa nodded her head as she processed what I said. She was trying to believe me, and I could see it in her face the moment that my subterfuge worked. She looked over her shoulder towards the parking lot before she started speaking again. "Detective Rumsfield was in here earlier in the day. About lunchtime. He had a lot of questions, mainly about you and that man you were in here with a few days back. He came in earlier in the week and asked around, which I thought was odd, of course. But today was different. The last time he was in here, he seemed worried about you. He was more interested in the guy. Today, he was interested in you. Like *you* were a suspect."

"A suspect? In what?" I acted shocked, even though I was under no illusions that I'd heard the last of Detective Rumsfield. The medical examiner's office had ruled the hunter's death an accident—a bear attack. Mom and I had listened to the radio news on the way into town. Not a common occurrence in Arkansas, but not impossible. The state had a large and thriving black bear population, nearly three thousand by the estimate of the state park agency. Normally timid around humans, the bears ransacked a few campsites and quite a few gardens every year. I'd even seen one while out on an afternoon horse ride this past summer. Of course, the bear hadn't bothered me. It had shuffled away no sooner than we'd laid eyes on each other.

"He didn't mention any specifics, just that he was following some leads he found in the woods. I assumed he was talking about that hunter, but like you said, the state medical examiner was clear that the man died of a bear attack. So I'm not sure what the detective was referring to. I mean what could you possibly have to do with that?"

More than you know, I thought. For starters, a dead neighbor with her throat ripped out, a dangerous and supposed ex, a certain Detective Rumsfield, who'd been thrown around in what appeared to be my empty yard by an unseen force, and a hand-carved wooden stake next to a clothing-filled grave.

The stake. If my heart had been beating, it would have sunk in my chest. My entire future was wrapped up in a piece of wood that I'd accidentally left in the forest after I'd staked Asa. I'd planned on going back for it as soon as I had awoken, but after seeing Ellie and Mom, I'd forgotten it completely.

I shook my head at Lisa and raised my hands questioningly. "Lisa, honestly, I have no idea what has gotten into Rumsfield's head. There was a break-in at my house last week, and from the few meetings I've had with him, he acted like I was the criminal. I think he's warped or something. But thanks for the warning. Although I imagine the detective won't be too happy that you've told me." I appreciated the fact that she'd gone out on a limb to help me.

"You are okay, right? I don't need to worry about you," she asked. In the parking lot, a two-door sedan had pulled in and parked. She turned around and smiled, telling the couple that she was glad they'd come. She'd have their drinks in no time. The couple must be regulars, I thought, but I didn't recognize them.

Lisa sidestepped in front of the couple, pulling open the heavy door as she did so. The motion put her back to me; the breeze of the opening door blew the hair away from her neck and her scent hit me hard. I sucked in air as if I'd been harpooned, and I felt myself go rigid as the hunger spread outward from my chest, flooding my arms and legs with a surging want.

The entire world was reduced to one girl holding a door. For a short time, I forgot about the crowd in the restaurant, my daughter sitting at a table waiting for her mother to come back, the waitress I'd known for three years who had a child of her own, or a detective who was eyeing me for murder.

All that existed was a girl. Her name was immaterial, and my left hand pushed the door from her hand with a resounding boom. The floorboards shook under foot. The parking lot was barren, and no one inside the restaurant had made a move towards the slamming door. The wind could be strong this time of year, so how were they to know?

She wanted to turn, but she was frozen, a statue in clothing. Her diaphragm hung up somewhere between breaths. She didn't swallow, and I doubted she could even blink. The only active muscle was the one left of center in her chest, and it was racing.

11

I'd come so close to her that I could feel the static electricity bouncing across the hair on her arms. My hands moved to her shoulders. It was only a short sprint to the dark corners of the parking lot. I could be done and back before anyone noticed we were missing.

"Annalice, your family's waiting for you." Her voice was little more than a whisper, and it shook with the knowledge that death had its cold fingers on her. Where she found the courage to speak I will never know, but hearing my name brought some sort of remembrance to me of who I had been—who I still hoped to be. I thought of Ellie watching the door for me to come back, and I wondered how my mom would care for her around the clock if I wasn't around.

My hands pulled away from Lisa's skin, her shoulders falling in relief. "I'm fine," I said, answering her previous question. "I'm just fine."

I walked around her, my shoulder knocking her roughly out of the way as I pulled the door open and went back inside. She was still standing out there, her heart rate slowly returning to normal as I sat back down at the table with my family.

The rest of dinner was stilted except for Ellie's lively chatter. Lisa had eventually returned to waiting tables, but she'd given our table the slip, and we had a newer, younger waitress. I caught a few frightened glances from her in my direction that eventually morphed into confused looks as logic began to convince her that what had happened could not possibly have happened.

Mom asked a couple of times if I knew why Lisa had ditched us, but I just shrugged my shoulders and mumbled about how my last tip might not have been big enough. Mom eyed me suspiciously, continuing to glance back and forth between Lisa and me as she worked the other tables.

But I couldn't think about a frightened waitress anymore. I spent the rest of the meal obsessing over the stake, and once dessert was finished, I was very grateful to leave the restaurant and head home.

I left two tens on the table when we left. One for the new waitress and one marked for Lisa.

Chapter 2

*T*he highway home was quiet, the road nearly empty. And while it was cool outside, my windows were covered with the fog from Mom's hyperventilation. It was bad enough that I had to turn the wipers on. I tried to ignore her fear, but all I managed to do was become more irritable by the second. Her fear made me angry, which was ridiculous. She had every right to be wary.

The only one who'd managed to remain calm was Ellie, who'd plucked away at her smartphone the entire trip home. We passed a couple of semi drivers who were still brave enough to drive the Pig Trail, the winding road that led north out of town, and a few local cars owing by the amount of dust and mud on them, but otherwise the highway was abandoned. Once I turned off onto the dirt road that led to my house, the already scarce traffic died away completely and the deafening silence between my mother and myself became all the louder. By the time I made the first curve on the one-lane road, my mom was a terrified mute, and I was a powder keg holding a firecracker.

Only a handful of houses dotted my dirt road, and all of them were scattered along the first two miles. After those brief marks of civilization, there was nothing but the dead quiet of the Ozark National Forest. The dirt road would end in my front yard—my house cocooned by the woods. In the height of summer, the canopy of trees was like women's petticoats turned upside down; you could scarcely see the sky. In winter, they might as well have been skeletons with their naked white arms held up to the moon in some sort of pagan dance, and Mom acted like I was delivering her as the sacrifice. She startled at every shadow that fell across the car, her hands gripped so tightly they looked like wax in her lap, ashy white and devoid of blood. The dash lights lit up her face, her lips moving in a silent prayer.

I tried to think of something to say, failed, and instead looked over my shoulder to check on Ellie, who'd fallen asleep, when a string of blue lights met us as we rounded the next curve—the kind of blue that can only indicate bad things. *Someone's died. Someone's had a wreck. Someone's been turned into a vampire.* Tonight, those lights were parked and flashing at Ms. McElhaney's house.

Mom looked at me for the first time on our drive home, her eyes wide and questioning. "Another break-in?" she asked.

"I don't know," I lied as a patrolman stepped out of a Madison County Police cruiser positioned roadblock style across the dirt road. He held up a hand for me to stop and ran a large spotlight across my car. There were four police cars parked—the one in the road and the other three lining the edge of Ms. McElhaney's drive.

Tonight, her house seemed out of place against the backdrop of the forest. I'd never seen the place look like this. Ms. McElhaney had gone to bed every night at seven o'clock, season and time changes be darned. This evening, the lights were on in every room, and her front door was thrown open to the wind. She would have been appalled at the waste of electricity. She'd always been a welcoming woman, and despite her advanced age, she'd kept the front door open in the summer with only the screen door to protect her. Ellie would press her face against the screen, peering inside for her when we'd stop in for a visit.

Tonight, the flimsy screen shuddered and shook, defenseless against the wind. *Probably the way Ms. McElhaney looked in Asa's grasp,* I thought. She'd suffered at his hands, and now dead, she still wasn't left in peace. Ms. McElhaney would be outraged that all these men were stomping around in her house with not even the good sense to shut the door. *They should have some respect for her.* I turned back towards the officer as an excuse to look away from the sight of the house. It brought back too many raw emotions from the last several days. *Hold it together*, I told myself. *You can't help her now.*

The officer took his sweet time getting to us. He turned once like he was coming to our vehicle but then disappeared back into the darkness of his car. Probably running our tags. *Not exactly legal*, I thought, but I was no specialist on police procedure. Either way, he kept us waiting for several minutes, and I was getting angrier each time a minute ticked by on my dash clock.

"I don't need this shit," I hissed under my breath. Mom sucked in her breath at my language but stared straight ahead. I don't think she needed this shit either.

Finally, and only seconds before I threw the car door open to ask what the hold-up was, the officer emerged from the front seat of the police cruiser, his form a dark shadow behind the high beam of his flashlight. It danced around in front of him as he walked before landing square in the front seat of my car. In a split second, I was staring into a painfully bright light. The leather casing of the steering wheel balled up under my fingers as I struggled not to bolt from the car. I felt trapped, and I'd gotten a bad case of the jitters after the incident with Lisa at the restaurant. Where the ride home with Mom had ratcheted my nerves to the next level, the spotlight pushed me fully over the edge. I shut my eyes tightly and looked down towards the floorboard. Mom lifted a hand to shield her eyes and rolled down the window.

"Where are you two heading?" the officer asked, leaning down towards the window. He was a tall, lank man who could have passed for the ripe old age of twelve. I wasn't convinced he could even grow a beard yet. He used the flashlight to check out the floorboards and the back seat as well as our laps and the dashboard.

"Aren't you up past your bedtime?" I asked through the window, bringing the flashlight back to the front seat. I winced but didn't look away.

Mom was mortified. "What has gotten into you?" she whispered under her breath as she turned towards me. She still didn't make eye contact when she spoke to me, but she did at least look in my direction. It was a start.

"That's real funny, ma'am. I haven't heard that one before." He brought the light full into my face, one hand resting casually on his left hip. "I'll ask again. Where are you two heading?"

"There's three of us actually," I said, motioning into the back seat. "And she's asleep. So can you keep that blinding light to yourself?" Cops can be bullies, I'd always thought from my interactions with them in the ER. But then again, if my job was to always be in the line of fire, I might be a bully, too.

"Just being safe, ma'am," he said flicking the light into my back seat. Ellie cringed but didn't wake up. In a split second, I was more than just nervous, I was simmering. The spotlight in his hand didn't help anything nor did the little smile that played across his lips when he flicked the light back to my eyes. *Keep it together. Keep it together.* I struggled to hold on to logic over emotion.

"People who are afraid of their own shadows shouldn't be cops," I answered. Like doctors who live in fear of malpractice attorneys, they lose their effectiveness. Mom's eyes went supernova at my smartass remark.

"Where are you three heading?" he asked again, his tone harsher, but he turned the flashlight off at least.

"Home."

"You live around here?"

Isn't that what I just said?

"Nah, we just thought we'd see what you boys were up to out here and ..."

Mom cut me off mid-sentence. "She lives at the end of the road, Officer. I'm her mother, and I'm staying with her for a few days." Mom cut her eyes at me while she smiled sweetly at the baby-face cop. I was still simmering. It was an antsy feeling, like having poison ivy between your fingers.

"Oh, you're the doctor Detective Rumsfield's been looking into," he said, a big smile spreading across his face. He eyed me more closely as he bent closer to the car. "I should've recognized the name."

16

"You mean when you illegally ran my tags?" I asked.

"Reasonable suspicion, ma'am."

"The only thing Rumsfield shares with reasonable is the letter R," I answered.

He smiled a little too smugly, raising his eyebrows sarcastically. "Sure thing, ma'am." He turned and hollered over his shoulder. "Hey, Rumsfield, that *doctor* you were looking for is right here."

I exhaled harshly. Just my luck. The teenage cop smiled sweetly, winked me a good-bye and walked back towards his car.

"Son of a bitch," I whispered.

My mother looked at me like I'd sprouted horns, and for all she knew, maybe I had. Directing her eyes off of me, I pointed to Rumsfield striding towards my car, smiling almost as big as the baby cop.

At least he rescued Mom and me from our awkward silence. "Annalice, what a surprise," he said. He'd leaned down to block my window, his hands resting casually on the doorframe like he owned the thing. The warm vanilla of his aftershave and the oddly beautiful smell of horses and old barns floated through the car and made my mouth water. My gut clenched, and I didn't dare look him square in the face. The steering wheel leather balled up further in my hands. I couldn't afford another incident like the one I'd had with Lisa at the restaurant. The fact that *he* could get this reaction from me only made it worse, so the edge in my voice came easily.

"Really, Detective? It's a surprise? 'Cause you know I live out this direction, right? You were at my house just yesterday morning. How *do* you keep your job with that kind of memory?"

He laughed, a low rumbling sound that said he found no humor in my sarcasm. "It's a surprise because I thought maybe you'd split after they found that man's body." He leaned even farther towards the car. I could have told you within a millimeter where his carotid was hiding among the lean muscles of his neck. I leaned a couple inches away from the window and tried not to think about how badly I wanted him. Why did it have to be him? He irritated the hell out of me.

Beside me, Mom was about to come out of her skin. "What?" she demanded. "What body?"

I chanced one glance at the both of them.

"You didn't tell her, Annalice?" Rumsfield's expression was one of extreme piety, but I could feel the sarcasm in his eyes. They hadn't left my face. "Yes, ma'am," he said across the car to Mom. "They found a man's body out behind Annalice's house this morning. I *cannot* believe she didn't mention it."

"We heard about the bear attack victim, Rumsfield, on our way into town. I didn't mention that he was found so close to my house because I didn't know. I read it in the paper tonight at the diner where I had a very normal dinner with my *mother*." I narrowed my eyes at him before I turned towards my very normal mother. "I didn't realize he had been so close to my house." But she had eyes only for the detective.

Rumsfield continued before I could defend myself. He wasn't fighting fair. "That's really odd, Annalice, that you live in this small, close-knit community and yet didn't know that a man had died less than a couple miles from your house. Everyone else around here has already heard, and I suspect they've all delivered a casserole and paid their respects by now."

"I was sleeping. Remember, Detective, I work the night shift."

"Oh yeah, about that ..." he started to say, but Mom cut him off.

"I told her not to buy that house, Detective. It is absolutely *no* place for a woman to live alone. But she won't leave. I've spent two years trying to convince her. Why would you think she would leave now simply because a man was attacked by a bear?" Mom was picking up on the detective's undertones.

Rumsfield cleared his throat and leaned down farther towards the car like he was trying to contain the rumors about me and wasn't the one spreading them in the first place. I gripped the steering wheel harder in annoyance. "Well, there's been a lot of tragedy associated with Annalice recently. Ms. McElhaney's death, and now this man is dead. It's a little strange, don't you think?"

I'd had about all I could take. "It was an *animal* attack that killed that man!" I said.

Mom ignored me completely. "What happened to Ms. McElhaney?" Her voice had ascended an octave. She looked back and forth between me and Rumsfield, each turn of her neck ratcheting her eyes wider.

"Annalice, you didn't tell her that either?" Rumsfield was looking pious again as he searched my expression, then he turned the full gaze of his butter-wouldn't-melt-in-my-mouth expression on Mom. "Ms. McElhaney died nearly a week ago. Somebody assaulted that poor elderly woman in her own home. Ripped her throat out with God only knows what. I showed the crime scene photos to Annalice." Finally, he broke eye contact with Mom and looked at me. "They were terrible pictures, I have to say, even for my line of work."

Mom was shell-shocked quiet for a couple of seconds while she tried to figure out how I played into this story. Then it was rapid-fire questions. "Why on God's green earth would you have done that? You're thinking it's the same man who broke into Annie's house? Have you found anything out yet from your investigation the other day? Annie said the police had been out. Any fingerprints or anything? Was it the same man? Still, why would you show the crime scene photos of Ms. McElhaney to Annalice? That seems a bit excessive for a break-in at Annie's house."

Rumsfield looked surprised then smiled briefly in my direction. It was so quick, I don't think Mom noticed his enjoyment at her state of shock, but he recovered quickly, the smile turning down in disappointment. His forehead crinkled in mock distress at having to tell my mom the bad news. He had me, and he knew it.

"Ma'am. I, um, I don't know how to break this." He paused for effect. "I hate to be the one to tell you this. I'm not sure what Annalice told you, but we *didn't* investigate a break-in at your daughter's house. No, you see, we had a search warrant. The suspect in Ms. McElhaney's murder was your daughter's boyfriend. They were seen together at the Screamin' Eagle around the same time that Ms. McElhaney died."

His words hit nothing but our stunned silence—mine as I tried not to say anything incriminating, Mom's as she slowly absorbed his words. Thankfully, Ellie slept peacefully in the back seat. Mom continued to add things up in her head, but two and two didn't quite make four. More like three and a half. Rumsfield waited for the message to settle in, and I waited for the other shoe to drop. Would he arrest me here?

Mom held to the daughter that had once been, the things that logically she knew to be true about me. Finally, she spoke. "My daughter doesn't have any man in her life except her ex-husband, and he lives miles from here. Annalice, what is he talking about?" she said, turning towards me. I guess concern overshadowed her fear of me.

But I had no answers. I wanted to look her in the eyes so she would know that I was innocent. One look is all it would have taken before because I'd never been able to lie to her. She'd have known I was telling the truth. But now I was afraid. Afraid that she'd feel the inhumanness in my expression. Afraid she'd see half-truths. I stared straight ahead, my lips pressed into a thin line. Finally, she looked away and back at Rumsfield.

"Ms..." Rumsfield asked, fishing for her name. I guess he couldn't call her "ma'am" forever.

"Lovelace. I'm her mother. But please call me 'Jacquelyn.'" She reached a hand across me towards Rumsfield but drew it back quickly. She couldn't stand the close contact.

"With all due respect, Jacquelyn, I think there's a few things you don't know about Annalice."

If you only knew the half of it, I thought. But I did know I couldn't sit here any longer debating this with him. I could feel Mom's suspicions growing along with Rumsfield's need to prove he had me.

"There's a few things I do know, Rumsfield," I said. "And the first one is that you don't have any proof of anything. Secondly, you can't even tie my 'boyfriend' to this, and he wasn't my 'boyfriend' anyhow. It was one date. And the man's death in the woods was ruled an animal attack. Not a homicide. If you had anything at all on me, I'd be in jail. All you have is a blinding desire to incriminate me in something I had no part in. You're grasping for straws."

Rumsfield leaned farther into my car, using the door frame to support his large frame, the metal of the door squeaking in response. His breath was a warm haze on my cheek. "The only animals in the woods last night were you and your boy-toy. Couple of freaks, the two of you, and I'm going to prove it." His voice was a whisper that Mom couldn't hear. "Turns out, Annalice, that I've got more evidence than you think," he said, louder now. And then ignoring me, he looked at Mom. "Ms. Lovelace, you be careful," he said.

I looked at him now and let the restrained hunter in me slide to the surface. I knew better, but I was angry, and part of me wanted him to know what I wanted to do to him. I'd like to think that the better part of me wanted to warn him. I'd spent the evening blocking out the sounds and smells of humanity. For a brief moment, I let myself listen to the sound of his heart. The four chambers beating in circuitous fashion. The valves opening, the pulmonic valve splitting open just before the aortic valve as his lungs filled with air. I could hear the blood rushing in and out of his heart. I'd never realized how truly inspiring the sound was until now.

Everything suddenly seemed brighter, sharper. The trees lining the road became crisper, their outlines pearly against the darkness. I knew where every human stood and how slowly they would reach me. I noticed the heat coming from my mom for the first time and recognized each grain of the leather-wrapped steering wheel under my fingertips.

The detective tensed and held his breath. He didn't even swallow. I could almost hear his muscles tightening up, and I could definitely see them doing so in his jaw. The fine hairs on the backs of his hands rose to my threat. In the seat beside me, Mom caught her breath, a garbled cry cut off. Behind me, I felt Ellie stir, and I was ashamed, ashamed that I would risk my daughter seeing me this way.

I forced myself to relax—forced myself to move again— simple things like running a hand through my hair, swallowing, and looking away from the man I wanted to kill. I reached one hand across the seat, slowly, and squeezed Mom's hand. I hoped it would reassure her. She jerked once but didn't pull away.

"You be careful yourself, Detective," I said, turning back towards Rumsfield. "We're going home now. If you have any questions, I live at the end of the road in case you have trouble remembering. And if you want to talk to me again, you better come with another search warrant."

The window was up before he could come up with a reason to stop me, but I watched for blue lights all the way home.

Chapter 3

I carried Ellie into the house, but she woke up as I crossed the threshold into the living room. "It's time for bed, babe."

She nodded. "I'm going to get a drink first," she said. I cringed at the words. My mother whistled through her teeth from the corner of the room. The fridge was empty. Nothing drinkable would be found in there unless you counted the pickle juice I left sitting on the back shelf after I'd devoured everything I could get my teeth on over the last week. And I hadn't even thought to go grocery shopping.

Ellie had already opened the fridge and looked in before I could make an excuse.

"Seriously, Mom? You need to go to the grocery store. And hire a maid." If she thought more about the messiness, she didn't say anything. Instead, she popped a cup under the water dispenser on the fridge and took a few long sips. "See you in the morning, Grammy." Kissing her grandmother good night, she held my hand as I walked her to bed.

I pulled the white lace coverlet up under her arms once she was comfortable and feathered the hair back from her eyes with my hand. "I've missed you terribly," I whispered as I leaned to kiss her forehead.

"I was only gone a week, Mom," she giggled, rolling her eyes. "You were supposed to have some grown-up alone time. Maybe go out with a boy, even. Didn't you have any fun without me?"

Kids. There was a time I'd have said the same thing to my mother, but then Ellie had come into my life, and then and only then was I able to comprehend how much someone could love another person.

"Boys?" I leaned back on my elbow, regarding her with a suspicious face. "And what do *you* know about boys?"

"I know that you don't ever talk to any," she said, pointing an accusing finger at me.

"Uh whatever. I talk to them like... all the time. Because they're everywhere. You can't escape them." I rolled my own eyes thinking of Rumsfield. "I'm serious. You can't escape him."

"You can't escape who?" Ellie asked, her eyes bright.

"You can't escape *them*. Boys, I mean. That's what I was talking about. You can't get away from them. They're like bad pennies. They just keep turning up. So, yeah, I talk to boys, you know, all the time."

"You talked to a real boy, Mom?" She looked at me skeptically.

"Yeah, of course. There's lots of male nurses these days, and I talked to Dr. Thompkins the day before Grammy picked you up."

"Mom, he's like seventy."

"Well, he's a *boy*."

"A *dried-up* boy."

"You didn't specify that they had to be young. Or cute or something."

She rolled her eyes. "You're dodging, Mom. You were supposed to have fun. Not miss me."

"Like I could have stopped myself from missing you," I laughed, pinching her nose. "I'm genetically programmed to miss you."

"Well, I missed you too but don't tell Grammy. She'll think I didn't have fun with her."

"No worries. Your secret is safe with me. Mom's promise," I said, crossing my heart with my index finger. "Sleep tight, babe," I added, giving her hair one last tousle as I stood and turned towards the door.

A very human reaction, I took a relaxing sigh. *No worries*, I told myself. *I've got this. I'm going to survive. This whole vampire thing is do-able*, I thought, using my new catchphrase. *As long as the police don't come for me.*

The bad mojo from the encounter with Rumsfield had dissipated some. My emotions had calmed down. Logic was beginning to surface in my brain. If the detective had anything, he'd have already tried to bring me in for questioning, so I was starting to feel better about talking to Mom, who was waiting in the living room for me. She was pacing in small circles in front of the fireplace, her footsteps tapping out a rhythm of unease on the old hardwoods. But with Ellie's smile still fresh in my memory, I felt I could conquer anything—even my eagle-eyed mother.

"Hey, Mom. Wake me for pancakes?" Ellie asked from behind me.

And then the world fell from underneath my feet. I'd been so happy to see her that I'd put off explaining my all-day absences. With a sick heart, I walked back to her bed and sunk down onto my knees beside it.

"Ellie," I started, but then I lost courage, and for several minutes, I could think of nothing to say. Cool tears rolled down my cheeks, and I looked down at the floor, wiping them away with my fingers before Ellie could see their red tint. A small, warm hand touched my shoulder. I leaned into it for strength.

"What's wrong, Mom?" There was worry in her voice. Not something I usually heard in Ellie's voice. She was always such an upbeat child. I wanted to keep her that way.

"Ellie, I won't be here in the morning. I know this seems so sudden, and it's really hard to explain, but something happened while you were gone. I got this really strange sickness that makes the sun hurt me now. So I have to stay completely out of any sunlight. I'll be hidden away and not just in the house in the bedroom but really *away*. But I'll be okay every night, I promise. And grandma will take care of you during the day. We may have to move to be closer to her, but otherwise, it'll be like I'm working the night shift again. You remember that? When I worked the twelve-hour night shifts. Only this time, I won't switch back to days." It all poured out in one long, continuous breath. It was the only way I could keep going. The only way to get all the hateful words out.

"What happened? How sick are you? Will it get better?" She sat up in bed, her little arms stretched out behind her. She looked so fragile, and I hated to scare her.

"I know it sounds crazy, but I caught some sort of virus and my skin blisters in the sun. It affects what I eat and even how I look. And, it won't get better, Ellie." Confusion crossed her face along with a bit of pity. She'd have questions. If not tonight, then eventually. I'd need to come up with better answers. "But you'll be okay," I added. "You won't catch it from me. You and grandma will be safe."

"So it's a virus, like a cold?" she asked.

I nodded. "Yeah, some kind of virus."

"So that means I *can* catch it," she said. Typical doctor's kid; sometimes they know too much about things they shouldn't know about.

I combed back a lock of hair that had fallen across her forehead. "But you won't. Because I won't let you catch it. I'll be very careful. No drinking after me or things like that."

"Can you still hug me?" she asked, a small frown beginning to form.

"Oh my God. Of course I can." I pulled her into my arms. "Catching this virus is harder than the average cold. It takes a lot of exposure, and it's nothing you can get from hugging."

I held onto her like a life preserver, drowning in my own self-pity. But Ellie, like a typical eight-year-old, was ignoring the bad and looking firmly at the positives. "It's going to be okay, Mom. It'll be fun. Remember how we used to stay up all night on your days off? And go to the late-night movies? And have slumber parties," she said, remembering my short stint on night duty at the hospital. "We can do all of that stuff again, and we'll have pancakes before the sun comes up. But not tomorrow because I'm really tired. So just let me sleep this time."

I smiled through the tears. "That sounds perfect. You sleep in *really* late, okay?"

She nodded, a yawn overtaking her. "See you tomorrow night, Mom."

The vampire and her daughter. I couldn't help but smile. "It'll be great, Ellie. Trust you to make me think about the good side and not feel bad for myself." I kissed her cheek one last time, tousled her hair and turned out the light.

Chapter 4

Mom was pacing in front of the fire when I returned to the living room. Usually she's a muted-light kind of person, preferring soft lamplight and candles to overhead lighting. But tonight, the place was lit up like a Christmas tree. Every light that could be turned on was burning brightly all the way through the house. Even the television was on, the picture glowing above the mantle. From the kitchen, the radio was blaring. The glare of the lights hurt my eyes, and the radio was irritating. I put my hands to my ears.

"What's with the radio, Mom?" I asked, but I already knew the answer. She was looking for background noise, something normal like televisions and radios to make her feel better. As if she could light up all the darkness she was sensing from me.

Forcing herself to stop pacing, Mom started to spin towards the fireplace, her hands outstretched for warmth, but in the space of a breath, she caught herself and turned towards me instead. She couldn't put her back to me, I realized, and the knowledge was as sharp as a needle. She warmed her hands behind her back; her eyes were hooded, but the fear on her face was as plain as day.

"Never mind the radio, Annalice. What really happened here?" she asked, her eyes taking in the scene of the room. The house had an open floor plan so the kitchen was fully visible to the both of us. I didn't have to look around to know what she was talking about.

The kitchen was littered with the trash of living a week in

captivity. Empty boxes, jars, and containers rose out of the sink in a jumbled mass. The cooktop was stained with the burnt spaghetti that I was cooking the night Asa intruded into my house and my life. The stench of the scorched pasta still hung in the air. I briefly wondered if Mom could smell it too or if it was only me.

I could just make out the outlines of my own bloody footprints across the kitchen floor, the ones I'd hastily cleaned up after Detective Rumsfield's first visit. I knew Mom couldn't see them since even I barely could. The kitchen island was a minefield of knocked-over empty cans, peanut butter jars half emptied and dried out, and stale pieces of bread. I didn't have to open the refrigerator to know it was, for all intents and purposes, empty. In the corner lay the tumped-over trashcan; the contents spilled across the tile floor. Something sticky and green had leaked out and stained the baseboard.

The living room had fared better. At least, if you didn't notice the near empty curio cabinet in the background. Which of course, Mom with her eagle eyes, did. She was staring at it now. I closed my eyes briefly against the flood of memories, thinking about the cause. I'd brought the shelf over on top of myself on purpose to make myself bleed—a blood sacrifice for the sake of my daughter.

"Look around, Annalice. I've never in my life seen anything like this. It's disastrous. And what happened to all of the knickknacks on the cabinet? Why is your bedroom littered with a week's worth of clothes? And why are some of them torn? Your hair is all over the bathroom. Walking on that floor is worse than walking barefoot in a hair salon. The bottom of the shower is covered in what I can only guess at. And now I find out there was no break-in. You lied to me, which is a new thing as far as I know, and suddenly, your old flame is a suspect in a murder. I didn't even know you had an old flame."

I started to speak, but my mouth was only beginning to open before she assaulted me again.

"You don't even look like yourself, Annie, and I'm not just talking about your hair. You're so pale it's like looking at porcelain. Your eyes aren't the same. I've tried to act like everything is okay, but I can't. I turn away from you and I feel like I've put my back to a rabid animal. The police clearly don't trust you, and yet you never had so much as a speeding ticket. And what happened to Samuel? That dog is Ellie's most beloved friend, and he's nowhere to be seen."

A sick feeling crept across me when I realized I hadn't thought of Samuel in days. I hadn't thought to break the news to Ellie tonight, and now it would be left to Mom tomorrow, as I'd be dead come sunrise. Greatest mom of the year would never grace my tombstone. If I had a tombstone that is.

"I totally forgot about Samuel," I said in shame. Mom looked at me incredulously. "You forgot about Samuel?" She could hardly believe her ears. Samuel had been with me for years. He'd been an important part of our little family.

"Your *father* gave him to you as a puppy. How could you forget about him?" she asked. To Mom, Samuel was a little piece of himself Dad had left behind. The last vestiges of a man protecting his daughter.

Strike daughter of the year from the gravestone too. "Yeah, I guess I did. I didn't mean to, Mom. Everything has just been so awful here that, honestly, Samuel was the least of my problems." Mom stared at me as if I'd just told her I was a serial killer. "Samuel died the night after you left with Ellie. He died protecting me. He was a hero till the very end."

She caught her breath, reaching one hand to the mantle to steady her balance. "Protecting you? From what? You said it was just a little break-in. Although the detective didn't seem to know anything about a break-in. 'Nothing to worry about,' you said. Well, *this*," she said, pointing to the disarray around the house, "looks very much like something to worry about." Her voice was as loud and accusing as it could be without waking up Ellie.

And here I stumbled, looking for words to make sense of the happenings that had left me as changed as a being could be. No longer human. No longer a member of the same species as the woman who'd labored to bring me into this world. I started to spill out the terrors I'd seen. For a split second, I wanted nothing more than to describe the harrowing things I'd experienced. To tell her how I'd scraped and fought to live, and how I'd won against all odds. Watching that man die in the woods and seeing the haunting face of Ms. McElhaney in the pictures the detective had showed me were so painful that I couldn't imagine how I was going to keep it bottled up inside me.

I ached to tell her the things Asa had forced me to do and how I'd done them. I needed to tell her how I'd lied and schemed and yes, even been party to murder. And even more, I needed to confess that I'd enjoyed some of them. I needed absolution. I needed forgiveness. I wanted to tell her all the awfulness I'd been through and feel her soothing hands on my forehead like when I was a little girl, hands that could wipe away my every wrong and heal most any pain.

But clarity came quickly, and I realized I could hardly open up such a void between us. Could her love survive the gulf of immortality? Could it survive knowing that her daughter was a different breed, a blood-drinker who lived off the life of others? Would she think me irredeemable? Or would she see my transformation like a religious parent hearing of the death of their atheist child. A divide that could never be spanned, a permanent separation, a choice that could never be unchosen. I wasn't ready to acknowledge such a gulf in our relationship. I don't think I could have said the words if I were forced to.

She asked again, irritated by my silence. "Protecting you from what?"

"A man," I finally said. "A monster really, and as good a man as the detective is, he was wrong. There was a break-in. But I lied to you about the police. I didn't call them because the monster threatened to kill you and Ellie if I did. And I thought he would because he *did* kill Ms. McElhaney. He killed her to shut her up and keep her from checking on me. So I knew he was capable of it, Mom. I didn't have any choice but to lie to the detective and to you because I never wanted you to know any of this."

Mom had gotten quiet. It hardly seemed she was breathing even, she was so still. "Where is he now?" she finally asked.

Dead and buried in a shallow grave, I thought.

"Gone," I said quietly because I couldn't tell her I'd killed him. I doubted that murderers ever confessed to their parents. Everyone needs someone to think they're innocent, to see their best side. Besides, she wouldn't be able to lie effectively to Rumsfield.

And there will be no body. But there will be a stake, and I have to make it out there tonight, I reminded myself.

Mom was nearly beside herself with fear and not just fear of me. She'd always been terrified of this house and now with what I'd told her, she could hardly stand still. She resumed her pacing, her hands fidgeting nervously behind her.

"We can't stay here, Annalice. We have to leave. You wake Ellie up, and I'll pack some clothes for her. We can find a hotel in town, and tomorrow, you two can move to Missouri with me. Forget the house. We'll hire a moving company to pack it up. They can sell the place on the auction block. Just grab the essentials tonight."

I stood absolutely still, knowing the moment of reckoning had come. At first, she was too busy to notice. She was still pacing in front of the fire while she made plans. For the moment, her fear of me had been pushed to the back burner. Her mind was busy planning the drive home. How long it would take us to get to her house, which bedroom would be mine, and where Ellie would sleep. Logistics like that. Moments later, she realized I hadn't moved.

"Annalice, time is of the essence. Why are you just standing there?"

"Mom, you said it yourself to the detective. I won't leave."

Her eyes widened, and she threw her hands apart widely. "I know what I said, but I thought surely to God you would have come to your senses after what the detective showed you, and you just told me that a *monster* broke into this house."

"I also said that he's gone."

"He could come back." Her voice hissed with a potent combination of fear and anger. "Two people are dead. Right here in your neighborhood if that's what you can call this backwoods hellhole."

"Mom…"

"What, Annalice? What more reason do you need? What this time? What could possibly hold you here now?"

"I can't leave." The words came out louder than I meant them to, echoing around the room.

A statue stared back at me, a heartbroken, confused, angry statue.

"I want to, Mom. More than anything, I wish I could strike a match to this house and walk out the door. I'd leave it all behind if I could." I nodded, acknowledging the truth to myself for the first time. "But he changed me. In ways that I can't really explain but I know you've picked up on."

"I don't know what you're talking about." She finally found her voice as the stone mask of her face splintered with suspicion.

I looked at her sadly while in the breadth of that second, I heard her heart beat pick up. Down the hall, Ellie shifted in bed; the sheets slid across her legs. The ticking of the massive wall clock pounded in my ears. The tree branches tapped the upstairs windows. I could feel the stirrings of hunger, and it wasn't for food.

Should I tell her it was the racing of her heartbeat or the quickness of her breath that gave her new fear of me away? The fine hairs that I could see standing up on her arms? Should I say, "You've been crying and I can smell the salt of your tears?" Instead, I called her a liar. "I think you do know, Mom. You just don't want to say it."

She ignored the truth in my words. "That man could come back, Annalice. How can you risk Ellie like this?"

"He's *not* coming back," I said. My gaze dropped to the floor. My emotions were high. Looking directly at her wouldn't be the greatest idea.

"*How* do you know he's not coming back?" she asked.

It was a leading question. The detective had said there were things about me she didn't know. But he was wrong. She knew. Mothers always know.

Unable to stop myself, I met her gaze and the violence inside me reached out to her. I felt it swell out from my heart and fill my arms and legs with blood lust. Not for her. It was a remnant of what I'd felt for Asa and the human he'd killed in the woods his last night.

Her breath caught as reality settled in, a silent "oh" on her lips. Most people say they could kill someone who threatened their family. Everyone feels brave from a distance, but knowing your daughter possessed the ability to kill is another thing entirely.

"I was only protecting myself, Mom, and the two of you. But if I leave now, I'm more of a suspect than ever. I have to see this through, or Ellie will never have a chance at a *normal* life."

How strange this must all be for her. When she'd left a week before, I'd been a typical working mom living a boring but happy life, and now I was someone with secrets she didn't recognize. Lots of secrets.

The fingers of her right hand clenched around a small bottle she'd concealed in her hand; her nails slid across the metallic canister. Mace. She always carried it in her purse. She took one last frightened look at me and started to turn away to leave the room. Then she remembered the fear of having her back to me. I saved myself and her the embarrassment and left before she had to back out of the room.

Chapter 5

I sat on the back deck staring at the night sky, waiting for Mom to go to sleep, needing to know that she'd find a little rest. The next few weeks would be tricky, and she needed to be able to sleep a fearless sleep. I knew she wouldn't leave Ellie. Nothing could drive her away from her only granddaughter.

Ellie had dropped into a deep sleep only a few minutes after I'd left her room. Sleeping like only a child can rest, safe and secure in the knowledge that Mom and Dad—or in her case Mom—had it covered. Ellie's heartbeat, quiet and calm, brought me a little peace. I might go to jail. I might fry in the sun, but she'd live, and Mom would be with her. I'd survived the worst even if I didn't make it through the next few weeks.

I'd realized tonight at the restaurant when I'd stood next to Lisa that I'd have to have blood soon. The thirst wasn't bad. *Yet.* But it wouldn't be long. Some innate knowledge told me that. I had a day or two at best, and then something bad was going to happen. Not all vampire knowledge was inborn, it seemed, but thirst was inherent.

Everything else clearly had a learning curve. I had great hearing, but it was new to me. I couldn't determine distances very well. Smell was easier, and I'd adapted to that heightened sense easier. I was stronger, but how much I couldn't tell. I was faster, but how much I didn't know. I needed to readjust to my new boundaries.

But tonight, the stake I'd left beside Asa's grave was a burning priority. My new strengths would have to wait. Impatiently, I sat tensed on the back deck while Mom tossed fitfully in the bedroom above me.

As restless as Mom was, the night sky was the opposite. The evening had quieted, the earlier wind dying down so that it barely rattled the trees. No clouds blotted the sky, and Orion was awake, his stars burning brightly, his bow poised in the eternal search of Scorpio. My yard spread out from the house and then transformed into the rougher terrain of the pasture. In the distance but quite plain to my sight, I could pick out the individual pine trees that formed the perimeter of the national forest.

Even after twenty-four hours, I could still see plainly my path from the night before as I'd run from the brutality of the sun. Certain that it had been visible to even a human last night, I wasn't sure now. To a highly experienced tracker yes, but to the average human untrained in such things, I was doubtful.

While I studied my day-old path, Mom finally drifted off into a semblance of sleep. Her breathing was labored as she struggled in her dreams, her heart thumping out erratic patterns. She tossed and turned. I could hear an occasional word as she talked in her sleep; it took very few of her whispered words to know that I was the subject of her nightmares.

Wishing them a good night, I began to retrace my steps back across the frozen ground to where the nightmare with Asa had ended.

The woods were quiet and I, even quieter, as I jogged through them. It's a strange thing to suddenly have speed and strength, and I felt the way a ninety-year-old woman must feel if she was to wake up in the body of an eighteen-year-old. The sensation was almost overpowering, and it seemed the woods brought it out that much more. The air was cold, the forest silent, and any animals I heard bowed to my presence as I rushed past. *Hunt*, my mind urged. *There's something out here for you.*

I fought the urges. As much as I wanted to streak through the trees and enjoy my newfound strength, I wouldn't allow myself. Surely it was akin to laughing in a funeral home—something taboo—and I struggled to believe that those rules still applied to me. *I wanted* them to apply to me. To feel human. To *be* human. If I acted like one, wasn't that half the battle? A man had died here less than twenty-four hours ago. A death I'd watched and done little to stop. It was too early for running.

I searched the forest, my eyes easily making out tiny details that I'd never noticed. The rough bark of the pine tree housed thousands of bugs; I could hear their bodies clamoring over each other in the search for food. Dead leaves clinging to winter's branches whispered to me in the small breezes. Tiny bright eyes peered out from under fallen tree limbs and then disappeared into the dark as I came close.

I slowed as I passed less than a hundred feet from the unfortunate human encampment Asa and I had come upon last night. Two of the camping trailers were still there, the metal siding creaking with the occupant's movements. From within one, I could hear the low sobbing of a man. The third human must have packed up and left him alone in his grief.

I listened momentarily, understanding in part what he was going through as I'd nearly lost everything myself. *He could be yours. Probably wants to die anyhow.* My forward motion stopped at the thoughts that popped into my brain, and I turned towards the camper. *Wouldn't I be putting him out of his misery? Answering the questions of what happened to his son?* The thoughts came easy. Too easy. I hadn't intended to think them, and yet they were there. *NO!* I screamed back at my own self. *I will not be this thing!*

Disgusted, I turned and ran deeper into the forest, leaving the man to his tears.

Another quarter mile and I slowed again as the smell of human blood began to blend with the smells of the forest. The scent was old but still recognizable—still delicious. And although I knew I needed to focus on retracing my steps to Asa's grave, I couldn't ignore the blood.

And I had died here too. I couldn't ignore my own death site any more than I could ignore the blood. Like dying and getting to go to your own funeral. It was irresistible.

As I had the night before, I let the scent lead me like a ribbon of red through the woods until I stood over the spot where the human's blood had soaked into the ground, leaving a large dark stain that would soon be decayed by the forest. Tonight, however, the smell was still potent.

The blood had painted a portion of the sandy soil a deep ruddy brown color; burgundy spatters flecked the nearby fallen leaves. There were hundreds of footprints encircling the stain, but none had threatened its border. No one had blurred the proof of my sins into the ground. Maybe they'd had no desire to smooth out the last traces of a man's life, as if leaving his blood pooled on the ground kept him present on this earth awhile longer.

Either way, it remained visible proof of what I'd been party to. It was an awful sight to me, but I couldn't look away. As decayed as it was, I'd have drank it now if I could have swabbed it from the dirt. My vision blotted red at the sight and smell. Reality lost its focus. I felt confused, and my thoughts were disheveled. My chest got tight, claustrophobic almost. *Why had I come here?* For a second, I forgot completely. *Think,* I reminded myself. *It's important.* But I couldn't remember.

Against the backdrop of mountains in the distance, the tree that I'd staked Asa to stood out. An oak, its thick trunk reached upwards and dissected the night sky as it gave way to thousands of brown leafless tributaries. The surface was marred by a hollow spot where my stake had pierced the trunk, bark scattered on the ground below. I'd let Asa dangle there for a while, his eyes hollowing and sinking in, my hand-carved stake pinning him in place. And it had felt good.

I started to turn away from the tree and the memories that it dredged up, but as I did, the ground at my feet began to bubble blood. What had been absorbed from the man the night before ran across my shoes. I stared at it in horror, a silent scream finally becoming real as I tried to take a step back. But my feet were rooted, and I could do nothing but watch the blood as it pooled around my ankles. I was still screaming when the blood turned and snaked up the tree. The trunk went red as the blood traced its path through the branches of the tree like millions of capillaries. The red fluid reached the terminal branches and dropped off in a heavy rain on my skin. I cowered under my hands, using them in a futile effort to protect my face from the blood, but it was no use. It dripped from my eyelashes and ran in rivulets down my cheeks and across my lips. I wiped at it with my hands and forearms, but I couldn't keep it out of my eyes and my mouth. I shuddered at the taste; the blood was old, dead and not fit to drink.

"You should not have survived. You should not have killed me," Asa's voice whispered from behind me. I spun around, arms flexed to fight, but legs coiled to run. But no enemy was waiting. Just the naked arms of winter's oak trees. I wiped at the blood in my eyes again.

"Face me you coward," I hissed as I turned back towards the blood-soaked tree. But my bravado was false; I was shaking like a leaf. I guess human reactions don't simply disappear overnight because my breath was chugging like a freight train. I wanted nothing more than to race home.

"And do what? Hide in the bed with your mommy? She will not comfort you; she knows you are a monster." Asa's voice mocked me from all directions now. He pounded in my ears, which I covered with my hands, my fingers digging into my scalp.

I searched the shadows for his hidden form and studied the tree limbs, expecting to find him stretched out on one as he laughed at me. But the forest was empty. He was nowhere to be found. *You killed him,* I reminded myself.

Logically, I knew that. I searched for calm and closed my eyes against the vision. I thought of Mom back home and Ellie sleeping safely in her bed. I reminded myself that I was a scientist at heart and all of this was a hallucination brought on by the scent of the blood, brought on by my rising hunger.

I walked a few steps away, taking deep breaths as I did so. The fresh air washed the smell from my lungs, and when I opened my eyes, the blood had evaporated from my skin. The forest floor was the simple browns and greys it had been, and only the small stain remained from the man's spilt blood. I would be careful to keep my distance.

I left the oak tree and the blood-smeared ground and retraced my steps from last night to where I'd buried Asa. After I'd staked him, I'd carried him nearly a quarter mile away before stopping to bury him. I was paying careful attention to the ground at my feet and little else, still in shock at the hallucination I'd experienced when I heard a hard and familiar voice to my left.

"Looking for something?"

Oh God, I thought as I recognized it. *Some vampire I am. I let a human sneak up on me. And not just any human. That human.* And then, *When did I begin to think of them as a different species?* I wondered.

I turned towards him, not bothering to hide my irritation. "The only thing I'm looking for is a little peace and quiet, Detective. Unfortunately, I find *you* here," I answered.

Rumsfield watched me from a thicket of trees to my left. He was well hidden, his back ringed by the scratchy limbs of cedar trees, and he looked more than a little nervous. While his body was glued in place, his eyes darted back and forth as he searched the forest around us. His pupils were dilated in the darkness; he smelled of anxious sweat and fear. A leather bag was slung across his chest, the strap melding the leather jacket he was wearing to his body; his right hand was poised above his gun.

"You a little trigger happy tonight, Detective?" I asked. I was hoping he'd put the handgun away. How would I explain it if he shot me and I walked away, alive and well tomorrow night.

"Do not bother with explanations. Just kill him now," Asa whispered. I jerked towards the sound of Asa's voice, studying the forest behind us.

"What?" Rumsfield questioned. "Did you hear something?" He jerked his gun from the holster.

The clarity of the hallucination was astounding. I reminded myself again that I'd killed Asa. That's why I was here and most likely the same reason the detective was here. "I thought I heard a voice behind me. It's nothing. Probably just nerves," I answered.

He nodded and swallowed, his held breath pouring out in a rush and then sucked in slowly as he struggled for control of his voice. "Did you hear that sound a few minutes ago? Sounded like a banshee screaming." The gun hovered above the holster, and I couldn't help but be impressed at how little his hand shook.

"I didn't hear anything, but I would have no idea how a banshee would sound," I answered. *But I know what I sound like,* I thought, remembering the blood curdling screams from a few minutes back.

"That was the God-awfullest sound I've ever heard, and I've spent a lot of time out here in these woods." He swallowed hard, looking past me and into the woods again. Finally, he re-holstered his gun and slid his palm down his jeans, wiping away the stress sweat.

"Maybe it's the same animal that got that man last night," I said.

His eyebrows lifted slightly as he cocked his head to the right. "Which makes me wonder why you're out here, Annalice. Don't you agree it's a little odd that you're wandering around in the woods with some wild animal on the prowl?"

"No odder than you, I guess."

"Don't play stupid, Annalice. I knew you'd come, eventually. If I waited long enough, I knew you'd come for it. Turns out, I didn't even have to wait that long. Mind you, I'd have come every night if that's what it took." The detective's low voice drifted across to me on the night breeze, each sound wave exaggerated by the stillness of the evening. I could hear the knowing in his voice, and I hated him for it.

"You knew I'd come for *what* exactly?"

"Come on, Annie," Rumsfield murmured. "I have to admit, I've never understood the criminal psyche. The evidence is right in front of their face, and they'll lie like the devil, come hell or high water, every time. Looks like it doesn't matter how educated the criminal is; they're still too stupid to just come clean. Sure save a whole lot of time and taxpayer dollars if you'd hang up this charade."

From the bag on his shoulder, he pulled a plastic bag, slapping the side of it with one hand. The sound popped in the air. Inside, I could see the outline of my hand-carved stake. I raised my eyebrows and aimed as condescending a look at him as I could muster. "What are you going to do, Detective? Stake me? Won't they question that down at the station?"

"There'll be a lot of questions, ma'am, but they won't be directed towards me because this is evidence." He lifted the bag up to look at it while he spoke.

"Evidence of what precisely? Wait. Let me guess," I said, holding my hands up in the universal language of back the f-up. "The same kind of evidence that you collected from my house? Oh, wait a minute. You didn't actually find anything at my house, did you? The search warrant got you nowhere. But you came back later that night. Collected a few fingerprints. Stuff like that. Any of it pan out?"

He started to speak but changed his mind, one hand lifting to run his fingers across a couple-days-old scrape on his forehead. "Wait a minute. How did you know about that? You weren't home. I knocked on the doors. Unless... unless you were watching me."

He was looking at me expectantly for answers, and I didn't have any. What was I going to say? *Yeah, I watched you get attacked, and I did nothing to help you. But don't worry, Detective, it was only because I was being held hostage by a vampire. Otherwise, I would have come to your aid right away.*

"I have a security system with cameras. I check it every night," I lied. "You came back that night after the search warrant and took fingerprints. Checked the house out. Again."

He rubbed his forehead a second time, wincing as his fingers grazed the broken skin. "Did, um... well did you see anything really strange on the footage by any chance?"

"Besides you acting a fool? Or maybe you were drunk, the way you were stumbling around my pasture. Nice cut you've got there on your head by the way. What were you expecting, Detective?" I asked hatefully. Of course, I was lying. I'd never set the cameras on my security system. They were as blank as the day they'd been installed.

He dropped his police guard momentarily, looking slightly vulnerable. "Did you see anyone else? Anything else ... I'm not sure what I'm asking. Just anyone else on the footage?"

I aimed another condescending look at him. "Who's the detective here anyways, and what are you asking me, exactly?"

His patience was wearing thin. I could see it in the way he rubbed a hand roughly through his hair. He hadn't shaved in a couple of days, and he looked tired. I felt sorry for him, knowing what it was like bearing the brunt of Asa's handiwork. Having seen things that made no sense and having no one to tell them to. But pity was for someone who had the luxury to care. And I didn't.

"There was no one there except you, Detective. I guess you tripped over your own feet. Served you right being where you weren't supposed to be. Did you find anything, by the way, on your little illegal run?" I laid the sarcasm on thick.

Vulnerability wasn't an emotion he was used to. He wiped it away quickly and put on cocky again. "Yeah, you might say I found something. I found some fingerprints that night. From a fifty-three-year-old cold case, and I found them on your doorknob and in Ms. McElhaney's house. Don't you find that odd?"

I laughed out loud at the question. "I've found a lot of things odd about you, Rumsfield. Aren't you starting to feel a little stupid yet? Or have you always been the laughing stock of the station?" I was being hateful, but I didn't care. It was in his best interest. The more insane this whole thing seemed to him, the better off the both of us would be. He needed to forget those fingerprints.

"No one's laughing at me, Annalice. I've got lots of evidence, and you know that. That's why you're out here in the middle of the night, right? You didn't come all the way out here just to take a walk and commune with nature. You were hoping that us 'good old boys' wouldn't find this. But this good old boy did," he said, pointing to himself.

His voice was confident, but I could detect a little hesitancy; more anxiety colored his scent, and it wasn't a pleasant scent. Like sweat on steroids. So I'd hit a nerve. Maybe he was getting a little more ridicule at the station than I realized. And then, I finally saw the truth staring me in my face.

"Well, if that's true, Detective, why isn't that little piece of *evidence* in the hands of the state crime lab right now instead of in your hands?" I asked, making quotation marks as I spit out the words.

The tinge of anxiety became stronger as my question hung unanswered. It was going to be hard for him to explain. Beads of sweat ballooned on his hairline, and his heart surged forward as he struggled to come up with a plausible explanation. Oh, the scents and sounds of lies.

"There's plenty of reasons I haven't turned this little beauty in yet," he said, pointing to the stake. "I tested it myself already. Your fingerprints," he said, jabbing a finger in my direction, "are on here. And I found clothes in a hole in the ground with a stab wound in the chest that is the same size as the end of this wooden stake. And a wedding ring. The shirt's pretty ripped up. In fact, I bet the person wearing that shirt was in a lot of pain. Want to explain that? It's a grave, isn't it?"

He was really getting worked up now. Pacing back and forth and pointing to the hole where I'd buried Asa. But there was nothing there now except more unanswered questions for the detective. I laughed again as if all this was ridiculous. "I don't have to explain anything, but I sure as hell don't have to explain some old trashed out clothes in a hole in the woods. Calling it a 'grave' is really going overboard."

He stopped pacing, his hands on his hips, one hand still holding the evidence bag. It rocked back and forth a few times on his hip when he swung towards me. He nodded his head slowly as he stared at me. "So you admit it. It's yours."

"I'm admitting nothing. I'm just saying if it was my handiwork, it wouldn't mean a damn thing."

"You killed him," Rumsfield said. He crossed his arms like Superman surveying the evil plot he'd just foiled.

I sucked in my breath at his accusation. Hearing the words out of someone else's mouth was even harder to accept. Luckily, he was still basking in his own glow and didn't recognize my "oh shit" moment. "I killed who, Detective? So you found my fingerprints on that piece of wood. What else did you find? Any blood? Any body tissue? If I'd killed someone, wouldn't there be some blood? And who do you propose that I killed by the way? Where's the body? Do you actually think that I'd have been any match for the young man who died out here last night? That I could have shoved a wooden cross through him? And what exactly would have been my motive?" I shot back, sneering in his face.

His eyebrows lifted in mock surprise as the corners of his mouth turned up in a feigned smile. "Whoa. Simmer down, Annalice. Interesting how that little tidbit shot out of your mouth so quickly. I didn't mention anything about the man that died last night. Strange that you brought that up. They ruled it an animal attack, you know. And Ms. McElhaney's cause of death was ruled the same thing. Don't you think it's strange this many people dying of animal attacks around here, and all of them so close to you. What, with your neighbor being killed and now this kid attacked practically in your backyard and all. In my entire career, I have never filled out a report of a death from an animal attack. Have you? I mean you are a doctor. How many death certificates have you filed as a result of animal attacks?"

Smart aleck. I'd verbally linked myself to the crime. Had I learned nothing in malpractice class in medical school? Number one rule, keep your damned mouth shut. Had I just hung myself by getting angry?

He waited for me to come up with an answer, his smile getting bigger. "Oh don't strain your brain if you're trying to think back, Annalice. I checked with the Arkansas State Health Department. You've never filed a death certificate with animal attack as cause of death. Which was a relief by the way. It did cross my mind that I'd stumbled across a doctor serial killer."

"Again, what's my motive in all of this, Detective?" I asked, ignoring his jabs. *He's just trying to get me riled up. Don't let him.*

"I'm not sure. But you can bet your bottom dollar I'll figure it out. The man in the restaurant with you the other night, your old flame, this is his grave. There's no body but these are his clothes. I know that because they match the description from Lisa at the Screamin' Eagle," he said, pointing to the smoothed-over hole

45

behind him. "Not that I blame you for killing him, mind you, because by all accounts, yours included, he must've been a real son of a bitch. But I didn't write the law; I just enforce it whether I agree with it or not. And you *were* out here when that boy died last night. I'm not sure why yet, but you were there. Your footprints were all around the crime scene. The two of you followed that kid. We've got casts of a woman's footprints and a man's. Both followed that kid out here but only the woman walked away." He pointed at me again. "You. Now everybody else, they can't see past all the signs of an animal attack. Makes them think those footprints don't mean anything. But you're not fooling me."

I shifted angrily in my place. A rage was brewing. I could feel my very unnecessary breathing pick up further. My hands clenched at my sides.

"Exactly how you fit into that man's death last night remains a mystery." He rubbed a hand through his blond hair as he continued, "But you had some part. Tell me, Annalice, what really happened to your neighbor? Did you get in over your head with that old flame of yours? A cult maybe? Drugs?" Staring at me, he waited a few moments before throwing his hands up in exasperation. "I just don't get it, Annalice. I really don't."

He didn't seem to understand how upset I was getting. Was he so lost in his evidence that he was missing what was right in front of his face? I tried to calm down as I opened my mouth. "Let's get back to the evidence and drop your insane questions for a moment, Rumsfield. You know they're my footprints because ..." I let my voice drift away to silence. "Oh, because you found my matching shoes, right? Yeah, it's all making so much sense now. De. Tec. Tive." I emphasized each syllable hatefully.

He took a step towards me, his handsome features warping with anger. "I'm not just some country bumpkin, ma'am. I've lived here my entire life, and I know these woods. I'm a damn good tracker, and I followed those footprints all the way back to your pasture. If I'd gotten there sooner, I probably could have seen your trail in the dew. But nobody's perfect, and we didn't find that kid's body until around ten this morning. So I made it to your place around noon and the dew was already gone. Interestingly, so were you. I bet I rang your doorbell for an hour. Wouldn't mind telling me where you were, would you?"

"I don't owe you any explanations. But if it makes you feel better to know, I was asleep. I usually work the night shift so I make it a point to not hear doorbells from pesky people who don't care about my work schedule."

"Ms. Creed, you were supposed to be at work at six tonight, but you didn't show." He let his words sink in. I couldn't keep the look of surprise off of my face. In my vampire angst, I'd completely forgotten about work, and it was a big deal. "In the doctor world, that's called patient abandonment and if anyone wants to push it, you could find yourself in some hot water with the state medical board," he added.

He'd found an angle and was pushing the point as far as he could take it. "I called the chief of staff of the hospital to find out a little more about you. He was happy to talk about you. Pretty pissed, you not showing up and all. Seems like that sort of behavior just doesn't fly, and I don't think he's going to let It slIde so easy once I got finished filling him in on the chain of events out here. You are planning on going back to work, right? Of course, I guess it's hard to return to a normal work schedule after staking men and burying them and all the weird crap you've been up to the last few days. Wandering around in the dark, looking for left-behind weapons from your latest crime and things like that. But I suggest you be available when I want to talk to you. Understand what I'm saying, *Ms.* Creed?" he asked as he closed the distance between us.

"That's *Dr.* Creed to you, and you better get what I'm saying Detective. You've got nothing. Those footprints, if they are mine, don't prove anything except that I've been hiking. You don't even have the shoes that you think made those prints. And your so-called 'tracking ability' would never hold up in court. And if anyone believed your ridiculous story, you'd already have a warrant and be searching my place, and that 'stake' you're holding would be in the state crime lab. Not out here in your bat-shit crazy hands. But you don't have a search warrant. Truth is, you wasted your only shot with a warrant on me a couple days back. Now I know you're a big shot in that one-horse town, but you can only push old favors so far before the judge starts to worry about his rep. It's hard to keep risking it on nothing more than crazy theories. Isn't that right, Detective? But you tried, didn't you? But you just can't get crazy separated from your name down at the station, huh?"

His face fell for the second time. *So they really are calling him crazy,* I thought. I guess I'd found the kryptonite because Superman had lost his composure. I'll give him credit for regaining it quickly though. He was looking confident again in a matter of seconds.

"And I'll keep trying, ma'am. It's just a matter of time, and I'll have everything I need," the detective replied as he turned on his heel. He shook his index finger at me as he did so. The movement only fanned the scent of his body towards me more.

Was he a madman? Couldn't he feel my loss of control heading towards him like a freight train?

"*Kill him!*" Asa screamed a demon's cry in my brain. "*He is a liability!*"

I was losing control. The hallucinations were back, and I could hear Asa's voice in my ear, and truth be told, he was speaking logic. Like the rare schizophrenic whose pathologic auditory hallucinations actually make sense.

Somehow, Rumsfield remained oblivious. He just kept talking. Like a dog with a worn-out bone.

It was a few miles to the highway that bisected the forest. He walked away briskly, heading north; I supposed his vehicle was parked somewhere up ahead. He made it a few feet before he stopped in mid-step, fine hairs beginning to rise up on the back of his neck. His diaphragm drew a breath in a sharp jerk and then slowed down to suck the air in slowly in the reaction of dread, each movement exaggerated by the innate knowledge that the slightest movement could be his final one. It was an age-old reaction of the prey. To lie still, blend in, bring no attention to oneself.

Finally, the reaction I'd been expecting. My instincts and Asa were begging me to kill him. He was a danger to me. A threat to Ellie. He stood between me and any chance I might have of living a halfway normal life with my daughter.

How simple it would be to end him and his endless questions. How easy he would die. I could bury his body so deep that it would never be found. Maybe I'd be a top suspect, but what did it matter? No one could prove anything. In the end, Rumsfield would be remembered as a good detective, but one who had finally been destroyed by the stress of the job. He'd let a case get to him—a missing person that would never be found.

"Eventually, he will only be *your* memory because everyone else will have died," Asa said. "And you will not remember him as any of those things. Only as your first kill. Your first taste of human blood and the first of many. He will remain special in that way alone," Asa's voice seemed real now. So embodied and full. I looked to my left and found him standing there. "Kill him," he urged.

"He's not real. He's using your own thoughts against you," the logical part of my brain tried to reason with the portion that wanted Rumsfield dead. The battle seemed lost, but still I kept fighting. I forced the air out of my lungs and closed my eyes so I couldn't see the fear-paralyzed form of Rumsfield.

When I opened them again, I was staring directly into Rumsfield's dilated gaze. I realized then that I'd followed him and jerked him around to face me without me even recognizing that I'd moved.

All seemed lost. My future, my daughter. Everything that I held dear evaporated like a hazy mist in early morning.

Rumsfield staggered backwards, struggling to pull himself from my hands. He was a tall man, towering above me, but now in my grasp, he looked small. I pulled him towards me, the momentum lifting him momentarily off his feet. My fangs cut into my tongue. All was definitely lost. I wouldn't have given a plug nickel for his life at that minute.

And with some inner strength that I hadn't recognized in him, he found his voice. "For God's sake, Annalice." His voice cracked on my name. Sensing the seriousness of the danger, his training had kicked in. He tried to make some type of connection with me—a human connection.

I'm not exactly sure what saved him. Certainly not my self-control or my lack of thirst. Maybe he survived because of expectations that had been pre-destined by my ancestors for the last two centuries. I'd been raised to be a good girl, a southern female curse that we pass from one generation to the next. We're brought up to be kind to a fault, helpful to the point of hurting ourselves. Ever apologizing for things that are out of our control, and I was still, at least in part, the woman I'd been raised to be. Or maybe, whether you're human or not, you don't become a killer overnight. But I made no mistake in believing that it had anything to do with any shreds of my own humanity. If I had any left, they were only fragments borrowed from my mother and daughter—a leftover code from a bygone era.

Either way, he was likely as surprised as I was when I gave him a shove and shouted, "Leave!" There was a moment's hesitation before he took a halting step backwards and finally flew away from my hands and into the darkness. I closed my eyes, hoping that the old saying "out of sight, out of mind" held true.

I didn't watch the detective disappear into the woods. I'd already spun on my heels and streaked away into the protective cover of the forest. Thinking of the event later on that night, I realized that I should have waited for him to make it to his parked car before I sprinted out of sight, but I'd wanted to put as much distance between me and his fear-tainted, delicious bloodstream as possible. My only salvation was that he'd probably been too frightened to stop and see the inhuman speed at which I had fled.

Moments later, I made it back to the spot where I'd staked Asa, and in the distance, I heard the roar of his patrol car and the bump of his tires on the potholed county road as he drove back towards town. He was out of sight, but he was not out of mind. I could think of nothing but him as I walked back towards my home.

Chapter 6

*I*t was four a.m. when I stepped out of the shower. Almost forty-eight hours had passed since I had staked Asa. His death was my way of marking time. A sick way, but so far, it had made sense. The wall clock's chimes had reverberated through the house, and I'd listened and cringed when I heard my mom stir a few rooms down. I waited, my breath held, as though I were still human, until she rolled over and her breathing had returned to a deeper rhythm.

I'd come to clean up, wash the forest and rain from my skin and change clothes. And as badly as I wanted to stay here, spend the day in my own bed, I knew that could never happen. I couldn't risk sleeping anywhere Rumsfield could find me, and so, after pulling on a fresh T-shirt and clean jeans, I soundlessly slipped into Ellie's room, kissed her forehead and left out the back door.

The yard was heavily dewed, and I regretted that I hadn't put on my mud boots as I walked in the direction of the pasture. The wet grass seeped water into my shoes, and I clicked my tongue at my stupidity, hoping vampires didn't get athlete's foot. I'd be spending my day, asleep, with wet feet.

Two nights previous, when Asa and I had left on our hunting trip and I'd died as a human, we'd crossed through the field behind my house. His smell had hovered on the air as we did so, and I suspected then that his hiding place must have been somewhere in my own pasture. Since I couldn't sleep in my own house, my plan was to sleep wherever Asa had spent the daylight hours. He'd managed to stay out of humans' reach during the day for over a century and a half, so I doubted I could do any better.

Still I was dread-filled at the thought of entering Asa's hiding spot as I leapt the barbed wire fence that separated the yard from the pasture. My emotions were mixed. He'd been a bastard and a murderer. Regardless, I found myself missing him in some ways over the last night.

Two days ago, I'd craved some human companionship, and now, I craved something I couldn't quite put my finger on. I can't say I craved a vampire specifically, but I did crave something, someone to talk to maybe or just to tell me how to be. It was like I was going through puberty all over again without the benefit of someone a few years older to tell me what to expect.

I followed Asa's scent, now mine as well, until I found the strongest point. The scent coincided with a small knoll in the pasture that eventually flattened back out near the fence line. I surveyed the ground but saw nothing I recognized as out of the ordinary. I'd crossed this same spot a thousand times while catching horses or taking a hike with Ellie.

Tonight, the horses had moved to the back of the field, wanting to be as far from me as possible. The cows had taken their lead and were trying to make themselves inconspicuous among the sleek, taller bodies of the horses. The gentle swell of the knoll drifted away towards the edges of the national forest that bordered my property. The rye grass waved gently, the green fluorescing in the moonlight. In the west corner, I could see a piece of fence that needed mending. A tree had fallen six months back and had taken the top strand of wire down. Along the eastern border, pine trees rocked in the breeze.

But nothing stood out or screamed, *"This is where the monster slept.'* Still, I could smell Asa. His scent floated on the air, coming and going like he did every night of that last week I'd been human. I whistled through my teeth in frustration as I walked away from the spot and then back towards it when his scent got weaker. Following a spiral, I worked my way out and then back in again. But still nothing. I studied the ground and finally the trees out of sheer desperation.

"Even in death, I make a fool of you," Asa whispered. His voice sounded so real, and for a slightly too hopeful moment, I looked around for him. Of course, he wasn't here. I'd killed him, shoved a stake through his heart, and siphoned his blood out so I could live and have a life with my daughter. *I'm alive and Asa is dead*, I reminded myself. *He can't hurt me now.*

I returned to scouting the surroundings and tried to ignore the feeling of unease that had settled into the pit of my stomach. Maybe Asa had just traveled through here many times and that was why I could still smell him. His hiding spot was probably miles from here, and I was wasting my time, I argued with myself.

But I continued to search. What else could I do? My internal clock was raging in the background. I only had about an hour left till dawn, and I needed a place to go. *If only I hadn't made such fun of Rumsfield. I could sleep in my own bed,* I thought. But that bridge was a pile of embers. I could see the proverbial smoke from where I was standing.

I was giving up and turning towards the barn to sleep buried in the hay when my eyes caught again on an outcropping of rock that seemed, on my one hundredth glance, too planned. The stones were well hidden in the dead space between two ancient oaks, the branches of which had intertwined in a battle of wills over the years. The tree on the left was winning as the other tree was forced to drop armfuls of bark onto the ground as it lost the struggle. It was in the roots of the left tree that I could just make out a corner edge of an old and decaying structure.

I approached it slowly, pushing past the overgrown bushes that obscured it. The visible edge was about six inches tall and built of rectangular shaped rocks held together by mud. It disappeared into the ground as the knoll lifted higher in elevation. I traced the roofline down with my hands until I could feel the fibers of a door recessed into the hill.

A forgotten root cellar, I realized as I felt the door through the vinery that had grown down across the entryway over the years. I started to rip the years of overgrowth down, my fingers closing around thick grapevine and the sharp thorns of blackberry brambles, when I realized Asa must have left it hidden for a reason—a reason that I now needed as much as he had. Sliding to the side, I let the thorns and branches scratch across my body as I crawled as close to the rock wall as I could. Blood welled up on my arms and face, but I paid the scratches no attention. They healed almost as quickly as they had occurred.

During the two years that Ellie and I had lived here, we'd never found the root cellar, although we'd both spent hours in this field riding horses, looking for arrowheads, and any other activity I could think of to keep us out of the house. Over the last week that Asa had been with me, I'd agonized over where he could be hiding. The answer had been only a few hundred feet away from where I'd waited for him each night.

The wood was soft in my hands as I pushed the door open, but it held together, screeching as it scraped on the earthen floor. The smell of my maker rushed up to meet me in such thickness that my nostrils burned. More thorns tore at me, welling blood up on my skin, but I brushed them away absentmindedly as I crossed the threshold.

The door opened into a small room about ten feet by ten feet. It was old. Older than the house even. By looking at the stone walls held together by hand-mixed mortar, I would have estimated it to have been built well over a century ago. The rock walls still held back the dirt except in a few places where the stones had been spat out by the occasional groanings of the earth since the cellar had been built. Here the wall bulged forward slightly, a moist and cool reminder that I stood a good eight feet below ground level. As a human, I'd been somewhat claustrophobic, but now, this cellar felt comfortable. Safe. Even Asa's scent brought me more peace than it should have.

The corners of the room were littered with petrified droppings of the nocturnal animals that had made their dens in here over the years, and cobwebs, thick like curtains, draped the walls. Years of moss, accumulated on the rocks, shone green and moist. A stale odor of the onions and potatoes that the cellar had once housed rose from the floor and laced the air, but I could smell no lingering scent of any humans.

I doubted if any living man or woman had crossed the

threshold in several decades, so it was easy to understand why Asa had chosen it. Human eyes would be unlikely to see its ancient outlines deeply embedded into the dirt, and it was even more doubtful that any human who'd known of its presence still lived.

Leaned up in one corner was a rotting corn stalk broom, in another, a pile of rancid blankets, and in the far back corner stood the swaybacked remnants of an old iron bedframe. Yellowed feathers from the mattress ticking lay trapped in the cobwebs of time. All items from another era, but across one bedpost was slung a modern-looking leather bag, and although the leather was worn smooth, it stuck out like a sore thumb amongst the other relics.

The bedframe hadn't been suitable for sleeping in generations, so squatting down on the uneven dirt floor, I ran my hands under the frame, my fingers falling into a packed depression where Asa's body had lain day after day. To the left of the frame, the dirt had been thrown where he'd dug down deeper into the ground to hide from the coming sun. Like vermin, I thought, and overwhelmed by anger, I tore the packed dirt from the hole. In handfuls, I flung it behind me, spraying the walls and the ceiling as I did everything in my power to rip all traces of him from the ground. Finally, I came to hard-packed clay and rock which broke even my hard vampire nails. Fingers dripping large drops of blood, I rocked back on my heels crying and beat the ground around me. I could tear the impression of his body from the ground but not from my life.

I cried then, not the light weeping that I'd done when I put Ellie to bed, but deep chest-racking sobs; my vision going ruddy as I faced the reality of just how close he'd been to me. "I could have killed him," I said out loud to myself, "if I had …"

I could have finished that thought in so many different ways. If I'd only known. Or if I'd only been brave enough to walk out my door and search. If only I'd realized sooner. If only I'd gotten an apartment in town. There were so many "if onlys," and I'd missed each one of them.

I leaned up against the bedframe and let the tears run down

my face, not bothering to wipe them away or to try to shut them down. There was no one to see them anyway, no human for whom to act human. No one to notice that they were bloodstained. No one to be embarrassed for.

But it was useless to cry. I needed help, and sobbing out my own blood was not going to help me at all. It would just make me hungrier, and I was really beginning to feel it. A pain in the pit of my abdomen burned like a coal of fire. Asa had never mentioned this kind of burn, but he'd probably never burned. He'd only consumed.

Through the red haze of my tears, I could see the blurred outline of the bag Asa had left on the bedpost. All that remained of him on this earth was waiting for me in that bag. It was rather plain looking really. Heavily worn, the brass eyes were beginning to pull away from the leather, but the material remained intact. It was zipped. Of course it was; Asa was not one to be open with anything. Even in death, the bastard left me struggling to know him.

And opening it, it was just as I'd expected. Absolutely sterile. There was nothing in here to identify the man, to separate him from anyone else. A well faded but expensive pair of jeans and a couple of shirts and some underclothes. One shirt was very worn, but the other was tailored, obviously expensive, and essentially unworn. Pressing it to my face, I could pick up on the soft hint of a human, the spoils of a recent crime. He'd never worn it, or I wouldn't have been able to make out the previous owner's smell.

I threw the clothes on the bed and swept my hand around the base of the bag, coming back with some cash, a woman's wedding band, a few other assorted pieces of jewelry, and a couple of watches. A pocket watch was among the collection. Not having been re-wound, the watch had stopped on March 2. Five days back. Asa had killed the owner of this watch while staying with me. My hand felt dirty just touching it, so I laid it aside with the clothes.

I ran a hand around the lining of the bag a final time and found an unexpected ridge. The lining shredded with the flick of a fingernail, and I found a fragment of the human life that Asa had left behind a century ago. A picture. An ancient tintype so faded that I could barely make out the image in the light filtering in from the outside.

Walking out of the cellar, I leapt up to the knoll to study the picture in the ambient light of the star-lit sky. A woman sat straight in a high-backed chair, her hands folded in her lap. The length of her dress skimmed her shoes and masked most of her curves. And still she was beautiful. Soft and feminine. On her left hand was a gold band. She wasn't smiling, but despite that, I could see the kindness in the gentle set of her jaw. Her eyes were soft and understanding, the kind of eyes that could make you tell her anything. Eyes that you couldn't shock and that held no judgment no matter what you confessed. It had to be his mother—the one human Asa had kept any affection for.

Next to her stood a handsome man; Asa before he'd changed. Before he'd lost all humanity and his conscience. One hand was resting on her shoulder, and he was smiling. He looked happy. When she died, she'd carried his soul with her into the grave. A part of me could understand why he couldn't come back from that kind of loss. Could I if I lost my daughter? I wasn't sure.

Back in the cellar, I laid the tintype and the jewelry aside and gave the bag another close inspection. One more ridge was palpable behind an inner pocket, and I ripped the rest of the lining out. A business card twisted into the air, and I plucked it from the breeze before it fell to the ground. It appeared fairly new and written on its back was a phone number. I didn't recognize the area code, and there was no name with the number. The front held the logo of a bar in Denver.

Why would Asa have a phone number? He'd obviously tried to conceal it. But from who? From humans in the event that he was discovered? Was he protecting the identity of the owner of this number or the owner of the bar? After having spent a week with him, I couldn't imagine him having formed any kind of cordial relationship.

Slipping the business card into the other back pocket of my jeans, I threw the old bag into the corner of the cellar and stepped back out into the pasture. My every desire was to go back to the house and join my sleeping family. And I seriously considered it, my heart trying to convince my brain that I'd be safe in a closet in my own home.

My internal bickering was at a stalemate as I sat down on the grassy hilltop overlying the cellar and watched the darkened windows of my house. The distance was too great to listen for their heartbeats, but in a window, I saw the shadow of my mother. Featureless and dark, I could make out only that she watched for something. Most likely for me, her lost daughter. She searched the darkness for a handful of minutes before giving up and returning to bed.

Like a sentry, I watched the house for what was left of the night, knowing that my life was becoming too narrow, knowing that I was losing myself, that every aspect of the life I'd lived was slipping between my fingers.

Just before the sun gilded the distant mountains, I crept into the cellar. As much as I hated the idea, hated the thought of laying where Asa's cold dead body had slept, I knew that it was for the best. After running into Detective Rumsfield in the woods, I was more sure than ever of how deeply obsessed he was with this case. I could envision him knocking on my door and demanding that I come to the station. My mom would point to my bedroom at a loss as to what else to do. He'd pull the door off the hinges and drag me outside to his patrol car. I wouldn't even get to see the shock on his face when I burned in his hands.

So I prepared myself mentally, dug into the same dirt that had covered Asa, and waited for the coming dawn.

Chapter 7

I woke to the smell of clotted blood. Cow's blood. And it was revolting even to a blood drinker. I tried to bury my face in the blankets lining my hole, but it didn't help. The cellar wasn't airtight, so the scent seeped in through the crooks and crannies. But the worst of the odor was coming from the hem of my jeans. Dried and stiff, the denim scratched against my ankles where they'd soaked up the blood the night before as I'd slit the throat of a cow in the pasture. The memory seemed remote now, like it had been days ago that I'd stooped to such measures and not just the night before. Maybe I was subconsciously dissociating. Maybe I was just losing my mind.

The animal had been terrified, running to the far side of the pasture as soon as I'd emerged from my hidey-hole. I'd been dangerously hungry and on a timeline. Not that I wasn't dangerous right now, twenty-four hours after my botched kill, but I'd been more on edge last night. I'd hatched a great plan after the failed evening with my mom and the run-in with the detective. I'd decided to kill a cow for its blood, and it had to be done and over with by the time Ellie came home. Then I could finish a relaxed evening at home with my family. Wouldn't that look good on a to-do list hanging from the fridge?

I'd looked first to the house before my bovine attack, grateful to find all the windows darkened except the porch lights. No one was home. Thank God. If I remembered right and hadn't lost too much track of time, tonight was the parent-teacher's conference and book fair. I'd signed up over a month ago to volunteer, and

Ellie and I were supposed to have worked the booth together. That had been when I was normal. When I didn't live like an abandoned animal in a forgotten den or chase frightened animals around in muddy pastures for the blood running in their veins.

The animal had fought, its large girth making it difficult to catch and hold. But finally caught, I managed to find a good artery, my mouth filling with hair and dirt, and I'd drank mouthful after another of sickeningly sweet blood until I could take it no longer. I'd puked it up onto the ground beside the animal in a dark maroon swath that stretched for several feet away from the animal's heaving form. It hadn't died as easily as I'd hoped. I'd crawled away in desperation, hoping some distance from the animal would help me keep the blood down. It hadn't worked. I'd heaved until every last drop soaked into the ground. Finally, I'd pulled myself up to stand, long wispy trails of drying blood waving in the wind, but I didn't bother to wipe them away. I'd just gone back to the cellar and spent the rest of the night trying to forget this had ever happened.

The house was still dark that night when I'd crawled back into the cellar. And I mean that literally. I crawled, still vomiting up bits of dark blood, back into my hole. For once, I'd been glad Ellie wasn't home. I was happy to look towards the house and see only the glow of the night-lights. The last sight I wanted my daughter to ever see was me hunched over a dead animal, blood smeared across my face and dripping from my hands. Better an animal than a human I had thought, which was why I had gone after the cow. Lesson learned. Animal blood was not the same.

Tonight, my thoughts were more of the same, like selected movie frames in a repeating loop. What I craved was one normal moment with my daughter, but the crater in the pit of my belly felt like a hot coal and a hollow emptiness at the same time. I tried to picture her, to think about what she'd be saying after a day of school and imagine her face as she talked excitedly about her friends in classes.

But closing my eyes only brought images of blood that flowed like waterfalls from opened carotid arteries in faceless people. And then just as quickly, my subconscious would blur those faces to that of my daughter, my eyes would startle open, and I'd ache on the inside in a way that I never thought possible. Vampires had exquisite moments it seemed—powerfully good ones and those that were as equally bad.

I wasn't completely alone, however. Asa hadn't changed his rhetoric from last night either. Except now, I could see him, and he was as beautiful as ever. Maybe even more beautiful to my lonely, hungry mind. He leaned back against one wall, his arms held stoically across his chest. The only difference from the Asa that haunted the last few days of my life was that this one smiled more.

"I'm losing my ever-loving mind," I said to him. Asa raised one eyebrow and nodded his head. "If I have to hallucinate, why does it have to be of you?" I asked.

"Because you need me," Asa said, pulling away from the cellar wall as he took a step in my direction. I studied his movements. They were smooth and natural. Not dream quality at all. "It is ironic that you killed me and now have no idea of how to survive. It seems you are the butt of your own joke."

"Whatever," I muttered, turning away from him and burying my face in the blankets again. "Surviving is easy. If I wanted to be like you, at least. I'd just start murdering my way through Arkansas. But I don't want to barely survive. I want to ..." I started to say but stopped, closing my mouth against my own crazy talk. The truth sounded sort of ridiculous to me. It would sound like utter nonsense to Asa. *And why do I care what he thinks,* I reminded myself. Further proof, I was worse off than I gave myself credit for. A glance over my shoulder confirmed that he wasn't standing where my hallucination had left him.

He'd walked right past his last known location and was knelt down beside my sleeping spot. "And you thought you would perform so greatly compared to me. Disappointed in yourself, Annalice?" he asked. "You judged the Children of Israel and find yourself as lost in the desert as they?"

His body felt real under my hand as I pushed past him towards the door. Outside the cellar, the sky was dark, the sky obscured by a drapery of thick grey clouds. A light rain was falling, just enough to dampen my skin and knock down the odor of the cow blood. I licked my lips for the moisture. They were so dry, but it made no difference, my lips remained just as dry. Parched from the inside.

The light from my house barely reached my skin as I stepped away from the cellar, but it was enough to make me homesick and add to my emptiness. I wanted blood, but I wanted human contact with my family just as much. I walked towards the house, reaching the fence that separated the yard from the field before I stopped. I was afraid to go any farther. The last thing I wanted for Mom to see was her daughter coming in like an animal from the field.

The bay windows of the kitchen faced the pasture, and behind the stained-glass figures of angels and butterflies, I could see two figures walking around the kitchen. One stopped and peered into the pasture, maybe to look for me. Maybe they were just nervous. I hoped it was my daughter craving my company. I strained to see who it was since my mom was a small woman, only a few inches taller than Ellie, but I couldn't tell who was who.

At first, it didn't seem strange to strain, very human and so normal to me, and then I realized that my vision wasn't as good as it had been, dulled by starvation like my resolve. And the less resolve I had, the more dangerous I became. It was time to eat. If I didn't, I knew the chances of hurting someone were going up night by night. Asa said I wouldn't care, but he was wrong. I was still human enough to care, and that's why I needed to do it tonight. Before I lost the ability to care.

"It is time to hunt," Asa whispered from beside me. He smiled, his lips parting to reveal fangs that a week ago had terrorized me. Tonight, the sight didn't produce a lick of fear. They were pure temptation. "Let us start with them," he said, inclining his head towards the house.

I started to spit out harsh words and threats but then reminded myself that there was no reason fighting with ghosts, or at least what I thought was a ghost.

"Are you real?" I asked him, starting to turn towards him. But then I changed my mind. "Forget it. Don't answer. I don't want to know." There wasn't an answer he could give me that would make me feel better. If he was alive, then I was screwed, but knowing I was hallucinating wasn't much solace either.

Sparing one more glance back at my house, I could see the two figures, grandmother and granddaughter, one at the stove and the other at the kitchen sink. Making lasagna I decided based on the smells coming from the house. Mom's secret recipe being handed from an older generation to the younger. I could hear Ellie laughing, enjoying this extra time with her grandmother. I wanted to be there with them as a family, but it was impossible, at least for now. I wished them a silent good night and turned towards the back of my pasture.

Chapter 8

ort Smith, Arkansas, lies along the banks of the Arkansas River on the western border of the state and within a stone's throw of the eastern border of Oklahoma. "Hell on the Border" they called the fort at one time. That had been when the hanging judge, the Honorable Isaac C. Parker, had presided and the fort squatted tenaciously on the border of Indian Territory and civility. It had been a rough and tumble town of hard men and even harder women.

In some ways, the town hadn't changed. "Hell on the Border" was still an applicable name on a few Saturday nights. Downtown Garrison housed a number of bars, as did Towson Avenue and Midland. The kind of places where remaining anonymous could be bought and sold. And so could anything else for that matter.

I'd worked in Fort Smith many nights as an emergency room physician, and I was familiar with every place in town from the swanky to the downright seedy. They'd each contributed, in their own way, to my job security over the years.

It was to one of the seedier bars that I went tonight. Fast, quiet and unseen, I weaved through the forest, nearly untraceable, I would imagine. What tracker in their right mind would look to the trees for clues? I crossed the mighty Arkansas River by way of the Van Buren railroad bridge around ten p.m. It was a half-hour after I left my house that I emerged out of the trees to walk across a poorly lit parking lot at the back of a motorcycle bar on the edge of town.

Housed in a long, squat building with windows so darkened it appeared closed a good part of the time, this bar was nearly out of sight and, to the cops, frequently out of mind. Or so they wished. It was a rough place, and I could hear several arguments going on inside. At least one of them would probably end with bloodshed.

The establishment had been temporarily shut down in the past due to the unusual amount of violence. Somehow, the club had always managed to get their license back, and we in the emergency room would shake our heads when the latest disturbance would end up strapped to one of our gurneys in the middle of the night. At one point, I'd gone to the city council along with a few other physicians to try to keep it closed. We'd lost. As it turns out, money *is* more important than public health. My guess is the owner was good at greasing palms. Tonight, I was hoping the place lived up to its reputation. Dark, seedy and out of the way were exactly what I was looking for.

Two heavily muscled and dangerous-looking bouncers guarded the door. The policy was pretty simple. The rougher you looked, the quicker they'd let you in. Show up in a dress suit and, like as not, the bouncers would carry you right back to the car, and probably not very gracefully. They'd turn your money down flat. It was better than paying your doctor bills. If you were going in there, you'd better be able to take care of yourself.

I knew I didn't look the part as I walked up to the door, but I didn't look good—at least not my usual clean-cut self. I hadn't changed clothes, and the bottom of my pants were stained with the cow blood and the mud from the forest. At least the dewy grass from the pasture had wiped the goo from my boots. I was wearing a short-sleeved V-neck T-shirt, which was odd for February, and no jacket. The skin of my arms glistened with the fine mist that had dropped from the overcast sky. My hair was a knotted mess, windswept and damp. Strands clung to the sides of my face and snaked across my neck and chest.

A pair of motorcycles had pulled into the parking lot as I walked up to the front door. I could hear the chatter from the women passengers as they climbed off from behind the two male drivers. Their speech was un-slurred; they'd make good witnesses so I hung back, letting the women and their dates make it to the entrance first. I needed to remain anonymous. Nondescript.

The smaller, but clearly more aggressive, of the two bouncers stepped forward when he saw me approaching. The muscles of his arms and chest flexed for show as he bowed up for my benefit. When I got closer, I flashed him the briefest of my "I'm going to eat you" gazes, just enough to convince him I could take care of myself but not enough to send him screaming inside. He started to protest, thought better of it, and finally shrugged his shoulders as if to say, "it's your funeral," and allowed me to pass.

Inside, smoke hung like a veil from ceiling to floor. It parted, resealing behind me as I pushed myself through the thin barrier. The place was packed, the room crowded with clusters of people gathered at the bar, which ran nearly the entire length of the far wall. Other groups, louder than those hanging around the bar, were gathered around the pool tables towards the south of the building. Between the bar and the pool tables was a dance floor. You couldn't have forced a hand between most of the dancers. The ceiling of the bar was dropped, adding to the secretive, guarded feel that made the bar known for its "anything-goes" reputation.

The combined scents of the sweaty bodies, smoke and alcohol made me dizzy, and I felt drunk on the heartbeats and the pheromones that floated in the smoky haze. My imagination ran wild, and my mood became more erratic. I could feel myself losing it. I paused and thought about leaving but decided I'd rather "lose it" here than back at my home. I stepped farther into the building determined to find a cure to my crazy.

Someone knocked into me as they passed, and I harshly pushed them back. Another drunk tried to slip an arm around my waist, flashing me a big smile as he did so. I smiled back, my teeth bared, eager for the human contact. Maybe my smile was too big or too desperate, either way he went absent into the crowd. I started to follow, but then got distracted by a girl standing a few feet away. She smiled invitingly, and I started towards her.

Asa had disappeared when I'd made the decision to come

here. I'd rushed through the forest alone—just me and the animals. But now he was back, and as I pushed myself through the pockets of people talking and playing pool, I caught glimpses of him on the other side of the building, and then unexpectedly, he appeared beside me, pointing to different humans that he thought would make good targets. He didn't say much, or maybe it was just the din of the crowd that overpowered the voice of his apparition. But he watched me; I could feel his eyes on me. I frowned at the woman and pushed farther through the crowd as I tried to outrun his following gaze, but it was impossible. Asa was a vampire; he could trail me anywhere. Maybe I'd been wrong about him. Maybe he was very much undead and alive. I decided I should get out of here. I started towards the door but then remembered again I couldn't go home without blood.

The music from the band on the small corner stage howled in my ears. The smell of blood hung in every corner, around every human that walked past me. I struggled to keep my hands to my sides, my fangs hidden. There were too many. Too much blood. I couldn't think, but I could hear Asa from across the room. "KIll them," he urged. "There's plenty to go around."

I was whispering to myself to ignore Asa. "He's not here," I kept repeating to myself, my index fingers burrowing into my ears to drown out the sound of his voice. Over my shoulder, I shot him another threatening glare when I stumbled into a man, knocking him off-step and into the bar behind him.

"You all right?" the man asked. He'd stopped his fall with one unsteady hand and pushed himself back upright.

I looked at him blankly. *Was it a rhetorical question?* I wondered. But he appeared serious.

"Hell, no. I'm not all right," I answered back. "Are you blind?"

"Nope. Just drunk. But sometimes if you get drunk enough, it slows everything down, and I can actually see more. And you, my dear, act like somebody's chasing you," he said, knocking the drink in his hand back. The empty glass disappeared from the bar behind him as quickly as he set it down.

"Somebody is," I answered. "I think."

"I'll protect you," he said. I looked at him doubtfully. Late thirties I guessed as I stared into what had been, at one time, a handsome face. Now it was aged by years of alcohol. Still, he smiled a friendly smile that brightened even more with handsome dimples. *I bet he was a heart breaker when he was younger. And healthier.*

Something about him didn't smell quite right, but I couldn't put my finger on it. It was like breathing in a beautiful aroma of bread and then detecting an aftertaste before you even tasted it. His bloodstream had to be nearly pure ethanol, and he was unsteady on his feet. He reached for my arm, and I let him keep his sweaty palm on my skin.

"What's a pretty thing like you doing here?" he asked, bringing my attention back to our conversation.

"I'm hungry." It was a simple statement, but it was true. The crowd was dense and kept him from sensing just how hungry I was. Or maybe it was the alcohol. Probably both, I decided. Over the man's shoulder, Asa was eyeing me from the back wall.

"The food stinks here, but the drinks are good," he said, lifting another glass in mock salute.

"You're not kidding. Everyone in here smells wonderful."

The man looked at me oddly. "Well, I guess the people here are okay, but I was talking about the drinks."

I nodded. "Yeah, I was too."

"Oh, I thought you were talking about the people smelling good."

Was this a riddle? I knew I should understand, but I couldn't quite wrap my head around it. "The people smell good. I want to drink them," I answered.

"Sweetheart, I believe you're as drunk as me," he said.

At that, I laughed a little, that crazy hysterical laugh that would frighten most people. He was unfazed.

"I have had absolutely nothing to drink. And I'm so thirsty," I added.

"Then you've came to the right place. Let me buy you something. What'll it be?"

"You," I said. He seemed an easy target. I ran one hand down his free arm. Gooseflesh, and not the bad kind, bunched up under my fingertips.

"Hey, whoa girl. I don't even have to pretend to get to know you? What does a pretty thing like you want with an old man like me anyway?" he asked.

"I don't care if you know me or not, and the only thing that matters is that you walk away from this deal still breathing."

"Come again?" he questioned as he took another swig of his glass.

Either he hadn't understood or he didn't care to. Maybe both. Maybe the liquor was making him brave. Whatever the reason, he didn't have the natural fear of me that Mom and the detective had.

Asa had materialized beside me. "Remember, I told you that crowds make it easier to blend in. Humans will not notice you as quickly, and the spirits he has consumed are beneficial as well. Even still, try to appear more relaxed. You seem every part the deranged killer."

Across the room where Asa had been standing was now just a small flock of people. I watched them briefly as they played with their phones and talked, no idea a killer was in their midst. But beside me, a woman was staring at me with narrowed eyes. I was starting to draw attention.

"I don't want to hurt him," I said to Asa. "Annalice, you are much too far gone for that to be your prime concern. At this point, he is undeniably a dead man. Just try not to get caught."

"Okay. Who are you talking to?" the drunk human asked, looking around to see if he'd missed a hidden boyfriend or a drinking buddy.

Asa smiled beside me. "Buy him another drink. Get him out of the building."

"No worries," I said, redirecting the human's attention back towards me. "I drink alone. He's just here to gloat."

"Who's here to gloat?" the man asked again. His expression was starting to turn concerned.

"I don't think he's real, but it's getting hard to tell."

"Well if it helps, I don't see anyone," the man answered

before he drained his glass. Holding his hand up, he signaled the barkeep for another.

"Bring two," I signed to the bartender. I'd been reduced to taking Asa's psychotic advice.

The bartender nodded at me as he pulled a young woman's cash off the bar. I smiled by way of thanks and turned back to the human I was stalking. "Then for now, I guess he's not real. All the better because you wouldn't have liked what he was saying about you," I answered.

"Whatever you say, babe." The man smiled pleasantly, warmed by the fires of whiskey.

Asa shifted his position beside me and leaned his long body up against the bar. He was as tall, dark and as handsome as I remembered. I rubbed my eyes. Maybe I hadn't killed him. Or maybe I'd staked him but he'd regenerated. Was that why his grave was empty? Asa nodded towards the door. "Ask him if he can see Detective Rumsfield over there?" I followed the direction of his inclined head to see the detective squeezing himself through a group of giggly girls in the doorway.

"Crap. How does he do that?" I hissed.

"Girl, what are you talking about now?" the man asked, putting the first drink I'd bought down.

"What's your name?" I pushed the second drink towards him.

He drank the whiskey quickly, not swallowing until he'd downed the entire double shot. I could see some fleeting thoughts cross his mind. Did he really want to give me his name? Something was definitely wrong with me. I smiled, took a deep breath to highlight my anatomy, and licked my lower lip in anticipation.

"Jonas," he answered in a quiet voice that was completely out of context to the spike in his heart rate and the quickening in his jeans. I had him. It didn't matter what I said next. My body had done all of the talking for me.

"Jonas, here's the deal. I'm a wanted girl. See that man over there wearing the leather jacket and blue jeans with the cowboy hat on?" I pointed to where Rumsfield watched me. He was *always* watching me.

Self-doubt crossed Jonas' face at the thought of competition, and he hesitated for half a breath before he turned away, leaning back against the counter, lifting his chin to scan the room. He was grinning at his good luck when he faced me again. "Girl, every man in here has on a leather jacket, but not a one of them is wearing a cowboy hat."

I looked over his shoulder at Rumsfield again. He was talking to a bouncer and pointing in my direction. "He's right there. Just like the devil in a country song," I said, pointing to the detective.

The human searched the room again to further convince me but shook his head with a definite no. I glanced back, and sure enough, Rumsfield was gone. Another hallucination, I guessed. Through the smoke that covered every person's head like a halo, I searched the entire building, looking for the telltale hat. But this time, I couldn't find him in the crowd. Maybe Rumsfield was here and maybe he wasn't. I couldn't be sure.

"He's a tricky son of a bitch," I said. "I honestly don't know if what I'm seeing is real or not."

"Somebody gave you some bad shit tonight," Jonas answered. He, of course, meant drugs.

"Bad shit is definitely one way to describe it." I smiled back at him. "What I need is fresh air, and for the two of us to be alone. I think you're going to be able to clear my head."

"I'll clear whatever you want me to, babe. Bad memories, bad shit. The sheets off a bed. It doesn't matter," he said.

I lifted the shot glass from his hand, tossed a twenty on the counter, and pulled him towards the front door. He put up no resistance at all. My luck was looking up. Leaned against the bar, Asa smiled at me, baring his fangs as he did so. I pulled the human a little faster.

"So what are you wanted for, or is that all part of the drug haze paranoia?" Jonas asked as we squeezed through the crowd. The bar had picked up, and the bouncers were having a hard time keeping an eye on the people coming in and going out. New customers were sneaking in under the guise of having just come out to get fresh air. Two men blocked our way as I was trying to guide Jonas out the door.

A couple of "excuse me"s didn't extradite them, so I shoved them roughly out of the way. They both turned, hot angry words on their lips as their drinks spilt in their hands, but one look at my desperate eyes and clenched teeth made them retreat wordlessly back into the crowd.

"Hey," Jonas said again. "What are you wanted for?" The first bit of fear had crept into his voice. Frowning at the way I'd pushed the men, he watched them walk away as he lagged back a bit.

"Nothing serious," I answered, jerking him slightly to catch back up with me. "Minor possession."

"Been there," he answered as we walked out the door and down the steps, placated once more into believing that I was simply a small-time drug user.

Outside the bar, the parking lot was a maze of cars and bikes attempting to either pull in and join the melee or escape it. I, for one, was very glad to be escaping it without having killed someone in plain sight. Several small fights had broken out while I'd worked to secure Jonas. Nothing major, but enough to bring the heaviest of the bouncers through the room in a show of strength. He'd easily subdued a couple of rowdy drunks fighting over a woman who'd been toying with the both of them the way a cat bats at a ball of string. I'd seen the bouncer circle his pointer finger over his head in the sign language meaning "call the police 'cause somebody's about to get their butt kicked." Two pool tables over, a woman had swung at a man, and he, in the process of trying to be nice, had taken his very own ass whooping. And some people say bikers can't be gentlemen.

The cops were parking as I pulled Jonas farther into the parking lot, zig-zagging him between cars. "You lost your car?" he asked. "What's it look like?"

"I didn't drive," I said, still pulling him forward.

"You walked here?" He was shocked, since the bar was on the outskirts of town. The nearest residential area was a good ten blocks away.

"A friend dropped me off," I lied smoothly. "Let's go down by the river." I was careful to keep my back to him. No reason to terrify him so early in our game.

"Why?" he questioned but still not getting overly suspicious.

"Don't you like it by the water? Think about it. The river and the fog. The misting rain on our skin."

"The bugs. The snakes. The snapping turtles," he answered back.

"Don't worry. I'll protect you," I whispered. I stroked the inside of his wrist with the hand I wasn't using to pull him farther towards the back of the parking lot.

"You're a freak," he said, but he kept following. "But I like 'em that way."

I couldn't keep from laughing. "Well, it's your lucky day."

The Arkansas River snaked through the darkness on its constant mission to meet up with the Mississippi. There, at that juncture deep in the Delta, the river was fat and lazy. But here, as it poured between the mountains, the river was cantankerous and dangerous, with hidden currents and undertows that took many swimmers to their death.

Despite its dangers, the Arkansas was no more lovely than in the dark hours of night when the gray-black eddies were silvered by the moonlight as the river coursed along rich bottom land to slice through inky Arkansas forests. My ex-husband and I had spent a few nights peering nervously into those forests when we'd first moved here. We'd tried to take up the night fishing that is so popular. We'd failed miserably, and while I'd never understood why anyone would want to fish at three a.m., I'd easily appreciated the natural beauty of the river.

Tonight, the lights of Fort Smith glittered on the turbulent waters. At the other end of the railway bridge, the Van Buren lights looked so much homier. Maybe because that's the way I planned to escape when this was all over. After I'd showered this human with my very powerful saliva and had my way with him—my way being to drain him of a couple of pints.

He was still holding onto my hand as we reached the rocky shore of the river, and as he tried to stop, I pulled him a little farther until we were standing on the wide portion of a sand bar jutting into the water like the broad end of a hatchet.

I could feel his nerves starting to build up as I turned to face him. He looked back towards the bar and lights from the club. Asa was right. The alcohol had numbed his senses, and he still didn't recognize me for what I was. This fear he was feeling was no more than a human fear, afraid of the dark and being out of his element. Not able to see well in the night and unaccustomed to the silence of being alone.

"We're not far at all," I answered his fears, wanting to reassure him. "I can still hear the music. The band's playing Skynard." Not a lie, but I certainly didn't add that it was vampire hearing that gave me such an edge.

"I can't hear anything," the human said, glancing nervously back at the bar once more. He'd told me his name, but I couldn't remember it.

"I can hear the sound of your heart," I said. The words slipped out before I even realized my mouth had opened, and I couldn't hide my lust for him. It crept up like a riptide and pulled me under. I stepped closer, my hand sliding farther up his arm. His muscles stiffed and his skin turned cold and pimply.

My words got his attention. They were more effective than a cup of hot coffee or flashing blue lights in bringing him to a semblance of sobriety. His eyes widened as I leaned into him and inhaled deeply. Our eyes met fully for the first time that night, and I watched as the irrational fear of my presence finally eclipsed the alcohol and his logic.

In the mere span of two seconds, his heart was off and racing—irregular and much too fast. Atrial fibrillation. I'd treated it a thousand times but had never appreciated how odd it truly sounded. He was taching at nearly one hundred eighty beats per minute. The man's expression became nothing more than a mask except a funny named muscle, the orbicularis oculi, twitching in the corner of his right eye. I studied the muscle closely and listened to his heart.

I could smell the sharp scent of fear and adrenaline, and the combination of the two set my lungs ablaze. His fear smelled the way it should, but it was heavily tinged with something that I knew I should recognize yet I couldn't name. I was too hungry, and I didn't care that he didn't smell exactly right. But my brain kept whispering to me to think harder. I batted the ideas away. I didn't want to think. I wanted to drink and to kill, and this man was going to have to suffice. Still, I hoped he wouldn't die. I hoped I was strong enough.

To my right, Asa materialized. He was smiling a very gloating smile, pointing out that I was such a fraud. "Are you not a physician, Annalice? Should I not call you 'Dr. Creed'?"

"Why are you still here? Haven't you gloated enough?" I hissed.

Asa just shrugged. "Think, Annalice. Look at him. I do not think your patient is doing well. Is not the heart rhythm strange for one so young?"

"You're not a doctor, Asa," I said. "How would you know?"

"My name is Jonas," the man managed to say while I was talking to Asa. I turned back towards the human and snarled. The sound shut him up pretty quick; his breath was going in and out in short wheezes.

"Think, Annalice." But this wasn't Asa's voice. Detective Rumsfeld stood to my right now. "Something's not right with this picture. A man this young shouldn't have atrial fibrillation. Taking any amount of blood is going to kill him."

I looked back at Jonas, frozen like the proverbial deer in my headlights. He was only in his thirties. His blood should be fresh but there was something about his scent that reminded me of cleaning supplies. It wasn't enough to keep me from doing what I was about to do, but it was enough to tell me that nothing about this evening was going to go well. He'd leave me wanting for more. The logic of my hallucinations was undeniable. He was too young to be going into this irregular heart rhythm from fear, and the sucking sound in his heart was no coincidence.

"Strange," I said back to Rumsfield and Asa. But my mind wasn't really on my former dead vampire lover, the detective, or what they were trying to tell me. I was concentrating on the damaged sound of Jonas' heart. Unfortunately, I wasn't listening in a doctorly sort of way.

Jonas' eyes were still riveted on me when his legs started to go out from under him. His brain hadn't even registered the movement when I reached out, my reflexes like the sharp jabs of summer lightning, to catch him. He started to open his mouth, but before he could utter a syllable, I opened an artery in his neck.

I hadn't meant for it to happen this way. When I imagined how this was going to go down, I'd soothed and calmed him with my lips, filled his veins with my powerful saliva until he had, in some fit of passion, given me his blood willingly. Then while he lay drunk from my pheromones, I slipped off unknowingly across the river after laying him gently where others of his kind would find and care for him.

What actually happened was that I crushed him against me, my fangs buried in his neck. As I did so, his brain and reasoning power finally kicked in. His fists flailed against every part of me that he could reach as I drank from him, but my jaws were a vice against his neck. His legs went rigid but soon gave way until all the joints in his body went lax and it was only my strength that held him upright. His neck lolled to the side; his hands went limp, slipping from the side of my face, and dropped to his side.

At some point, his heart thudded itself silent; I only noticed the organ's failure because it stopped pumping his blood into my mouth. I pulled my lips away from his neck when the flow stopped, jerking his face around to look into his now cold eyes. I should have been sorry, but at first, I was so angry that I shoved his body away. His limp form flew backwards, arms askew, before pirouetting like a bizarre, overdressed scarecrow, and dropped, dead weight, onto the damp riverbank. The left side of his face sank into the mud, cold river water creeping into the depression where he landed and lapping at the dark hair curled against his forehead. One white hand landed across the toe of my left boot.

I stared at the white of his dead skin mutely before jerking my foot back and stepping away from the body in the sand. I'd thrust him aside so quickly that bloody saliva was stringing from my lips. I wiped it away as my brain processed what I'd done and what I should now do. My first instinct was to call 9-1-1. It was short-lived, and then my second instinct was to dive into the river. I could be gone and already dried off from the swim before anyone noticed this man was missing. I turned to jump into the current when I remembered the security cameras in the building.

The owners had them placed a year earlier as a concession to the police, and they were everywhere. How many of them had caught sight of me luring Jonas out of the building, across the parking lot and out of sight? I could hardly leave him to be found by some passerby or early morning fisherman. Burying him would only open a missing person case that would lead straight back to me. Such behavior would do nothing but add fuel to Rumsfield's flames. I had no choice but to report his death. Still, I couldn't let anyone examine the body in such a state.

Most people think of death as a sudden, abrupt occurrence. You have a heart attack, and you're dead. Take a blow to the head, and you're dead. We all, doctors included, tend to mark the end of life as the cessation of a heartbeat. Time of death 3:12 a.m., Jonas' death certificate might read. But in reality, death is a process that starts when the heart stops, but there is so much more that has to die as well. Otherwise, how would we take an organ such as a kidney, unattached from its blood supply, fly it four hours across the state and re-attach it to another human? How could we do CPR and bring someone back twenty minutes after their heart has stopped if death wasn't a process?

It's very simple really. Cells remain active after the heart stops for some period of time, and it is during this nebulous period of time that humans sometimes work the impossible—heart transplantation, successful code blues, resuscitation after hours submerged in a cold lake, life from death, re-animation, whatever you want to call it.

This principle was foremost in my mind when I bent down and rubbed my spit into the wound on Jonas' neck. Some of the cells were still alive, and I used their final minutes to heal the small wounds that I'd created. Then I took a deep breath for good measure and did what any good doctor would do.

I leaned over and gave him two rescue breaths. Then I started screaming to beat the band while I began chest compressions. I gave him two more breaths and began the process all over again.

Finally, after getting the attention of someone who'd left the bar to smoke, and through a series of yells and hand signals, 9-1-1 was notified.

By the time the ambulance arrived, a crowd had grown around Jonas' body, and I appeared the very convincing innocent bystander caught in the wrong place at the wrong time. One woman had given me a handful of wadded up tissue paper to blow my nose into, and another was rubbing me on the back from the presumed exertion of providing CPR. A man who'd wandered down from the bar had handed me a beer. I pretended to drink it.

Chapter 9

"How is it, Annalice, that whenever you and I run into each other, someone has died? And always in your proximity."

Rumsfield was standing to my left, and the sheriff from Sebastian County, Sheriff Taylor, stood to my right. I'd met Taylor while working in the Fort Smith emergency room a few years back, and I'd liked him instantly. With Rumsfield standing beside me, I liked the sheriff even more.

John Taylor was on the right side of middle-aged. Still handsome, he worked out at the local fitness center several times a week. Somehow, against all the cliché donuts and fast-food joints prolific in cop careers, he'd managed to maintain the physique of a twenty-year-old. He was also nice, which never hurt any man's looks.

The three of us were staring down at Jonas' body. Me, with my hands on my knees, bent over deep in thought about how to explain my presence here while Rumsfield was racking his brain over how I'd managed to kill this man. Meanwhile, Sheriff Taylor was trying to figure *why* he was standing here on the dark banks of the Arkansas River with a local doctor and a detective from another county looking at what he clearly thought was the leftover corpse of too much alcohol. I, for one, loved him for not looking outside the box on this case.

"He was the town drunk, Mike," Taylor said beside me. He'd lifted his hands from his knees to stand upright. Done with the case and ready to write up the cause of death while he waited for the medical examiner to agree with him, Taylor looked over me at Rumsfield. Obviously, they knew each other. He called him "Mike." The shortened name just didn't sit right with my interpretation of Rumsfield because I couldn't imagine him in a friendly kind of way.

"So that rules out foul play? Him being the town drunk and all?" Rumsfield asked, still bent over studying the corpse.

"Look, Mike. I've personally picked this guy up more times than you can count the feathers on a turkey for public intox, bad debt, and misdemeanors. You name it, and I've brought him in for it. He's spent half his time in the hospital and the other half in a beer can. This is death by natural causes. Pure and simple."

Rumsfield, standing to his full height, motioned behind him. "John, can we talk a minute?" he asked the sheriff, pointing to a small grove of bushes behind us. The riverbank was too sandy to grow much here where the body lay, but a few feet back, everything was coming up green. I walked a few steps down the riverbank as Rumsfield and Taylor stepped away, pretending to ignore them as Rumsfield shot suspicious eyes in my direction. But vampire hearing has its perks, and I wasn't going to miss a word.

"Listen, I think you should put a little more thought into this case," Rumsfield said. "I've got a bad feeling."

"A bad feeling? You've no right to have a feeling at all. You're not supposed to even *be* here," Taylor answered. He looked at Rumsfield, his arms crossed on his chest. His jaw was shifted to one side, his tongue poking furiously into his cheek as he studied Rumsfield.

Rumsfield dug his cowboy boots into the sand as he pointed to the body. "So you don't find it a bit strange that this woman, who has been associated with two murders, just happens to be standing over his dead body?"

The detective wasn't wearing his cowboy hat tonight, and his blonde hair danced lightly in the wind while the warm vanilla of his aftershave wrapped his entire body in a scent that made me want to snuggle up against him. More like woller actually. That's a southern word that means get right on up in there and make yourself at home on somebody. Why did he have to smell so good?

"If you're trying to tell me that Dr. Creed snuck out here on this riverbank and killed this man, then I'm telling you that the only thing strange around here is you. And this is the first I've heard that she's been associated with any murders," Taylor said. The sheriff was starting to get angry. I could smell it on him like the lingering scent of a Roman candle.

Rumsfield was no idiot. He might not smell the anger, but he could feel it. "John, this is your territory, and I know that, but just think about this. A man was found in Madison County, a mile or so behind her house, dead. Her next-door neighbor, an elderly woman, was also found murdered in her home."

"I've heard all about the first case. A clear and simple bear attack, and in the second case, the suspect is a man."

"That's right. A man that she knew and yet she won't shed a light on about his whereabouts."

"And you can prove she knew him?" Taylor asked. His forehead was wrinkled with skepticism.

"Annalice Creed was seen with a man who roughed her up a little," Rumsfield said. "We have a reliable witness to that. Then her neighbor dies. Fits a certain picture, doesn't it? That this is the type of man who could have perpetrated the attack on an elderly lady?"

"And you have *reliable* evidence to say it's the same man?" Taylor asked like it was the cliffhanger in a comic book. He didn't get an answer, just a roll of Rumsfield's eyes.

"I have evidence, Taylor," Rumsfield finally answered.

"And?" Sheriff Taylor asked again, but no answer came. He waited the time it took Rumsfield to huff his breath out and shake his head. "Then you have nothing," Taylor continued.

But Rumsfield couldn't leave it alone. "*If* he's even still alive. I think she killed him, too," Rumsfield said. To anyone else, he probably sounded confident, but to me it came off as self-righteous indignation.

Taylor took a step closer at his words and dropped his voice. "Mike, I think you need to simmer down. Those are serious accusations. You can't just throw those kind around without something to back them up. I've known Dr. Creed a long time. She's a fine doctor and a fine lady. She's not a murderer."

"Taylor, you've known me a long time, too. I'll wager even longer than her. Have you ever known me to throw around false accusations?"

The space between the two of them festered for a long minute, and it was a relief when Taylor's cellphone rang. He pulled it smoothly out of his pocket and answered it. His eyes were still on Rumsfield when he turned and walked away.

With no one to protect me from Rumsfield's mouth, I watched him warily. He ran a hand through his sandy blonde hair. Locks of curls lifted and settled in the wind as he stalked towards me. "So, Annie, how'd you do this one exactly?" he asked. Maybe he was taking a class on diplomacy because his voice had dropped into the low rumblings that proceed spring storms—the kind that makes you eager for the rain.

With his blue eyes, rugged features and a body that made a girl gasp out loud, Detective Rumsfield was a dangerous man. I was going to have to be careful, but he should be more careful, too. His presence tended to bring out the worst in me, and these days, that was a bad thing.

"I didn't do 'this one,' Detective." I made quotations in the air. The angrier I got, the more I talked with my hands.

"But you *were* with him, Annie, when he died."

"Well, most people have someone with them when they die, and no one accuses them of murder."

"Not quite the same thing, and you know it. The bartender said you two were getting pretty cozy." He motioned towards Jonas' body on the ground. "Wanna tell me why you're slumming it with an alcoholic? This man doesn't strike me as your type. I pictured you with someone more... I don't know, debonair maybe."

I gave him a "come hither" wink. "Why have you been picturing me at all, Rumsfield?" I let his cheeks flame for a split second before I continued. "But I gotta say, it's flattering. You do that mainly at night when you're alone in your bed?"

His cheeks bloomed into a deep red as he cursed slightly under his breath. "That's not what I meant," he answered.

"Ahh, that's too bad. But as I've said before, Detective, you don't know me. You certainly don't know me well enough to keep calling me 'Annie.'"

"Then let's change that, Dr. Creed. You call me 'Mike' and I'll call you 'Annie.' Easy. Now we know each other." He knelt back down by Jonas' body and retrieved his camera.

Great. He'd unleashed the low thunder voice again. It rumbled all the way to the tips of my toes.

"So we're friends now, *Mike*?"

"Friends," he said. I swear his voice dropped another half an octave. His blue eyes danced a little from underneath a stray lock of blonde hair as he cut his eyes up at me.

I laughed out loud, but I couldn't stop myself from enjoying his flirting. "Is that how you catch the bad guys, Mike? Do you look at all of them like that?"

"Friends, Annalice, are not so suspicious of each other."

"Sorry, I forgot. Here's the deal, *friend.* I came here tonight to let my hair down a little. Relax a bit. Jonas is a former patient of mine. We met up by happenstance, and I was talking to him, trying to provide some direction."

"And you directed him right on into the afterlife."

"Now, Michael, my good friend, how do you propose I did that?"

"Guess we'll just have to wait for the medical examiner. And when I get the cause of death, I'll be the first to tell you about it while I'm serving the arrest warrant."

"So much for the friendship." I narrowed my eyes at him but kept a sarcastic smile plastered on my face.

"You know what they say. Friends who do time together stay together. Only difference is which side of the bars we'll be on."

"Let me tell you what the M.E.'s going to say. That way the 'not knowing' won't keep you up at night. I know he's backlogged and all because I talked to him about a month back at a medical conference in Little Rock. First, he's going to say that Jonas was suffering from cirrhosis, a dense fibrosis of the liver caused by long-term alcohol use. Then he's going to say he was suffering from congestive heart failure due to the direct effects of alcohol on the heart musculature. Also, he was anemic due to the cirrhosis and the bleeding gastric varices he had, once again, due to the cirrhosis. And when you combine that with the congestive heart failure, his heart simply could not take it. He then had an acute myocardial infarction, a.k.a., a heart attack. And that, Michael, is your cause of death."

I was ninety percent sure that was what the good doc was going to say because the theory was the most logical and obvious conclusion. I'd had time to put all the clues together now that my blood lust wasn't driving me to near insanity. I was still thirsty. Jonas' blood hadn't packed much punch, but it had put up a thin wall that would keep the beast at bay for a while. I hadn't had any hallucinations in the two hours since Jonas had died, so I hadn't seen hide nor hair of Asa. For the moment, I was rational. Calm.

The cleaning supplies scent I'd smelled on Jonas was the ammonia produced by his liver failure. He was already dangerously anemic, and that was why the adrenaline produced by fear caused him to develop the irregular heart rhythm. My only little white lie in the whole scenario was that I'd drunk what little bit of blood he did have left, thereby pushing him into a heart attack. Jonas had been a ticking time bomb, but I lit the fuse.

I should have been wracked by guilt, writhing with it actually. But all I could think about was how the sun would be coming up in a few hours, and I couldn't still be here dickering with the detective when it did so. There would be time for guilt later. That sneaky emotion always caught up with me.

"How convenient for you that he was an alcoholic. But the medical examiner is getting his mental workout this week. Lots of *odd* cases. Maybe he's going to be thinking outside his normal comfort zone?" His voice raised on his last words, his shoulders helping to push them even further up.

"Okay. I'll bite." My eyes went wide at my verbal mistake. I didn't mean to say it. It just slipped out. I pretended to wipe a lash away and continued on. "Tell me about these cases. I'm sure you think I'm involved somehow."

"How dare I make a supposition about the innocent, the sublime Dr. Creed?"

"Innocent, yes. Sublime, probably not. Just think of it as a sideline medical consult. Free of charge," I said.

He blew out his breath slowly, pulled a hand through his hair, and finally pinched his forehead between two fingers before he decided to talk. By his body language, you'd think talking to me made him a Benedict Arnold. "It's classified, but why not enlist the aid of a thief to catch one. So here goes. There's been a couple other cases in the last two weeks. One, a twenty-year-old frat boy at Arkansas State was found dead on the edge of campus. He'd just left his job at a local pull-through hamburger place. Death was from massive breakdown of blood or loss of blood. The medical examiner said he probably had bone marrow failure. He also said he could have a gastrointestinal bleed and been bleeding for days. Either way, the death was ruled natural causes. But then In the peaceful town of Brasshears, about eight days back, a farmer was found dead out by his henhouse. Time of death was estimated to be at two a.m. the morning before he was found. He lived alone, so why he was out at his henhouse in the middle of the night, God only knows. Brasshears is in my district, so I worked the scene myself. The body had multiple scratches, lacerations and multiple bruises. Looked like he'd gotten in a fight with a cat. I found a couple of dead chickens scattered around, but otherwise nothing out of the ordinary. Any guesses on the cause of death?"

He didn't wait for me to come up with a guess. "Anemia, disseminated intravascular hemorrhage vs. gastrointestinal hemorrhage. The same thing all over again," he spit out.

"Those are pretty common causes of death, Mike. Anemia just means they're low on red cells. So any type of bleeding, traumatic or internal, can make you anemic. Let alone the thousands of medical conditions that can cause anemia. Then you can throw in all of the viruses that can shut down your bone marrow. Anemia is a very generic term." *Did I just call him "Mike"?*

"And what about all of the scratches and bruises? Men who die of anemia don't usually get in a fight with someone, do they, Annalice?"

"Maybe his cat got him after he fell over dead. Or maybe he did have bone marrow failure, so he didn't have any platelets to stop the bleeding, and he bruised all the time. Or maybe a raccoon lit into him after he died. I had a patient once whose dog chewed their toe off after he died, but I didn't think we had a mad-dog killer on the loose. I could go on and on with the what-ifs in this kind of case, Mike. Do you really think the medical examiner is going to find something strange about this? Is that what you're looking for?"

I was hoping he'd see reason, and not just for my sake. Mike and I weren't friends, and I wasn't going to pretend we were, but I didn't want him to ruin his career. He was probably the only detective able to see any of these cases clearly for what they were, but I hoped he was able to realize how crazy this made him look before everyone else did or before he realized just how messed up I really was.

"Don't you think it's odd there have been so many deaths from anemia in such a short time span?" Rumsfield was exasperated. His voice sounded a little frantic.

Of course. Yes. Because there was a mad vampire lose in the area. And now there's another. Asa must have killed the Jonesboro kid before he met up with me, and the older man was part of the reason he'd managed to keep me alive. Another casualty for my benefit. I'd tasted his blood on Asa's lips one night, and I'd liked it.

"No," I lied smoothly. "I don't find it odd at all. Almost everyone in the hospital is anemic." At least that part was true. *It's just normally not fatal.* "I still don't understand what any of this has to do with me. ASU is in Jonesboro. I've never even been there. Brasshears is close enough to my house, but why in the world do you think I had anything to do with that? There's nothing at all to tie me to that man's death."

"You seem to have something to do with everything bizarre in my county these days," he answered.

86

"I didn't have *anything* to do with either of those two cases."

"Fine. What about this man tonight?" he asked, pointing to where Jonas' body lay on the ground.

I'd almost forgotten about him. The body hadn't been moved yet, and the dew of early morning was beginning to settle on his face. The light slick of liquid gave his skin the allusion of dewy youth. The effect was kind. His features didn't seem quite as flat and made it look like maybe the human was only sleeping, but it didn't soften my guilty conscience. I wished the deputies who were milling in the background would bag him up and carry the body away. No one wants to look at their sins any longer than they have to.

"I didn't kill him," I reiterated. *I wasn't lying*, I told myself. His heart had killed him.

"What *did* you do to him?" Detective Rumsfield was punching keys on his phone. He didn't look at me for the moment as he asked the question. If I didn't know better, I'd have said he was distracted.

"What do you *think* I did to him?"

There was silence from him as he fingered his phone screen again. For a man with man's hands, he was a quick texter. Who was he texting anyhow? Secretly, I was hoping for some other homicide to get his mind off of me. What a pathetic excuse for a person I'd become.

"What do you *think* I did to him, Detective?" I asked again, trying to bring him back to me. Knowing what he was thinking was still better than the not knowing. Maybe I could stay ahead of him that way.

"Hmmm?" he asked, still not looking at me.

"Forgetful much?" I asked, throwing my hands up into the air. Patience had once been one of my minor virtues. These days, it didn't even register on my personality scale.

He'd snagged his lower lip between his teeth and was making a light meal of it while he studied his phone intently. His texting hand had risen up to rub the back of his head. Rumsfield took a deep breath and shook his head. I watched the rise and fall of his chest under the chest-contouring T-shirt he wore. It was skin-tight under his leather jacket. He swallowed hard. So did I. As much as he annoyed me, he was easy on the eyes.

"I'm losing my fricking mind," he said under his breath. A human couldn't have made out the words.

Was he figuring me out?

"What are you losing?" I asked, hoping for once he'd continue to speak.

His eyes were wide, a little incredulous, when he looked up at me. A little scared even. "Um. Nothing. I've got to go. Something's come up."

Sheriff Taylor was walking back up to where the two of us still stood over Jonas' body. Behind him were a couple of paramedics and a woman I'd met before. She was the county coroner.

"John, I'm heading out. Something just came up in Crawford. Sorry I stepped on your toes, man."

"Nothing to apologize for. What's going on in Crawford? Anything big?" Taylor asked.

Rumsfield smiled as he waved a good-bye to the other officers. "Just more of the bizarre and unusual that has overtaken my life. See y'all around."

Nervous as a cat, I watched him all the way back to his police cruiser. But for once, he didn't give me a backwards glance.

The next hour was an uncomfortable one where I attempted to make small talk with the county coroner, who was a nice but predictably weird lady. I didn't want to rush off and make myself look suspicious in any way, so I fielded some questions from the coroner as well as from one of the deputies and Sheriff Taylor. Finally, I was all smiles with the bar owner as I told him how sorry I was about Jonas. He'd been a great guy, I'd lied.

The county coroner unit was loading up the body when I made my good-byes to Sheriff Taylor and walked towards the parking lot as though I had a car stationed there. No one had asked yet what I was driving. I hoped they wouldn't think to before I was gone and out of sight.

The parking lot was practically empty except for four dark police cars and three other civilian vehicles as I pretended to quickly walk across the black pavement. Inside, I was cringing at my slow progress. I did thank the gods for that morbid human curiosity that kept all the humans at the back of the building with the body, and I slipped out of the parking lot unobserved into the flood plains that grew corn in during dry years and mosquitos in the wet ones.

Only a handful of minutes passed before I picked my way through the shadows of a few abandoned houses and empty lots on my way to the river bridge. Finally, with an almost human sigh of relief, I grasped the slimy pylons of the train bridge crossing from Fort Smith into Van Buren.

The trains this time of night were few and far between. Still, I crossed the bridge quicker than the river water surging beneath me, careful to stay hidden in the crevices of the massive structure.

The entirety of my evening had been spent on finding blood, and I knew it had been necessary. Still, one look at my daughter's face would have been a sight for sore eyes. I craved that as much as blood.

I planned to take a shower at my house, change clothes and then to steal a kiss from Ellie's forehead before dawn took my remaining time away. But fate had other plans, and as I prepared to climb the steps of our back deck, I could see the silhouette of my mother stalking the living room floor.

After a long debate with myself, I went straight to the root cellar. I finally decided delaying the oncoming fight was probably better than having to run from the house in a frenzy to avoid the sun in the midst of the heated discussion I knew was coming.

Chapter 10

*T*he evening was quiet. Unusual for early spring when the call of the bullfrogs ushers in spring and the whistling breezes blow down from the mountains. The coyotes hadn't begun their evening songs, which can be so eerie as to bring you awake, eyes wide open and darting around in the dead of night if you aren't used to the lonely sound. Even the doves that usually wooed each other from deep within the forest were quiet tonight. Not a human sound littered the air as I stepped out of my hiding place in the root cellar, and I appreciated the beauty of the silence—a golden thing really, considering the strength of my hearing.

I couldn't hear any cars on the dirt road. Even the main highway was empty. No hunters searched the forest. No dogs barked for miles. The quiet added to the calm I had gained from the blood the night before, and for a few seconds, I felt like things were looking up. I studied my house, realizing how picturesque it really was from this angle, and I admitted that it had been a poor choice, but from this view, I might have bought it all over again. It was peaceful, tranquil.

Too peaceful, I realized. The washing machine, dryer, and dishwasher were off. Nobody flushed a commode. No water ran from the faucets. I couldn't make out a single alarm from a DSI or iPad. Even Ellie's normally pesky cellphone was quiet. But it was more than that. The gentle purr of electricity was absent. The normal sounds of a working household were gone. No normal sound of a heating system. The refrigerator had lost its hum. The house was no longer lived in. A house with no family is a lonely place. Just an empty shell.

Ellie was gone. I knew it before I swung open the kitchen door, desperately searching the room for my daughter and mother. I flew down the hallway, hoping to find something and yet terrified to do so. My imagination ran away with itself. Immediately, I thought of Rumsfield and blamed him. Perhaps he'd taken them. Or maybe it was Asa back from the dead. Maybe I'd been too confused to realize that he was real. It could be a simple intruder. Or Mom had finally had enough and left. That thought crossed my mind, but I refused to acknowledge the possibility. Cautiously, I stood still, listening for human or vampire sounds, but other than the constant creaks and moans of an old house and the tree branches scraping the roof, there was silence.

There had to be another explanation. They wouldn't just disappear, and as I rounded the doorway of Ellie's room, I dropped into a crouched position, half expecting and definitely craving a fight. But the room was empty, the light off, and her bed made. Nothing threatened me, and I couldn't find the scent of an intruder. The only scents I caught were those of my mother, Ellie and I. From a single look, she might have been at school. But to me, someone who knew Ellie like the back of my hand, it was a room emptied out. Too neat and very sterile. Not the room of a little girl who excelled in feminine clutter.

Asa appeared behind me. The blood from the evening before was already wearing off, and he was back. "I finished her. Did you really think you could protect her from me?" he asked.

I batted at his imaginary figure with one hand while I rushed to her closet. The door was shut. Momentarily, I argued with myself as to whether I should open it or not. Finally, I wrenched the door open, half expecting to find my missing family, more victims of Asa.

Instead, the shelves were cleaned out. Most of her favorite jeans and dresses were gone, along with her best boots and tennis shoes. Two old family quilts had been taken from the top shelf. Behind me, her dollhouse was missing, as well as her favorite stuffed bear—the one nearly as tall as her. I'd won it last year at the Washington County Fair.

Refusing to accept the most obvious explanation, the one that was slapping me in the face repeatedly, I cursed Rumsfield, blaming him for the disappearance of my family. I raced to the dresser in the corner of the room, jerking the drawers out two at a time. Empty. Cleaned out. "Damn you, Rumsfield!" I screamed.

"And you thought your mommy would understand," Asa laughed behind me. "You know the detective is not the guilty party. Your mother took your precious daughter and abandoned you."

"She wouldn't do that. She does understand!" I continued to scream, slicing at his laughing face with an empty dresser drawer. He dissolved as my momentum threw me to the floor, the drawer flying from my hand and disappearing out the window. I heard the split-second indecision of the glass before it gave way and burst, shards of glass flying in all directions. Some flew outwards, some backwards, burying themselves into my skin. Small drops of blood beaded across my face and arms but I paid them no attention. One more burst of anger caused me to pull the bureau over, but the resounding boom of it hitting the floor gave me no satisfaction.

Asa was right, and I knew it before I read the note on the counter. The flat sheet of paper appeared stark white against the granite counter. I approached the note cautiously, dreading to read the words she'd written.

"Annie, I have taken Ellie into town. I've rented an apartment so that she can finish out the school year here. There's been too much trauma to move her now, so we will stay here until the end of the semester. I know you loved her. She was your life. If there's any part of you that is still my daughter and still her mother, please try to understand that this is in Ellie's best interest. Please don't do anything rash."

The tile floor of the kitchen was no cooler than my skin as I

92

slumped down beside the kitchen island. The note was still drifting in the breeze blowing in from the forgotten open kitchen door as Asa slid down beside me, his back resting against the wood. "Do you not wish I had simply killed you outright?" he asked.

Chapter 11

The trip to town was windy and wet, but I didn't feel the rain or the wind as I slung my body between the trees. There was only one apartment complex in the small town where Ellie went to school, and I aimed myself straight for it. It never even crossed my mind to take the car. I realized how inhuman and alien it appeared as I stepped out of the tree line that ran in a horizontal line behind the apartment complex. Three sides of the two-floor complex faced small city roads, but behind it was an open field, the fence of which had collapsed not long after the farmer who'd sold the field had cashed the check.

Mom hadn't left me the unit number, not that they'd be hard to find. I could have simply sniffed at each door until I found Ellie. Of course, that would look really strange, but I didn't have to resort to that. I could see her stained-glass sun catcher hanging behind her curtains—a gift from her father the previous Christmas. She was in unit sixteen, a ground-floor unit. Unfortunately, she was flanked on both sides by other tenants.

I tried to calm myself down as I crossed the field into the parking lot. Would it look more bizarre to see a blur coming across the empty field or what appeared to be a person walking in from the woods? Definitely a blur I decided, so I forced myself into a fast but even-paced step. If anyone asked why I was on foot, I'd tell them my car broke down.

It was February; the rains had still not let up and a fine mist had fallen while I was in the forest. I ran my hands through my windblown, damp hair as I crossed the field. I smoothed my clothes down and tried to knock some of the mud off of my shoes. Normal was what I was going for. I *had* to appear normal.

The apartment door was a light green, a bright shock in an otherwise drab brick building. But apartments were slim pickings around these parts, and I knew they'd been lucky to find a place at all. To the left, I could hear a family making dinner. Something was boiling on the stove; the microwave was running. To the right, the two people who occupied number seventeen were watching TV—an old rerun from the seventies. Inside number sixteen, I could hear Ellie's cheerful voice. Things had gone well at school today. She'd gotten an A on her spelling test. Math was fine and she thought this little boy named Dillon was kinda cute. But just kinda.

Mom had made pizza. Not the frozen kind but the old-fashioned, deep-dish meat pie she was famous for. I could smell the peppers and fresh tomatoes from outside the apartment. I leaned my head against the doorframe, wishing I could eat pizza, talk about boys, and study for spelling tests. If only I'd left the morning after Asa had found me, then I'd be doing exactly those things. But when he said he'd track and kill my entire family, I believed him. *Always the gullible one*, I reminded myself.

"You are in this situation now because of your pride. Arrogance was your greatest flaw," Asa said from beside me. Two days ago, I'd have been startled to find him beside me. Now it was just old hat, and I didn't even bother to swing at him this time. He looked just like he had the night before I staked him.

"I'm in this situation because you were a monster," I answered. My voice was calm. Even I could hear that. It was sort of like I was standing outside my own body listening to the insanity. Part of me knew I was hallucinating. Part of me didn't. The rest of me didn't care. I rested my forehead against the rough brick of the wall.

"Is that what you truly believe, Annalice? Is it not more likely that you were partly a monster to begin with? Only another monster could have survived something as bad as me."

"No," I said out loud, but I nodded my head yes. My forehead slid up and down on the brick facing of the complex wall, and blood welled to the surface of my skin, but I didn't care about that either. I was much too focused on Asa's words. He'd said that from the beginning, that he could sense something in me. Some sort of darkness. I thought he was lying, but maybe it was true. Maybe it did take darkness to survive darkness.

"You are lying to yourself, Annalice. You are as bad as I ever hoped to be. One more monster in a sea of monsters. You were going to protect her from the world. But you cannot even protect her from yourself."

He'd gone too far again. I was about to fly into him when the door opened. My mouth was open and one hand was raised in anger.

"Annalice?" she questioned. Mom stood hesitantly, the door opened halfway in front of her and her body partially shielded by the door's bulk. "Who are you talking to?"

Beside me, Asa stood smiling. Handsome, cruel. A laughing son of a bitch. "A dead son of a bitch," I whispered partly to myself and partly to her. *He's just a hallucination.*

He gloated at me as he leaned against the wall.

"Quit smiling at me," I hissed at him. Mom glanced in the direction I was looking, her eyes getting wider. *Can she see him? No, he's not real,* I reminded myself.

"Annalice, you're scaring me. I think you need to leave." Mom started to shut the door gently, but I put my hand up like a white flag. I looked away so my eyes wouldn't scare her all the more.

"Please, Mom. You took Ellie. I don't have anything left. Please, let me talk to her. And then I'll leave."

"She doesn't want to talk to you, Annie."

"That's a lie, Mom. *You* did this. And that damn detective did this. I'm her mother." All the emotion I felt poured through in that one word. "Ellie!" I called around Mom's body. "I need to talk to you!"

"Think about what you're doing, Annalice!" Mom's voice rose only slightly as she stepped across the threshold and pulled the door shut behind her. Calm on the exterior, a human would have never noticed the slight shake in her words. But a daughter would, and I was that daughter. She was afraid, and that fear made me angry and so very sad at the same time. I stepped back to give her space.

"You think about what you're doing, Mom. You took the only thing I have left in this life." My voice broke and bloody tears rolled down my face as I shoved a finger in her direction.

"What did you think, Annie? That you could raise her? Look at yourself! You're in no condition to take care of anyone, let alone her. You don't even come home anymore." Her words were quieter now, but they rang in my ears like she was yelling.

"I'm her *mother*." I hesitated for a second before I finished. "You're *my* mother, and you know what she means to me." Unable to look at her, my eyes traced the cracks that trailed through the concrete walkway underneath our feet.

"You *were* her mother. You *were* my daughter. Only I don't know what you are now. I'm not sure that I want to know. But I do know that you are not yourself. Whatever you are, you're not right. You are not capable of looking after Ellie right now." She opened the door and took a few steps backwards into the entryway of the small rental. I knew she couldn't turn her back on me.

"I want to see her, Mom."

"No, Annie. She doesn't need the distraction."

"And you don't think it's a distraction that you took her away from me? Away from her home? I have nothing left, Mom. At least before, I had her. And it gave me a reason to keep trying. To fight this." My voice broke into loud, racking sobs.

"She knows you're sick, Annie. She understands more than you think she does, and she recognizes that you're not the same. She's not afraid of you. I'm not sure how you've managed that, but she knows you're in trouble."

"I want to see her. Now!" I said, my voice harsher.

"Like this?" Mom gestured at me. "Do you really want her to see you like this? When's the last time you bathed? You haven't changed your clothes in at least two days. Is that blood or mud on your jeans? I'm thinking both. You haven't even combed your hair, and you want to *see* her?"

If I were human, I'd have flushed with shame. I attempted to run a hand through the hornet's nest on the back of my head. I blotted at the mud stain on my right cheek. I could see it in the reflection of the window. My shoes were spotted with blood and mud, and I was still wearing the clothes I'd worn to the bar the night before. They were the same clothes I was wearing when I killed the cow. I tried to change the subject.

"I would never hurt her, Mom. Or you. What's happened to me can never change how much I love you both. I only did this for the two of you," I said, gesturing to myself. "I'm not evil."

"Are you sure, Annie? And are you willing to take a chance with her life? You're not human anymore. At least not completely. I can feel it even though I can't explain it. When I think about what my gut tells me, I feel like I need to have my head examined. But I have to trust my gut and not my brain on this one. My daughter, the one you claim to be would never endanger her child, so I have to wonder exactly what you are. Two nights back, you were gone again as usual. Ellie and I woke to the worst sounds I've heard in a long time. A group of coyotes were going nuts in the pasture. I've heard coyotes before, Annie, but nothing like this. I called you, but you never answered, so I called the detective. And do you know what he found in the pasture?"

I looked down at my feet embarrassed. I knew what he'd seen.

"A dead cow. A dead cow, Annie! Not that a dead cow is odd in and of itself. But its throat had been slit, and that's certainly out of the normal, don't you think? Something had to be done about it this morning. I told Detective Rumsfield you would take care of it. That you were a whiz with the tractor. I waited around for you this morning, hoping against hope that you'd be there, but of course, you weren't. You're never there. I stayed up all night waiting for you. I called the detective last night about the cow to see if he thought it was related to the other incidents. And guess what, Annie? Any idea what he asked me?"

I knew exactly what the detective had said and exactly what he was going to say because he'd pulled up behind me and parked. I could smell Detective Rumsfield's cologne as soon as he stepped out of his truck.

"The detective asked if I thought *you* could have killed the cow," she said, answering her own question.

Mom waited for my reaction, but I didn't give her one. I was too focused on Rumsfield walking up behind me. I pretended not to notice, but I could hear his every breath, the rustle of the hair on his arms against his jacket while he walked, and his heart beating in his chest. I could smell his strength and even his fear. But not the cowardly kind of fear that oozes out when you're turning to run. This was the kind of fear that only those willing to die for someone else can produce. For the second time in two weeks, I wanted to pour out all my troubles to him, break down and lay it all on his strong shoulders, but that would be a mistake because no one's shoulders were that strong, right? Why did my senses threaten to drown me any time he was near?

I turned my respect into anger. Rumsfield had no business getting so involved. *Why can't he just leave me alone?*

Mom's voice was starting to break. "And the sad part, Annie, is that I couldn't say no. Maybe you did kill the cow. I wouldn't have a clue because I don't know you anymore."

I felt my anger for Rumsfield solidify like a cloak around me. *If he'd just mind his own damn business.* "Did you call the detective when you heard me at the door tonight?" I knew the answer, but for some reason I had to ask.

Mom took a deep breath. "This isn't about him, Annie. Detective Rumsfield was only trying to help. It was him that buried the cow this morning. I have no idea what I would have done without him. He said to call him when you showed up tonight. We both knew that you would, and he's just here to make sure this goes smoothly."

I nodded my head but still didn't look directly at her. I refused to acknowledge Rumsfield standing a few feet away at all. "Yeah, you needed to make sure that you taking my daughter went smoothly. This is bullshit, Mom."

"Annie, I need you to leave."

Her words hit me like a ton of bricks. I was getting nowhere fast. I knew I needed to calm down and try a different approach.

Was now the time to explain that unbreachable gulf? Maybe I'd been wrong. What if she could handle the truth?

"Mom, let me explain. I've never told you everything that happened while you were away. Then you can at least try to understand what I went through—what I gave up to be here."

She held up her hand in front of her chest, warding off my words and pushing my explanations back. "I can't listen to any more of this insanity."

"Mom, please. I'm lucky to have any life at all," I said, beseeching her to listen, to give me a chance. I caught her eyes, but she shifted her gaze quickly away. I had to keep trying no matter if my hungry eyes frightened her or not. "Mom, I'm serious. Look at me. I'm lucky to be here at all." Still nothing. She looked everywhere except at me. My heart sank, and the sensation was the same as when I was human. It felt like it landed somewhere around my pelvis. Maybe more so because every emotion was doubled. I'd expected pity. But not this. She wished I hadn't made it out alive, and she was ashamed that she felt that way. That look frightened me more than any of Asa's threats or the detective's suspicions and warnings. It cut me off, divided me, from the person I'd been. I think it was the first time I realized that perhaps I couldn't get back to where my life had left off, or maybe her expression stripped all of that hope away. Either way, it shut me down, and for the first time since my conversion, I felt truly dead.

"I see." I took a step back and brought my hands to my temples, pulling my hands through my hair. "Wow! I see it now. Call me a river in Egypt because it took me a while, but I get it now. I'd be better off dead."

I waited, hoping she'd refute my words, but she only stared at me resolutely. Once the words were out for the both of us to acknowledge, there was no way to pull them back in, to *unspeak* them. There was no going back. Only one thing was left to be said. I couldn't raise Ellie by myself, not when I fell over in a stupor every sunrise, and the police wouldn't leave me alone. "Tell her I love her. Every day, Mom. Remind her of that. Thinking of the two of you was what kept me alive this past week. It was all I had. It's all I'll ever have."

Rumsfield, leaning rigidly against the stairwell to the second floor, watched us as we talked. I could see him from the corner of my eye. My peripheral vision was as sharp as my central. He tried to look relaxed, but I could see the outline of a small gun in his right front pocket, his hand resting nonchalantly, fingers half in, half out. His left hand was dangling suspiciously near his holstered gun on his left.

The sound of my mother's whispered voice reached me as I turned away. "Annie, I'm sorry. It's for the best." She took a deep breath, looking for the calm in the storm. "If any part of you really is my daughter and Ellie's mother, please listen to me. Don't come here again. Leave Ellie alone. Let her go. Let us both go. You should know that I'll take care of her because I love her like I loved you. And forgive me because you know I'm doing what I think is best for her or I wouldn't be doing it. And I *will* tell her every day how much you loved her."

Rumsfield peeled himself off the railing as I turned from the door. One hand was still fingering the hidden gun. He was just letting me know it was there, I guessed. Behind me, I felt the wind from Mom starting to close the door. Her heart was thumping against her chest so loud it nearly hurt my ears, and I went from being cut off from the entire situation to once more feeling massively betrayed.

Where had the cops been when I was fighting for survival? Why hadn't Rumsfield done more to protect me and why was my mother, the person who should be fighting the most for me, taking from me the only thing that mattered in life? Shouldn't they both be on my side? I'd done nothing wrong. Beside me, Asa reappeared and agreed.

"You should disembowel them both for their treachery," Asa said.

I looked towards him and he smiled, fangs bared and lips red—so full of blood and promise. Maybe Asa was right. Why had I killed him?

The door to the apartment was nearly closed when I thrust a hand forward and rocked it on its hinges. I heard the friction of metal on denim as Rumsfield pulled his gun. From the corner of my eye, I could see the small barrel pointed at me. The detective's hand shook a little; the muscles in his forearms were taut and gleaming with a little sweat. His nervousness wasn't from a lack of experience. His gut said something was wrong with me, and yet his evidence would never stand up in court. The logic in his brain couldn't quite convince him that pulling a gun on me was the right thing to do. I had to give him credit for his willingness to go out on a limb for my mother and child, knowing it might cost him his career.

Mom gasped to my right and tried to push the door shut. She might as well have been holding back a tornado. My head jerked around towards her as I held the door. She didn't let go, but she didn't back down. I didn't try to protect her from my eyes this time. My hungry gaze fell on her full force, and she shrunk back mouse-like. Her arms dropped down by her sides, and she stepped backwards, catching the door for balance.

My emotions were being flung from one extreme to the other. Where I'd felt betrayed and shut down and then angry, I now skipped straight to shame. This was the woman who'd held me through thunderstorms and washed my skinned knees. Rocked me to sleep when I was afraid of the boogeyman. She'd cheered for me as I crossed the stage to accept my medical degree. The awfulness of what I was doing dissolved my delusion of Asa, and his form faded away.

"I forgive you," I answered. She was still slack-jawed when I leaned over and pulled the door shut.

Rumsfield's gun was still leveled at me when I disappeared into the darkness of the parking lot. I didn't look at him as I left, and I could have cared less if he'd shot me. In fact, I wished he would. Maybe the pain would have lessened the fracturing pain from my heart.

Chapter 12

The walk home was a slow and lonely one. I walked because there was really no reason to run. No reason to hurry. Where was I going to go except back to an empty house? I had no one to visit and other than a few work friendships that ended once I drove out of the hospital parking lot, I had no one I could even talk to. I was completely alone.

Nothing but an empty house waited for me when I got there, and it was so cold and lonely without Ellie and Mom to make it feel like a true home that I couldn't force myself to go into it. Even the animals in the pasture were gone. Rumsfield must have taken the three horses, as well as the cows that had ranged the pasture, when he buried the dead one. And Samuel wasn't there to chase the birds that landed on the deck and bark furiously at the squirrels as they made dives towards the bird feeders. The windows of the house stared towards the lawn like empty eye sockets, and the front door, left open by me, gaped like a mouth opened in dread. I couldn't bear to go back into it.

The cellar where I'd been sleeping wasn't any more appealing, so I stretched out on the front lawn, planning to wait until closer to dawn before going to my sleeping hole in the cellar.

"You must be very thankful that you survived me for this," Asa said beside me. I didn't flinch at the sound of his voice. I'd come to expect it. He'd stretched out beside me on the grass and was studying the stars as I had been.

"I'm thankful for every second I had with my family," I answered.

103

Asa smirked his most annoying grin. "Yes, humans often speak of quality time. You are spending such large amounts of it with them now."

I rolled away. "Someday, things are going to be normal. I'll be a mother and daughter again, once I figure all of this out." The sliver of hope was sharp, and I just couldn't quit cutting myself with it.

"Nothing is ever going to be normal again, Annalice."

"Luckily that doesn't mean much coming from a hallucination," I answered. "I'm going to keep fighting for them no matter what you say."

"The effort is wasted."

"You only say that because you had no one to fight for. You had nothing to keep you sane, but I do, and it will make all the difference."

Asa had been alone in his second life. No friends and no family. His family had been killed by his maker, and he in turn had killed his fiancée. Only two days back, I'd found a picture of his mother that he'd carried around with him. Even he had been unable to empty his heart of all his human emotions.

He'd also had a business card, I remembered suddenly. I'd forgotten about it after I stuffed it down in one of my pockets. "You had a business card with a phone number on it in your bag. Whose was it?" I questioned him. I hadn't changed clothes since then, and I pulled the card from my back pocket. It was still slightly damp from where I'd swam the river the other day, the ink smudged a tad, but otherwise it was no worse for the wear.

"Who does this number belong to?" I asked again, looking back towards him. But he was gone.

"He isn't real," I told myself. Even so, I kind of missed him. Further proof that I was pathetic. I was so lonely that I enjoyed the company of a delusion.

Pointedly, I distracted myself with the card. Who could Asa have possibly known that would have given him their phone number? Some very lucky girl he never hooked up with or some woman who wanted to buy him a drink while he was stalking her? Maybe, but he'd have just thrown those kind of numbers away. He'd kept this number for a reason.

The card was an advertisement for a bar in Denver. The emblem was a large 'J' decorated with roses and a cowboy hat hanging off one crook of the J. "Jolene's," it read. The phone number was handwritten on the back. I didn't recognize the area code, so I asked my iPhone to search the web. Thankfully, I'd upgraded my phone recently and the voice commands worked. I sure couldn't work the screen, which was why the battery hadn't died, but the battery was about to go. Only a sliver of red remained.

The area code traced back to Maine—Boston to be exact. Asa had never mentioned going there, but he'd had years to travel. Curiosity got the better of me, and I asked Siri to dial the number before I lost my nerve. It was probably very unwise to dig into Asa's past at all, but I was aching to discover not only why he'd keep this number but keep it so well hidden.

The line rang several times with no answer. *It's four in the morning*, I chided myself. *It's a stupid goose chase anyway. Asa never had any need to know anyone.* I was just about to hang up when a strong male voice that didn't sound like it was four in the morning answered on the other end.

I was caught so off-guard at the sound of the voice that I didn't speak or even breathe. The man on the other end repeated "Hello," once and then twice and then went silent. The two of us sat like that for several minutes in a game of quiet tug-of-war. I didn't move at all. You couldn't have heard the rub of my jeans if you had a stethoscope on my butt.

"Only vampires can hold their breath that long," the man said, and out of surprise, I sucked my breath in sharply. He laughed lightly and then asked, "Is that you, Asa?"

I jerked the phone away from my ear like it had suddenly caught fire, pulled it halfway back to my ear again, and then laid it gently upside down on the ground, as if that would lessen the effect that I was trying to get rid of him.

I watched it for an hour until I was sure it was dead, expecting whoever I'd called to hit redial. They knew about vampires and they knew about Asa, and I couldn't shake the bad feeling that had crept into the pit of my belly. I regretted ever making the call.

But the phone remained silent, and long before the sun threatened to crest the mountains to the east, I sprinted back to the cellar, crawled between the blankets lining my sleeping spot, brushed a couple of spiders out of the way, and pulled the bed frame back into place. I was thinking about the voice on the phone when the sunrise claimed my thoughts and put them to rest for the day.

Chapter 13

"You should have taken my offer," Asa whispered to me. I looked up at him through the coils of the ancient springs that had once been a bed. How was the rusted metal even holding him up? I wondered. It was evening, and the sun was down for the day.

"You're not real," I spoke aloud for my own benefit.

The last two nights were perhaps the lowest points of my entire existence. Nothing I'd ever been through in my life could have prepared me for how I felt when I woke the evening after Ellie's abduction. Not the enormity of surviving medical school to the emotional roller coaster of divorce. Losing my dad had probably been the worst moment of my life until I'd met Asa, and then the almost certainty that I'd lose my life to Asa in exchange for my daughter's life now seemed pale in comparison to what I was facing.

An eternity of nothing. What does one do with immortality when they have no one to share it with? Losing my mother would be hard. Losing my daughter—insurmountable.

So when I became conscious the evening after the confrontation with Mom, I didn't bother to get out of my hole. I was still lying in the same pit of depression I'd gone to ground in when the sun oozed back behind the mountains. The sliver of hope was a knife like no other, and I'd cut my heart out with it. There was nothing left.

When the sun rose again the second day post Ellie's abduction, I didn't bother to open my eyes. The movement seemed pointless. There was nothing to see. There was no one to see. There was no Ellie to see. I knew I was wallowing, but I didn't care. I didn't care if I ever got up out of this hole again, and I had every intention of lying there and starving myself into a state of paralysis.

My only company was Asa. He'd joined me in the cellar again, or maybe he'd never left. I couldn't remember, and it didn't matter whether my eyes were closed or not, I couldn't escape him. His voice vibrated in my ears, and he laughed at my condition, tormenting me for my attempts to outwit him.

"I promised you a quick death. A dignified demise really, Annalice. You *should* have accepted my offer."

"You said that already." I glared at Asa through the springs of the bed again before I rolled away and dug myself a little farther into the ground. The hole I was laying in was now just a dirty packed-in pit. I'd clawed through the blankets I'd placed into the hole, and now my clothes were damp with mud and starting to mildew. The smell of the fungus was starting to overwhelm the decades-old scent of vegetables.

"I cannot see how this path you have chosen is any better than the one I offered you," Asa said.

Angry, I punched through the springs at his face, but he was faster than me, and he dissolved just in time.

"I didn't want to die," I answered. Sometimes when I answered his deranged line of thinking he'd leave me alone for a while.

"What *were* you expecting to happen, Annalice? Did you honestly expect that you could survive me and simply return to your former life? Surely, somewhere deep within, you understood that fantasy would never happen."

"Leave me alone."

"Answer the question and I shall."

"You're a damned liar," I answered back. "You'll never leave me alone."

Asa laughed at me, his face leering down at me between the mattress springs. "You are correct. I will never leave you alone. Still, answer the question. What were you expecting to happen?"

"What would it hurt?" I whispered to myself. "I don't know, Asa. Call me crazy, I guess, because I expected to help my daughter with her homework in the evenings and take her to the movies on the weekends. Normal motherly things. I certainly didn't expect to be laying in here with you."

"Foolish girl. It was insanity to lie to yourself that way."

"Why? Because you couldn't manage it?" I asked.

Asa smiled down at me with his cruel, albeit beautiful face. "Because you are a vampire. Because you are dead. Because you are not human, no matter how hard you try to convince yourself. Because you drink blood. I could go on with the whys if you need me to."

"Whatever," I said. But he was right. The truth burned as deep in me as the hunger that felt like it might eat its way through my ribcage. I was a *fool* to think I could be any different from him.

Chapter 14

I was attempting to ignore the monologue that Asa kept up in the background by arguing with myself on whether he'd returned from the dead-dead or was my own consciousness reflected back towards me. In my saner moments—I went with the latter. But here, now, with the deep-seated hunger singeing the lining of my stomach, I was leaning towards the argument that he was dead and well beside me and not dead and dead in the ground. I wasn't entirely sure I understood my own questions.

From the corner of the cellar, he was calmly talking about how I could put an end to myself, and I was considering the merits of his argument when I heard the rumble of a vehicle in the driveway. In the ground, all such sounds were magnified. The vibratory sense of vampires were as powerful or maybe more so than the hearing. The engine of the motor cut off, and I waved Asa into silence as I listened. For once, he listened and fell quiet. No other sounds reached me for about five minutes, and I was beginning to wonder if I'd imagined it when a door opened, the hinges protesting with a high-pitched grating.

The human who stepped out of the vehicle milled around in the yard for a few minutes before climbing through the strands of barbed wire guarding the pasture. The faint rip of snagged material could be heard and then more steps as he walked towards me. At least I was fairly certain it was a man. The footsteps were heavy and hard as they approached.

I listened as the human walked the perimeter of the pasture, the footsteps getting weaker the closer he got towards the fence that separated the forest from the pasture and then stronger as he walked back towards the house. He walked in circles and then took off on near diagonals. The footsteps meandered around the barn and then over to where I'd killed the cow. Here they paused for a couple of minutes before turning in the direction of where I was laying in the cellar. If there was a pattern to his walking, I couldn't discern it.

I wasn't alarmed that this human would find me, and even when he passed directly over my hiding spot, I didn't get alarmed. I even smiled a little at the stealth I could hear in the footsteps. I most likely would have laid there and ignored him, I was too deep in my own pity party to be disturbed, if the scent of this man hadn't floated down to me through the aged vent holes. But one whiff of his blood brought me to my feet, and the second whiff sent me leaping from the hidden doorway onto the ground six feet above.

It wasn't the smell of blood that brought me out but *whose* blood it was. I had to hand it to him; he was brave and dedicated. Or stupid and fanatical, depending on how you looked at it. Whichever, here the detective was, in the middle of the night, facing his own fears and knowledge that something wasn't quite right about me, clearly willing to risk his life for his convictions.

"I think you are overselling him. He is just nosy," Asa said. He was beside me again. Together, we watched the detective, who was now about thirty feet ahead of us. Deep in his studies, he was walking slowly, his shoulders hunched forward as he used a flashlight to search the ground. He was so intent that he had not, as of yet, noticed my presence behind him. The fact that he hadn't swung around at the sound of Asa's voice was further proof Asa was a hallucination after all.

Every few feet, the detective would bend down and pick at something on the ground. A twig, a blade of grass. I took a few steps in his direction, my curiosity burning slightly more than my hunger. He moved on a few feet, his flashlight bobbing brightly on the dark ground as he walked.

"What's he doing and why is he doing it at night?" I whispered to Asa. My thinking was foggy. I could feel the elusive answers hovering at the edge of my reason.

"This man is foolish. He should have at the very least come during the day," Asa responded.

"See, I told you he was dedicated. He works 24/7." The words had only cleared my mouth when I realized the truth. "Or he's working during the day, and this is his side project. Unsanctioned by the station, of course, so he's forced to do it on his own time."

"He is tracking you," Asa answered.

I looked at Asa for a second, my mouth opening to argue and then realizing that he was right. "Holy crap," I said. Instantly, I was simmering. Rumsfield was working off the record, which meant he had no business here at all. He was my own personal demon. Tracking me and ruining my life, adding fuel to my mother's flames. I felt the renewed desire to kill him; the urge slipped on as easily as a winter coat, and Rumsfield felt it immediately. I smiled as he came to a halt, my presence washing over him like a dark cloud across the warm summer sun. Still stooped from his tracking, he lifted up slowly. Did he actually think his quicksand movements would keep me from killing him?

"So you stuck around after all?" Rumsfield asked, turning towards me.

Where did he get the strength to face me? Grudgingly, I admired his bravery. Even if it was immensely stupid.

"Detective, what a surprise. What brings you to my neck of the woods? Official police business, I presume?" My voice was warmly sarcastic, and I enjoyed its effect on his expression. He had no right to be here, and he knew that as well as I did. "Maybe I'll just call down to the station and check on your warrant," I said, smiling at him again as I pulled my now very dead cellphone from my pocket.

"Don't bother, Ms. Creed. You know I don't have a warrant. But that doesn't change anything. You're as guilty as they come. We both know it, and I *will* prove it."

"And yet here I am still not in jail. Still not charged. Doesn't quite make sense, does it?" I asked. I pretended to peck at the screen of my phone, hoping he didn't realize the screen was dark from that far away.

He whistled between his teeth when I laid the phone to my cheek. "Just … just wait. Okay. Let's talk about it before you get crazy with that phone."

So I'd hit the nail on the head. "Fine," I said, shoving my phone in my pocket. "Sure, let's talk about it. Why don't you tell me again what you have exactly and what makes you think that I'm so guilty? Surely killing a cow isn't illegal?" I asked, spreading my hands out in front of me as I pursed my lips together in a sarcastic look. "And then I'll try to talk you out of crazy town and back into reality."

He didn't answer me, just stood looking at me with his arms crossed tightly across his chest. I continued to berate him. "Ah, come on. You can't tell anyone down at the station because they'd think you're nuts, but you can tell me. I already *know* you're crazy." My cold laughter drifted across to him in the dark. "I'm laughing at you, by the way, not with you."

He shrugged and blew out his breath harshly again while shaking his head. "We've already been through this, Dr. Creed."

"Humor me, Detective. Surely you didn't come all the way out here just to hike around my pasture," I answered.

Another sigh, one hand tugging its way through his sandy hair. "Fine. What's it matter? Let me build you a timeline, Annalice. That way you won't be so surprised when I do arrest you someday. You see, it happened like this. First, your boyfriend killed Ms. McElhaney. I don't know why, and I think you probably had nothing to do with it. But you knew about it," he said, pausing here for a moment for emphasis before continuing. "But you didn't call it in. In fact, you were still screwing around with him after he killed her. Now, that seems weird to me, Annalice. I personally showed you what I thought he did to her, and yet you were having dinner with him a couple of nights later.

"So after some sex and drinks, you two head into the woods. Ransack and rob a campsite and then track a hunter." Shaking his head, his hands dropped down to rest on his hips as he pinned ice blue eyes on me. "And this is where it gets really strange for me. You guys tracked him. No one else in the department seemed to notice that, by the way. Maybe because they haven't spent every free minute of their spare time out here in these woods like I have. But I followed footprints from this house," he jammed his finger towards the ground beneath his feet, "all the way to the crime scene. With no variance and no wrong turns, you both followed him until you trapped him and then killed him. "He tried to get away, but not from you. Your footprints seemto say that you held back, and at some point, you even knelt down. What for? Were you trying to help him or were you freaking out at what you were seeing? Got in a little over your head maybe? I'm not sure yet. But here's where it gets even stranger. One set of footprints, yours, leads away to a grave with clothes, an antique wedding ring, and a wooden stake but no body. And your footsteps were heavy, like you were carrying something. Or someone?" He stopped here for emphasis, his eyes pleading with me to fess up. "Any answers for me, Annie?" he questioned.

I stepped closer, needing him to believe me. "You have a stressful job, Mike. I get that. But you're desperate, and you think you're on to something here, but you're not. My boyfriend and I spent most of the day in the woods. We'd been hiking, so of course, we might have left footprints out there, and hiking is not a crime. Besides, the papers said that young man died of some sort of bear attack. There were *no* signs of foul play. The most you can prove is that we saw the scene of the attack. So let me spell this out for you, Mike. We might have hiked before the event, during the event, or after the event. The worst you could get us for would be not calling the attack in. But you can't accuse me of murder by bear. Besides, are you that good of a tracker? That you can tell me the exact hour of the day I was there? If you were, I suspect you'd be working for the Discovery Channel."

He ignored my remarks about his tracking skills completely. "That doesn't explain everything, Annalice. What about the one set of footprints leading away and the grave with clothes? Am I to believe there's nothing to that either?"

"Come on. You cannot actually believe that I went up against my 'boyfriend' with that stake that you were so ridiculously parading around the other night. And can you really call that hole where I buried my boyfriend's clothes a grave? It was empty, Detective, because there was *no* body."

It was his turn to laugh at me now. My story was a little ridiculous, but he couldn't prove it, and I knew it. "It was a really big hole. I could tell that as I dug it back out. And if not a grave, then why did you bury his clothes? And please don't forget to tell me why you'd punched holes through them. Holes that just happened to match in size and shape of the stake I found on the ground with your fingerprints on it. Please tell me because I just can't wait to hear this one. It could go down as the best lie I've ever heard." His blue eyes remained cold and hard despite the pleasantly condescending smile he held on his face.

"He was a vampire, Detective," I said matter-of-factly, watching as he rolled his eyes at me. Starting to turn away from me now, I raised my voice in anger. "No, I've listened to your crazy shit, and now you're going to listen to me! He *was* a vampire. He was sucking the life right out of me. And so I symbolically staked his clothes and buried them. I read about it in a self-help book."

He started laughing now. "That is rich, ma'am. Really rich. I'm going to write this crap down. It'll make a great story to tell my friends someday. Once I've nailed you that is, and I will. You're not going to take a step that I don't take; you're not going to as much as take a piss that I don't know about. I'll stay on you until I finally break you down."

"You can't handle my pace, Michael," I snapped back, saying his first name like it was a curse. "I'm just curious, are they starting to worry about you down at the station? You know, quit talking when you walk in the room? Look at you funny? You should be careful spouting all this crazy talk around, Detective. Never know when they might start 'testing you.'"

"Let me tell you about crazy," he said angrily as he walked towards me. Fear was making him overly brave. "I know that you're gone all day, and it isn't to work because you've quit your job. Hell, you didn't even give a notice. I doubt you'll keep your medical license. Your mom has your daughter. Suddenly, you're spending your evenings in bars, bars where men show up dead, I might add. Your house looks like crap, you're killing the farm animals, and your mom won't even say your name. You are ruining your life, and you call *me* crazy? I'm going to nail you, Annalice." Leaning into me as he emphasized his last words, he poked me in the shoulder with a strong index finger as he spoke each syllable.

"The only thing you're going to nail is your own coffin lid when they fire your ass at the station," I answered back.

"We'll see, Annie. We'll just see about that," he said. "I have a hunch that all I really need to do is to figure out where you go in this pasture when you leave your house." He'd turned away from me and was studying the ground again with his flashlight.

Finally, the truth of what he was doing in my field hit me, and I remembered my prints in the dewy field a few nights back. He was tracking me to my hiding spot, and if he got really close to where the cellar was located and studied the ground hard enough, he might find it.

In that one moment of clarity, I hated Michael Rumsfield as much as a person can be hated. Everything bad that had happened since Asa died appeared to be of his doing. My daughter was gone and my mother thought I was a monster— her opinion aided and abetted by the detective. He knew too much about my involvement with Ms. McElhaney, and he was too suspicious about my comings and goings. And now he was here, in my pasture, searching for my last safe haven. Add that to the hunger that gnawed at my backbone and Asa's encouragement in the background, and I lost all reason. Every ounce of my anger and angst landed squarely on his back in the shape of a hazy red target.

Without a conscious thought, I flung myself through the air at the detective's hunched-over frame. I don't remember making the movement, but the expression of surprise on his face as he jerked towards me in response to my ear-splitting howl registered for a fraction of a second before my fangs slid into his neck, and we crashed to the ground.

I hadn't eaten in days, and since I'd killed Asa, I hadn't taken my fill. I was weak, and Detective Rumsfield was a strong, skilled officer. He buckled underneath my momentum but still managed to flip his body over as we fell.

Landing with his back to the ground, he was silent except for the air being forced out of his lungs in a loud gush as the back of his head slammed into the dirt. One tiny vessel burst next to the iris on his right eye, but he remained conscious, although somewhat stunned.

With the rotation of his body, I'd lost my choke hold with my teeth, and I took the moments of his confusion to regain it as I went for his carotid artery again. Being bitten is a very unnatural feeling, and finally, he began to scream when his brain caught back up to what I was doing. He shot his left hand up, the palm catching alongside my cheek, and tried to force me away. With his right hand, he was landing right hook after right hook to the side of my head.

He couldn't dislodge me, and with every second that I had my fangs in him, I was getting stronger, and he was getting weaker. I clamped down harder, cutting off more of the flow of blood to his brain; his consciousness began to wane, and his eyes lost focus. The maneuver is predatory, and most great cats in the world use this trick, but it also delayed the blood flowing into me. So when I was convinced that he was no longer conscious, I let up on the pressure in my jaws and allowed his carotid to flow more easily. I wasn't thinking of anything except the kill. Not about Ellie or Mom, or about the man who was dying at the tip of my fangs.

I heard the bullet before I felt it and sat bolt upright on his chest as the hunk of lead slid through my spleen, dug through my diaphragm, traversed my lungs and then exploded out of my right shoulder. My arm flung outward before landing useless against my side. Knocked off balance, I fell backwards and rolled off of Rumsfield's heaving form, landing on my belly, just as a second bullet pierced my chest, burrowing through me before burying itself in the ground.

"Officer down! Officer down! I need back-up! I have just shot, I repeat shot, Dr. Annalice Creed behind her house. Send backup! 2332 Deerwood Drive. I need an ambulance," Rumsfield screamed into his radio.

The squawk of his handheld radio hurt my ears as he kicked his legs free of mine. He crab-crawled backwards a few feet and then with a loud gasp of air pushed himself to his feet. I hadn't moved as of yet. The pain of the shots was excruciating. The nerve endings of my core were lit up like firecrackers, too much in shock to move when he stumbled over, his right hand gripping the left side of his neck, and kicked my leg with one booted shoe.

The radio screeched again with the metallic sounds of sirens and an affirmative scratchy response of the officer on the other end. Apparently, there was another squad car about ten miles away. The ambulance would take nearly twenty minutes longer.

"10-4," Rumsfield spoke into the radio. "I think I've killed her. She's not moving."

I heard his grip tighten on the gun as he inched a little closer and rolled me over with his foot. I didn't fight him, just let his booted foot push me over, until he'd leaned over close.

He was searching my face for signs of life when I opened my eyes. He let out a cry of alarm, stepping backwards, both hands wrapped around the butt of his gun, the barrel pointed at my chest. I got to my knees, and he stepped back another few feet.

"Get down, Annalice. Get down, or I'll shoot again!" Both hands were shaking, his index fingers stretched out along the stock to help steady the weapon, but he'd quit backing away from me. "Get down!" he yelled again.

I didn't listen and got to my feet as he fired a warning shot over my head. He tried again. "Dammit, I mean it, Annalice! I will shoot again. Get down on the ground!"

I gritted my teeth against the pain. "Oh, I thought you meant it the first time."

He emptied the clip into me. The surprise factor was gone, and I took the bullets better this time, knowing what to expect, but the force of the impact was still a shock to the system. I was still standing when the last one hit, but I'd staggered backwards a few feet with the shots, my arms jerking backwards and forwards with each impact. Blood was dripping from my fingertips onto the grass and pooling at my feet.

A few steps in front of me, Rumsfield was looking like he'd just seen a ghost, the gun hanging limply in his hands, his eyes round and incredulous as he took in the impossible. In the near distance, I could hear the scream of a police siren. I didn't have much time.

"What the hell is wrong with you?" Rumsfield mouthed under his breath. His breathing was becoming very rapid, and he looked on the verge of a full-blown panic attack.

I advanced on him with a fury. "What the hell is wrong with *you*? Coming here in the dark to spy on me! Haven't you done enough to ruin my life? You've practically stolen my daughter, turned my mother against me, and done your level best to convince everyone I'm a murderer. You want to see how bad I really am? Huh? You're going to now 'cause you just went and made me hungry," I said as I backhanded him down. His body spun in the air and landed face down about five feet away.

I jerked him off the ground by his hair. One leg had snapped when he had hit the ground, and he yelled in pain as I pulled him to his feet. I sank my canines into him again and pulled out another couple units of blood. His lungs wheezed with the effort of breathing. His chest had flailed with the impact, and his right lung was sucking heavily, a section of ribs flailing out with every breath. His heart was struggling to pump what little blood he had left.

The sirens were seething up my driveway when I pulled my mouth away from his neck, and I was like a trapped animal. I surveyed the field, looking for a way out. I could make it to the back of the pasture and hide in the trees, but I had nowhere to go at dawn. The house stood beckoning, but I was certain it would be searched, and I'd burn in their hands. The ground at my feet was covered with blood—mine and his. All of it precious and desperately needed. Somehow, Michael was still breathing but barely, and even if he were dead, I didn't have time to hide the body.

My first thought was to rake my nails across his neck and chest and keep with the animal attack theme. Luckily, common sense prevailed. Humanoid nails do not make a pattern on skin that resembles any animal prints. Nor would his skin just disappear out from under my nails when at some point I was questioned and DNA tested. And I *would* be questioned and DNA tested. There was no chance I could just disappear without a trace, leaving my daughter behind. Running out on her was not an option. The best I could hope for was to keep making Detective Michael Rumsfield look like a crackpot.

So I did the only logical thing I could think of, which was to rub some saliva into the wounds on his neck and race away to my cellar, hoping to God none of the responding officers could track like Michael. At least he was alive, which was more than I thought possible a few minutes ago. My other saving grace was that all of my body tissue and blood would degrade at first light.

Chapter 15

My driveway was a tunnel of swirling blue lights when I slipped into the cellar. I pulled the weather-beaten door as tightly shut as I dared without splintering it and stood at the entrance, waiting for the worst. If they found me, they were all dead. I'd kill each one of them to protect myself. I knew it to be the truth, and although I didn't like the self-revelation, I couldn't deny it. Inwardly, I prayed that it wouldn't come to that and stood, not breathing and as silent as stone, at the doorway.

Three police cars had careened down my driveway. The first two came as a unit; the third running a handful of minutes behind. Like three voices singing the same part, the sirens echoed each other. Dogs bayed in the distance along with a pack of coyotes. In the darkness of the cellar, I couldn't detect any light, and I leaned my head against the door as I listened to the footsteps pummeling across the yard towards the pasture.

I'd left Michael's body about thirty feet from the cellar. His heart was beating desperately to keep him alive, his breathing shallow and rapid. Occasionally, he moaned, and I listened as at least five officers surrounded him.

"Secure the scene!" one officer yelled. Four sets of feet fanned out from his body as the hammers on the Glocks they carried were cocked. A couple of the officers cursed underneath their breaths; one whispered a prayer for safety. In the air leeching in through the air vent, I could smell overpowering fear and restless energy.

"Mike! Can you hear me? Wake up, man!" The voice belonged to the flashlight-happy young cop from a few nights back. "Stay with me, Mike. The ambulance is on its way. You just gotta hold on." In the distance, the ambulance sang the importance of its mission. "Officer down! Send more units to help secure the scene," he spoke into his handheld radio. The button got stuck, and he clicked it again with more force.

"Mike? Wake up. Can you hear me?" Another cop was asking. I heard Rumsfield rouse slightly. His breathing was labored, and his voice was muffled with weakness.

"It was her," Mike's voice wasn't much more than a gasp. "Find her."

"Who was it? Dr. Creed?" the first officer asked.

"I don't see anyone," the second officer said.

"There's blood everywhere. He definitely shot someone. Hey, Lyle, take some blood samples from several locations about two feet apart. Jeremy, get Mike's gun and document how many bullets have been fired. Find the casings. Bag anything you see. Williams, take two men when the next squad gets here and search the house and barns. Be careful."

I heard Officer Williams walk towards my driveway. Two more patrol cars were pulling in as he left the group gathered around Detective Rumsfield.

"Mike, you said on the handheld that you shot Dr. Creed and that you thought you'd killed her. Where is she? What happened?"

"She's a monster," Rumsfield said. His voice was hushed, and his teeth ground together. Most likely, he was going into shock and starting to shiver. He needed fluids and blood, a warming blanket. He needed a hospital. And a doctor. He needed me, and here I was, his near killer, locked in a black hole in the ground, unable to help him. The guilt was finally hitting me. He was right. I was some kind of monster.

The ambulance slid in only a minute or so behind the latest squad cars. In the background, the metal legs of a gurney dropped down as the bed was pulled from the ambulance. It made a rattling dance across the pasture as it was pushed towards the detective.

Rumsfield had quit talking by this point, cardiovascular shock had fully set in. His heart had sped up to a frenzied fight to keep what little blood he still had circulating. His breathing was so shallow, I doubted he could have filled the wings of a moth or wavered a blade of grass.

In the darkness of my underground abyss, I listened to the pieces of the laryngoscope being locked into place by a paramedic. He asked for cricoid pressure to help with the intubation, and I held my breath as he checked for open cords and slid the endotracheal tube into place. I couldn't see the movements, but I knew them by heart. Every swing of the laryngoscope, the slap of the stethoscope on bare skin, the rise and fall of human lungs—all were sounds I knew better than my own voice. I should have been out there helping him.

Now intubated, the detective was bagged, the air sliding in and out with a hiss. A paramedic was issuing orders for IV fluids and a heating blanket. Finally, Mike was loaded onto the gurney and quickly pushed back towards the waiting ambulance. His heart was still beating, the last I heard, as the doors to the emergency vehicle were closed.

After Rumsfield was extricated, the remaining officers went into overdrive. The house and barn were searched, the entire pasture canvassed. They searched my car. I listened as one cop called my mother and warned her of what happened. Had she seen me, he asked.

The young officer who'd gotten to Rumsfield first attempted to follow his footsteps. He began where Rumsfield had fallen and then walked a perimeter walk, increasing the perimeter by about one foot each time he did so. His path carried him across the knoll that housed the cellar many times, but he never stopped, never seemed to realize that there was anything under his feet except the gentle rise in the topography. Underneath him, I continued to hold my breath and hope my hiding spot remained exactly that—hidden.

Every little while, someone would radio in and ask about Rumsfield. He was in critical condition, the voice on the other end said. Only time would tell, the voice proclaimed an hour later.

It was nearly six a.m. by the time the voice came back over the radio. The detective was fighting an uphill battle, but he was hanging on. He had eight cracked ribs, a collapsed lung, a flail chest on the opposite side, and he'd suffered massive blood loss. He'd fractured his femur. They had already taken him to emergency surgery for a femur nailing. He'd been hypothermic when the paramedics arrived, and so he'd coded on the way to the hospital. A simple arrhythmia that had responded to IV meds, and he was still intubated and on the vent. But he was responding. Weak and seriously injured, but nothing he couldn't survive, I knew. As long as nothing unexpected happened. Like a ventilator associated pneumonia or a blood clot. Or one of the many hundreds of things that can kill you in a hospital.

I closed my eyes and whispered a thanks to the heavens. Not because he was alive and would be fine but because he wasn't dead, and it couldn't be blamed on me. I was shameless, pathetic, and I knew it.

Sunrise was coming, and the cops were still working methodically, removing anything that seemed like evidence when I dug deeper into the dirt floor, pulled the tattered remains of the blankets across my shoulders and entered oblivion. I whispered a prayer before I shut my eyes, hoping for Ellie's sake that they wouldn't find me but knowing I didn't really have any right to ask for such protection.

Chapter 16

I awoke in the cool, damp dirt of the cellar, which meant I hadn't been found. I was relieved. And not just for Ellie's sake. I didn't truly have a death wish. I wanted to live. I simply had no idea how to do so without Ellie in my life. I took a moment to be grateful to whatever god would keep something such as me alive. A monster. Isn't that what the detective had called me?

Outside the cellar, the field was quiet. A couple of mice played tug of war a few feet away; the frogs were beginning their evening chorus. I was surprised. I'd expected to still hear the police, but I guess they'd collected all of their evidence. Most likely, they'd left a couple officers posted along the roadway and some closer to my driveway. Surely, I was a fugitive by now. Detective Rumsfield had told the central office that he'd shot me. He was in the hospital, and I was nowhere to be seen. They'd probably been issuing all points bulletins about me since early this morning.

I pushed my senses out even further, listening for the sounds of traffic. I heard the low rumble of a semi on the highway and the higher pitch of some passing cars. About a mile up the road, I could hear the neighbor's dogs put up a ruckus, probably over a squirrel or raccoon, and in between these sounds, the static of walkie-talkies. The cops were out there, but they weren't close. Probably a couple hundred feet past my mailbox. No doubt they weren't expecting me to come in from the pasture, or to come in at all. A smart criminal would have been gone by now. I listened awhile longer but heard nothing more than the typical background noise of the forest.

I surveyed the house from outside the cellar. The windows were dark, the electricity still off, and from the back deck, I could see yellow streamers lifting up long yellow arms in the breeze. The outdoor ceiling fans spun incessantly, pushed by the wind. The remnants of last summer's roses scratched the kitchen windows. I could hear the high-pitched scraping from where I stood. It was an empty, forlorn scene, and I screwed up my mouth to hold back the tears, but a few, tinged red, managed to slip out.

I wasn't sure what to do or where to go. My first thought was of Ellie. I considered going to see her or checking in with Mom. I couldn't call her. I'd have to make a face-to-face visit. My cellphone had gone dead shortly after I'd called the number I found in Asa's bag. I hadn't charged it, and for once, I was happy my phone was dead. The police couldn't track it. But of course, I couldn't call Ellie either. I was, once again, disconnected from the world.

Logic told me I should leave my house. Counter logic told me to hide where they'd least expect me to be. I considered the options and decided to stay on my own property. Maybe it was the comfortable decision or maybe the most logical. I couldn't really tell anymore.

Either way, a shower seemed like a good idea. Filthy was not a strong enough adjective to describe me. Rank wouldn't come close either. I'd make it a quick one and pack a bag of clothes just in case I needed a quick departure.

I'd climbed the last step onto the deck when I noticed a message scrawled with my daughter's red chalk on the deck floor. "Who are you?" it read. The letters were large and wrapped around the house. Certainly not the small neat handwriting of my daughter. The police? I wondered, but that seemed unlikely. They knew who I was. Local doctor turned killer. Child-abandoning mother. Psycho at large.

So if not the cops, then who? The red chalk lay neatly on the patio table while the rest of the colors were scattered across the

126

concrete. I brought the chalk to my face and inhaled deeply but could smell nothing but my own hand. Had they worn gloves? And why were they asking me this question? Did they know what I was? Were they covering their scent intentionally? And if so, why didn't they ask *what* I was?

Suddenly the backdrop of the forest didn't look so inviting. The dark border of trees frowned back at me, a dark slash in the face of the pasture. The barns with their hundreds of hiding spots menaced me from the backyard. I'd begun to consider over the last few days that I knew essentially nothing of my new world. There were other vampires somewhere. Logically, I recognized that fact, but what else was out there? I'd read about vampire hunters on the web while I was housebound during my week of captivity with Asa. Maybe Rumsfield had been given more credence for his crazy ideas than I'd realized.

Jumping straight up, I took to the pergola and then flung upward even farther into the trees, walking catlike out to distribute my body mass across several small limbs. I held myself perfectly still except my roving gaze that searched the landscape for anything out of the normal.

The night was quiet around me as the light breeze had died down, and I listened closely, hearing nothing except for the occasional static of the walkie-talkies down the road and the creaking of the limbs around me. I hadn't realized until now that the forest around my house had become strangely quiet, an eerie silence without the natural sounds of industrious animals going about their nightly business. I wasn't sure when the ceasing of their movement had begun. I'd been too involved in my pity party to have noticed.

Not moving, I lay perfectly still except my eyes, which I kept constantly moving, looking for anything out of the ordinary. In the distance, I could feel something else do the same thing. It was probably more of a hunch than anything else, but I was convinced I was being watched. The words stared up at me from the deck. *Who are you?* They'd asked. Time became nothing more than a march to the rising of the sun and a waiting game of who would come out first.

As I watched the stars in their migration across the sky, I became more alarmed about my situation. Dawn could not be stopped; I could feel the beginnings of its searing power hovering on the edge of my consciousness. I was terrified to be trapped in my house. Where would I go with this something watching me? Did the penman know what I was? Was he mocking me? Did he know of my failings? I could only imagine that whoever or whatever watched me from the shadows knew something was amiss. But why the games?

I had little time to consider it further as the brilliance of the sun was beginning to glow on the horizon. Fear overcame me as I flipped down out of the trees, landing smoothly on the ground. I streaked to my hiding hole, more afraid of hiding in my own house than what awaited me in the woods. Having no more time to think of what stalked me, I cleared the fence in one leap, landing many feet on the other side, and without missing a step continued on to the ancient cellar.

I dared not even glance in the direction of the horizon. I raced across the pasture and reached for the cellar door hidden beneath the decades of brush. I wrapped my hands around the metal handle only a minute or two before the sun exploded into view.

I threw the door open, almost to safety, when powerful arms wrapped around me, keeping me from my haven. I spun to face my captor, bared my teeth, and hissed deep in my throat at who dared to keep me from the safety of the dark. If they'd been human, they'd have been dead.

But it was no human who held me. I found myself facing what I immediately recognized as another vampire. Fangs bared, he hissed back. I had only seconds before I'd be dead for the day, and I struggled to break his grasp.

My mind was clouded by an uncontrollable fear as I struggled and fought. I used every weapon available to me. I lashed out with my arms and legs, tore at him with my teeth, but I was unable to break free, my strength lacking compared to his. Didn't he know we were in danger? Was he a fool? Did he want to die?

"Stop!" he hissed roughly into my ear; taking hold of my face and forcing me to look at him, the first words that either of us had spoken.

"Are you a fool? Let go of me. We will die here!" I shrieked up into his face, but he simply laughed at me.

"You are very young," he stated as if it were a simple fact and I had no cause for concern. Finally, after what seemed like an eternity, he shoved me backwards through the door into the cellar. The last image I saw was the first golden glow, heralding the sun's approach, casting the vampire in black outline. Tattooed and burnt into my mind, I stared at the image as I fell backwards into the cellar. I was gone before I hit the floor.

Chapter 17

I woke to the smell of onions and potatoes. Too many nights spent sleeping on old mattresses in my grandmother's storm shelter waiting out Missouri tornados would forever associate those earthy smells with safety, and for the briefest of moments, I felt safe. A little girl whose worst fears were the cold walk back to the house in the rain after the winds had ceased and the pale, harmless lightning dancing across the sky. The calm after the storm. Everything was going to be fine. Daddy would soon light the kerosene lamp, and if the ground was really wet, he'd carry me in his arms back to the house, the lamp swinging in his left hand as we went. I laid my cheek back against the cool dirt and waited.

A sharp boot in my ribs destroyed the illusion. I jerked to a sitting position as I remembered the last moments of this morning and searched the darkness of the shelter. My eyesight was still dim, but better than it had been before the run-in with Rumsfield. Already, I was hungry again, and the blood from the detective would soon wear thin. I could make out the simple shapes in the utter darkness of the shelter, enough to know I wasn't alone. I could sense him a few feet from me. No scent, no heartbeat. Not human. I remembered the strength in his arms this morning. So he hadn't killed me after all. I was more than a little surprised.

"You're very young," the vampire said from the far wall of the shelter.

He'd said the same thing this morning. "You're repeating

yourself. Tell me something I don't know," I answered.

"How very brave you sound. How about I tell you that I can make out the color of your hair even in the complete darkness, while you could barely tell me where I was standing if not for my voice. That kind of hunger *is* painful, isn't it?"

The door grated against the dirt floor as he pushed it partially open. A booted foot came into view. Thankfully, it was a near cloudless night and enough ambient light from the stars bent around the door that I could see my captor.

He was leaning against the wall just to the left of the door watching me. His stance was relaxed, his arms crossed loosely against his chest, the foot he'd used to push the door open resting against the wall, knee bent, while the other long leg was stretched forward. But for all of his casual stance, his eyes were icy. I stared back just as coldly and did my best not to flinch.

I growled a low warning at him as he pushed away from the wall and took a step towards me, one that I was powerless to act on. He smirked and kneeled down in front of me. I'd gotten to one knee, my other leg and arms resting in a runner's position. I hissed another warning.

"You're no match for me. So keep the idle threats to yourself." His voice was calm but held an edge that was meant to be recognized.

Weakness gives some people a fake sweetness. Me, it just made surly. "Wanna make a bet?" I asked.

"Sure. I'll bet you I can pull your heart out of your chest before you can make it to the door," he said. The look on his face said he wasn't joking.

Marginally friendlier now, I asked a different question. "What do you want?"

"Answers."

"Well, there's always Google," I said.

"Cute," the man answered. "Here's a question: Do you want to live more than another ten minutes?"

I didn't say anything. My answer would give too much away.

"That's what I thought, so cut the crap. Next question: Who are you?" he asked. It was the same three words written in red letters on my porch. At least he was consistent, but I still wasn't sure I understood what he was asking.

"If you wanted my name, you could have read it off the mailbox."

"If it was your name I was interested in, I could have read it off the search warrant hanging on your front door. There were no less than six cop cars and a score of policemen running around here this morning after you went to sleep for the day. And you, nothing but a scared infant, in a big bad vampire's world. You're in no position to act so mighty, but given that you are obviously newly reborn, I will rephrase the question. To *whom* do you belong?" he asked, reaching out and forcing my face towards his.

"I sure as hell don't belong to you, so you better get your hands off me."

"Again, bold talk for a starving child." A smile crossed his features as his grip on the back of my head became tighter. "Have you been abandoned, or are you being punished by your blood maker and are being starved?"

I smiled hatefully. "I killed my blood maker."

I had his attention now, and he stared at me in clear shock for a couple of seconds, and I don't mean a good *wow* stare. This was more like an "I'm going to fricking kill" *you* stare. My muscles gathered to spring forward, but he jerked me to my feet before I could bolt. He bared his fangs, and I knew he could have severed my head from my neck in less than the time it had taken me to spit those words out.

His first thought really was to end me, but indecision played across his face momentarily, and he loosened his grip on my neck. I slipped from his grasp and landed hard on my knees.

"Perhaps I have miscalculated your strength if you killed Asa. Or perhaps you are lying, and you were left as a distraction for me."

"Or you miscalculated Asa's arrogance," I answered. "Why do you care? Who was he to you?"

"My brother," he said through gritted teeth.

Truly shocked, I stared at him speechless.

"Asa was your brother?" The shock was so potent that for a

moment I forgot how scared I was. "I ... don't know what to say. Asa never mentioned ... He told me about his mother and sister. And how he killed his fiance, but he never mentioned a brother." I studied his features, looking for a family resemblance.

"I'm not his *human* brother. I meant that we were of the same sacred bloodline. Asa cared nothing for family though, so you can understand my surprise now that I learn he had a child and even more worrisome now knowing that his child destroyed him. He must have trusted you, and how did you, after all these years, manage to reach him?"

"I'm not his *child*," I said, the words nearly burning my tongue. "He made me by accident. He didn't know what he'd done because he had no idea I was turning. I was his hostage—his blood whore. Nothing else. No one ever *reached* Asa. He was cold and hard to the bitter end, and he got what he deserved." I turned my head away so he couldn't see the red-tinged tears streaming down my face. He didn't say anything as I wiped the tears away with one hand. I was grateful. Knowing you're weak and having someone make snide comments about it are two separate things. "So what does that make me to you? Your niece?" I laughed.

In the bending light from the doorway, he lowered his gaze, and I saw his eyebrows lift and the corners of his mouth tilt up in a crooked smile. Maybe it was my imagination, but for a moment, I think he got my dark humor. But the moment passed quickly, and I felt the tingling of fear pool in my limbs.

"No," he answered quietly. "It makes you a target." His tone held a threat and so did his crossed arms and resolute jaw when he lifted his gaze to mine again. He wasn't joking. "In our world, a child who kills her blood maker is to be destroyed. As his brother, it falls to me to avenge him. The blood bond is sacred, and the penalty for such desecration is to burn in the first light of dawn."

Again, I considered bolting for the door or launching into an attack that I knew I stood no chance of winning. But I couldn't bring myself to move. Instead, I began to laugh the crazy, uncontrollable laughter of those who stand on the precipice of their own breakdown. One more step would take me completely off the deep end.

"Well if that ain't the pot calling the kettle black." I pushed up from the ground to stand in his face, all fear gone for the minute. My 'father' holds me hostage for a week, threatens to kill my family if I don't cooperate, then makes me watch as he kills some poor innocent man before he finally turns on me. But because he'd spread this disease to me, I should have been so grateful that I just let him kill me whenever the mood struck him. And since I chose to fight back, his avenging brother, who he never mentioned by the way because he didn't give a *shit* about anyone, shows up to punish me. That's about par for the course. Makes perfect sense." I jammed my finger into his chest with the last three words. Then, for good measure, I shoved him as hard as I could. He didn't move so I shoved him again.

"Watch it, child," he hissed. "Don't spread yourself too thin."

"I'm not a child, so quit calling me that. And quit threatening me. I'm sick of it. You want me dead?" I spread my arms wide and motioned to my heart. "Then get it over with because I am *ready* to die this time. Asa took everything else from me; you might as well take the leftovers." I closed my eyes, not wanting to see it coming. Talk is one thing, actions another.

I waited for the proverbial axe to fall, but the blow never came. I opened my eyes to find him leaning against the damp wall of the shelter looking at me as if I was a one-person jester act. "Hunger does make one dramatic," he said.

It was the last straw. My vision went red as reason left me, and I launched myself against him, fangs bared and fingers curled into claws. I'm ashamed to say that I didn't even land so much as a scratch. He caught me easily in his arms, and in a split second, slammed me to the ground. The sole of his boot tore into my skin as he ground his foot into my chest. I'd seen this move on the WWF. It never ended well, and despite my wrenching on his leg, I couldn't budge it.

"Child, you are too weak and starved to come against me."

"I'm not your child!" I spat back at him, writhing underneath his foot. As with Asa, I didn't want to die at this man's feet, but it was looking very likely that dying on my back was unavoidable. "No, but you're still *a* child. My dead brother's bastard child. He was little more than a bastard himself, and it appears history repeats itself. What to do with you," he mused as he leaned down and pulled me to my feet. "Do not lie to me. Did Asa want you for an eternal companion and you chose to betray him? Be careful. Your lips will decide your destiny. Lies come hard to the inexperienced, and I am quite *experienced.*" His eyes traveled down my body.

I shivered at the hidden meaning in his last word. He smiled when I caught his double meaning. Taking a deep breath as I remembered Asa's mocking face in my mind, I forced myself to not look away from his searing gaze.

"Screw you," I said.

"Poor choice of words, dear, because that could be arranged. Now understand that you're not going to anger me enough to kill you. But I'm quite willing to torture you until you talk, so ask yourself if your display of autonomy is worth the price."

I'd fought my fair share of fights for lost causes, but I had no penchant for pain, and I'd already spent a week on my back. I could think of no reason not to answer. "Fine," I answered. "Asa said that he thought about keeping me but decided a companion was just not his style. Surprise was my only advantage, and I staked him before he realized that I'd been turning. I'd been changing for days, but he never noticed."

"Any regrets?" he asked, searching my face.

"Yeah. Of course," I said.

His eyes widened slightly. He was waiting for the wrong answer, I knew. Only I didn't know what the wrong answer was. "I wished I'd just let him kill me."

He sighed heavily. "Back to that nonsense again."

I guess that wasn't the answer he'd been expecting. I'd had my fill with games. I tried to look relaxed lying beneath him. "Look, seriously, if you want to kill me, then I suggest you just do it already because I'm tired of hearing about it. In case you haven't noticed, I'm still standing, despite all the death threats and a week of being a blood bag. I certainly have no interest in crying on your shoulder. I'm a survivor, and I don't need a vampire shrink for moral support."

He smirked. "Actually, you're lying on your back in a hole in the ground. A truly *amazing* feat," he said, moving his foot from my chest.

"Whatever," I said, pushing to my knees and shoving past him as I climbed out of the shelter. My house loomed out of the darkness, looking as dejected as I felt. Still, I walked towards it since I had no other place to go. Mentally, I hesitated to put my back to him, but I figured he could dispatch me just as easily to my face if he'd wanted, so I kept walking.

"How did you find me?" I asked, already knowing the answer. It was his voice at the other end of the line when I'd dialed the number I'd found in Asa's bag. How many nights back had I made the call? Time was beginning to run together.

"You called me. Since I had your number, it was easy to trace the call back to you. When did you last feed?" he asked, switching subjects.

Ignoring his question because of my embarrassment, I just kept walking. "So you get a hang-up call, and you automatically know its Asa. How's that work exactly?"

"Asa was my brother, but he was very aberrant, even for a vampire. I only met him once, and that was by complete coincidence. I was living in Denver when he roamed through. As you may or may not know yet, all vampires take the scent of their maker. It's how we're marked. Imagine my surprise when I smelled my own scent too strongly in a bar that I hadn't been in for days. Our father had never mentioned him, and it didn't take long to figure out why. Asa was very broken. I gave him my number on the off chance that he might want to assimilate better into the human world. Since I only give my number to other vampires, it wasn't a great jump in logic to think the phone call was connected to him. What I didn't understand when I traced the number was how you were involved. It seemed unlikely he'd made a child. Since I doubted he'd call in the first place, and if he did, he'd have answered, I suspected he was dead. And so here I am now with my dead estranged brother's helpless child, who just so happened to stake him." His tone held that threat again. It was like he just couldn't get past what I'd done.

I stopped and faced him again. "What are you? The vampire police? Like I said, just kill me already. I'm tired of the innuendo, and I've been dying every night anyways."

"I remain undecided about your fate. Vampires are an ungoverned society, but killing your blood maker is the one offense that we hold each other accountable for. The cardinal sin you might say. But I am willing, for the moment, to give you the benefit of the doubt, as I witnessed firsthand the broken nature of my brother."

"Benefit of the doubt. Such a human expression," I said under my breath.

"We did start out that way. Human, each one of us. But we've ended up so much more. Which is why the blood bond is so sacred. The blood is what pulled us from the bland herd of humanity," he said.

I looked back at my house, remembering what he'd said about the search warrant. Benefit of the doubt was not a luxury I had with the Madison County Sheriff's office. He'd said there were six patrol cars here this morning, but at the moment, I could detect no one other than myself and my visitor. I guess the authorities had pulled the cop who'd been stationed a ways up the road last night.

The house was quiet and devastatingly dark—abandoned looking. The back door had been left cracked by the police, and the yellow police streams fluttered from the deck. *Just like a crime scene*, I thought. Oh right, it *was* a crime scene.

"Have the hallucinations begun yet?" he asked from beside me.

I feigned a lost-in-thought moment while I tore the yellow DO NOT CROSS ribbons down. This was one question I didn't want to answer. I hadn't seen Asa since I'd taken the detective down, and I preferred to keep all of that safely tucked away.

"We've all had them. You're not alone," he said.

I nearly snarled. "Yeah, I kind of am alone. So what's with all the Mr. Nice guy now? You were ready to stake me a few minutes ago, and now you're all concerned about when I fed. So I guess I'm not really buying the family love you're selling."

He moved into my personal space; I took a step back for balance, the yellow streamers floating out of my hand and across the porch. "Make no mistake; if I decide you're a saboteur, I will carry out the traditional sentence. But for now, you need to feed."

"Traditional sentence?" I asked. He said nothing, just pointed one graceful finger to the east.

"Rising sun. How could I forget?" I got the heebie-jeebies just thinking about it. "The hallucinations come and go," I answered, deciding I had no reason to keep it from him. "But I've had none in the last twenty-four hours."

"They'll get worse and stronger. Real enough that the thoughts can control you. When did you last feed?"

Shrugging my shoulders at him, I responded dejectedly, "I got the most amount of blood last night when I nearly killed a police detective. But since he shot me full of holes, I suspect most of it poured out on the ground. Before that, I'd say about three days back, and it was more like drinking alcohol straight from the tap."

"Drunks do not make for the best choices. Neither do policemen. They tend to complicate things. And before that?" he questioned.

"The night I killed Asa, I drank from him."

"And when was that?"

I shrugged. Losing track of time had gotten worse each night that passed. "I'm not sure. Several days back."

"Did you drain him?" he asked.

I nodded my head, afraid to put the confession into actual words. He took a deep breath, one hand flexing at his side. "That explains why you've made it this long. Asa's blood was potent. I'm certain he wasn't a fan of discretion, and he drank often, but you won't make it much longer on what you got from him."

"You mean I won't survive it? I can die from not feeding?"

He looked at me skeptically. "No, you can't. But you will wish you were dead because it's very painful. Feeling guilty?"

Obviously, he took this blood maker thing very seriously. It reminded me of the obligations of doctors to other doctors in the Hippocratic oath.

"Look, it's not what you're thinking. I'm not wanting to die over some soul-racking guilt over Asa. I have no guilt over him at all. But I'm probably going to be brought up on first-degree murder charges. My mom's taken my daughter. I'm no longer gainfully employed. So maybe my mom is right. Maybe I'm better off dead."

His body language changed at my words and I had an "oh shit" moment. How could I have been so dumb to have mentioned Ellie and my mother?

"You have a child?" Even his tone was different, sad sounding but resolute. "I mean ... I did. I had a daughter. I don't now because my mom took her and left. She cleaned me out. Took her clothes, her favorite toys." My voice cracked. I could say nothing else. I turned away and walked into the house, jerking more police streamers down with me as I went.

The house was as straight as a pin as a result of Mom's anxious energies. The "my daughter's a psycho-killer-monster of some sort, so I might as well clean the house" type of energy. I could have eaten dinner off the floor. If I ate dinner that is. As it was, I simply sank down in the comfortable leather of my favorite chair. Asa's brother joined me in the matching recliner; the one meant for a husband that had taken off a few years back.

"Where did she take her?" he asked.

"Do you have a name or should I call you 'Uncle'?" I asked, hoping for a subject change.

He frowned. "Definitely do *not* call me 'Uncle'. It's Levi."

"That's a nice name; I'm Annalice," I said by way of introduction.

"Yeah, I know. Got it off of the mailbox, remember? Where did your mom take your daughter?"

I hoped he'd forgotten this line of questioning. I tried again. "Is there a family name? Does your last name change to take into account the new vampire surname?" I asked.

He wasn't easily distracted. "Where did your mom take your

daughter, and don't try to change the subject."

There was silence while I tried to think of an answer. "I don't know," I finally said.

"Annalice, that's a lie."

"Oh, and why is that?"

"Do you love your mother?" he asked.

"What kind of question is that? Of course I love her."

"And you don't think she feels the same about you? If the situation was reversed and your daughter was the one who'd been turned, would you take her child and not tell her where you were going?"

"She said I was better off dead."

His smile was gentle. Understanding. "She didn't mean it."

I shook my head at his naivety. "She's not here, is she?"

"And neither would you be if the roles were reversed. You can't blame her for trying to protect her grandchild."

"Yes, I can," I answered harshly. But he was right. I'd have done the exact same thing.

"Where is she?" he asked again.

"I don't know," I lied again. "If I did, I wouldn't be sitting here with you."

"You're sitting here with me because you don't know of anything else to do. You have no plan, no strategy. You don't want to hurt her, and you don't want to leave her, which leaves you in a frozen state."

The laughter came out of me dark and soft. "No plan. No daughter. No future."

"If I want to find her, I will. You must know that."

I bristled, and our talk went deadly in an instant. "Asa threatened my daughter. Look where it landed him."

It was a quiet but deadly hiss. Not overstated and boisterous. The sound curled my toes, but I meant what I'd said, and I wasn't backing down. Weak, starving. It didn't matter. I would die protecting her.

He knew exactly what I was thinking. "You can't protect her if you're dead."

"And you can't kill her if *you're* dead," I responded.

"You're like a cat defending against a Rottweiler. You make a lot of noise. You try to look ferocious with your hackles up, and you mean the words, but you've no way to back them up."

"Asa thought the same."

A subtle intake of air, and he leaned back into the chair. "And that's where I get stumped in this whole affair. You had nothing but show, a small but loud Banty rooster, against Asa as well, and yet somehow you managed to best him. Logic would say he trusted you, and you betrayed him."

"I told you what happened."

He lifted dark eyebrows at me, his full lips coming together in a sensual pouty face. "Maybe you're a better liar than I give you credit for. If you were human, I would know in a second. With vampires, it's much harder to tell."

"Well, I guess we're at a stalemate then," I said.

"No. I just haven't called checkmate yet. But make no mistake, I have the upper hand."

And he did. We both knew it. He wasn't Asa. There was something much stronger about this man. It whispered confidence and control. But not Asa's kind of control. He was different. I'd have no choice but to try to prove my innocence. I was going to have to play nice.

"So then how's this going to work exactly? How do I prove my innocence and escape roasting in the sun? And is the traditional sentence ever commuted to a simple staking depending on circumstances, such as being held captive by your brother, the psychopath?"

He was all smiles now. "As it turns out, no. The sentence is always death by dawn. And if I detect any subterfuge when you are well enough to be questioned, then you will be stripped naked and hung from a suitable tree to meet the first light. Of course, there will be an audience. You see, we vampires believe in vigilante justice. It's kind of like the old west hangings. We invite everyone we know and make a party of it."

"Why naked?" I was appalled just thinking of the humiliation.

"It's just more fun that way," he answered without any hesitation at all.

141

"Nice to know that my new species are all a bunch of sick bastards." If I'd been human, it would have turned my stomach. Instead, I turned my face and stared at the wall.

"For now, let's focus on getting you fed. I won't question you in this condition. You need to be at your best."

"How can I think of dinner after such threats?"

A small smirk lifted his lips away from his teeth—bright red on white—and I looked away at the sight of his fangs. They did something strange to my insides. I considered leaving the room altogether, but the aroma of blood stirred the air and the sound of it dripping onto the leather of the chair brought me to my knees in front of him. This was not what I expected.

It probably would have been polite to not bite him since he had done it for me, but he made no sound of pain as my own fangs slipped into the skin of his wrist. Cool blood met my tongue where I craved hot, but still, it was like an oasis in the desert, and I drank until the fingers of his other hand wrapped into my hair.

But he'd let me get more than enough, and for a few hours, I had peace from the burn that had settled in the pit of my belly the night I awoke after killing Asa. When I lifted my mouth from his arm, my mind was clear, like waking up after going to sleep with a marvelous headache. For a rare moment, I forgot how much danger I was in. From the vampire beside me. From the police. In those moments, the memory of Asa was completely gone. No thoughts of him and no hallucinations of his face or voice. I was at peace. I let my body roll down onto the rug and closed my eyes. And for once since waking that night, my mind was empty of everything.

Levi said nothing during my cathartic moments, and I almost forgot he was there until I heard him breathe out slowly. I opened my eyes as he got to his feet.

"I'm leaving. The cellar is the safest place I can think of for the moment, and that is where you should spend the daylight hours."

I sat up quickly. "Where are you going? You're leaving me after all the threats?" I was dumbfounded, and although he'd spent the last couple hours trying to frighten me, his was the first contact that hadn't felt stilted and unnatural in nearly a week.

Besides, I was scared and maybe I preferred death threats to being alone. So far, alone time as a vampire had sucked royally.

"I'm not abandoning you, Annalice, and I meant what I said, that you have major explaining to do about Asa. I'll be back by tomorrow evening. The following morning at the latest. Either way, stay put and don't try to run. You'll never make it, and if by some miracle you did, the world is too small a place to hide. At least for immortals."

"But *why* are you going?"

"To drink. The responsibility of feeding you falls to me now, at least until I have decided what to do about Asa's second death. I must stay fed. Besides, I can't stay here with your saliva in my veins. It will cloud my judgment," he answered.

"What does that mean?" I asked, but he was gone before I'd finished the sentence.

Chapter 18

The next evening, I awoke the way I'd entered the death sleep. Alone. The name I'd given to what happened to me each dawn was morbid, even to me, but it was the most accurate description I could find. It was dreamless and as close to non-existence as I could imagine. I was alive one moment, thinking and feeling, craving and burning, and then I was not. But there was a definite break. Some point of time I could define as having not been around. Then the next moment, I was all of those things again. Unlike sleep, there was no "coming to." There was no slowly becoming aware. There was existence, and then there was not. It was creepy.

The bullets that had riddled my chest and belly clanked against each other as I sat up and dropped onto the dirt floor. I picked one up, the metal bullet exploded and curled backwards like a flower in bloom. "Asshole," I whispered to myself. Rumsfield had shot me with a hollow point. No wonder he had said I was a monster. What else could survive these?

The prior night's activities had been so insane that I hadn't even questioned how these little reminders of my evening spent with Rumsfield would come out. I gathered the metal fragments and laid them aside. More mementos that I wasn't human. I felt for the wounds, knowing they'd be gone, too. Levi's blood had been rich. I could taste that much. *Where is he?* I wondered. Why couldn't he stay with me last night? And more importantly, why did I care? Was I that lonely?

The hunger in my belly had returned, but it was only a warm

coal, not a raging fire, so I could deal with it. I felt like myself again, which meant I had to see Ellie. Maybe Mom might even feel somewhat normal around me. I didn't give Levi another thought.

Behind the apartment complex and melded into the shadows, I waited for courage. Just a few feet away through some thin brick walls, I could hear Ellie talking to my mother about school. Math was a little harder than she'd expected. There was a boy who was stealing her jacket. Mom said he was crushing on her. Ellie sighed and said that was just weird. Then she said she missed me. My mom said nothing, just turned back to the stove and clicked on the oven.

Immediately, I felt vindicated. Of course Ellie missed me, and I missed her desperately. I stepped out of the shadows, intent on seeing her tonight.

"Won't that just make it harder on her?" Levi asked as he settled into the shadows of the building beside me. I'd never felt his presence nor seen his movement.

"How did you do that?" I asked. Compared to him, I *was* a clumsy child.

He pointed to the side of his head. "You don't think like a vampire yet, and you're not in touch with the environment or your surroundings. That's the kind of thing your maker teaches you. If you don't kill your maker, that is."

I snorted. "Whatever. Asa never had any intention of teaching me anything."

Levi leaned back onto the wall of the complex, his long legs crossed in front of him. "We'll get to that later. As I said, do you think this is a good idea?"

"I'm here to hunt," I lied.

He raised an eyebrow. "Your hunting skills suck. You're here because this is where your daughter lives."

"She needs to see me. She needs to know that I still love her."

"Does she? Or is it you that needs to see her? To know that you are still loved."

In the apartment, Mom was helping Ellie cut her dinner. I could hear the knife sliding across the stoneware. They were making plans for the weekend. Mom mentioned going to a couple of antique stores in Fayetteville. My heart cracked, fissured. Maybe Levi was right. Maybe I needed it more than Ellie. "Is that so wrong?" I asked.

"Do you want to make this harder on her?"

I looked away from his scrutiny. "What kind of question is that? Of course I don't."

"Then walk away. Coming and going in and out of her life is the worst thing you can do to her."

I started to argue, but he put a hand up. "At least walk away tonight. You need to feed more and be at full strength before you go in. You'll feel more human. You'll look more human, and it'll help your relationship with your mother. Besides, the police have been looking for you. They've been here asking questions, and they're casing the place. You'd know that if you were being cautious."

"You afraid of the *police*?" I asked, dropping a large amount of sarcasm on the last word.

"I'm not afraid of any human. But you're a liability to me right now and a danger to your family. You *should* be afraid of the police. I can disappear and not be seen again for fifty years. You, being in the family way, are tethered here. At least you are mentally. A prison doesn't have to have metal bars."

His logic was flawless. Of course the police would be watching, and I wasn't skilled enough to fight them all, and if they had enough bullets, they could take me down. At least temporarily.

Resigned to listen to him, I followed him back into the woods.

Chapter 19

"**W**elcome home," Levi said as I stepped out of the woods into what had once been a central yard for several buildings that looked like barracks. To the north end, a couple of larger buildings were sagging with age. They all looked worse for the wear.

"Why did you leave me behind, and why are we here?" I asked. Once he'd glided out of the shadows of the apartment complex, he'd left me struggling to track him. If it hadn't been for his strong scent trailing behind him through the woods, I'd have never caught him. His speed was as amazing as my tracking ability was poor. He was lounging against the rotting remains of a front porch when I stepped out of the forest.

"First, you need tracking experience. Second you, actually *we*, need a new place to hide. And this is it."

"You want me to leave my home?"

"Well, actually, I want you to leave the hole in the ground behind what was *once* your home."

"For another hole in the ground, I presume?"

"Do you want to be taken in for questioning by the police? Because eventually one of those cops is going to stumble across the doorway to that cellar. You know the old expression 'even a blind squirrel finds an acorn now and again?' We can't stay there."

I looked around at the deserted campground, finding nothing redeeming about the place. "But why here? It's at least fifty miles away from my daughter and in the middle of damn near nowhere."

"And fifty miles away from all of those cops, and the one you nearly killed, who by the way, is fighting for his life in the hospital you once practiced at. Out of sight and out of mind is what you need."

"It makes me look all the more guilty," I said. I'd been rethinking my strategy while chasing Levi through the woods. I didn't look like I'd been shot. They certainly couldn't prove that I had. Wouldn't it be better to show up and make Rumsfield look like a man gone crazy?

"You couldn't look any guiltier if you went and stood over his bed with a machete. What you need to do is to lie low and let the dust settle. Eventually, if he survives, his story is going to start not making sense. When that happens, you can resurface and answer a few lingering questions. Right now, the police aren't feeling as generous as I am to dole out the benefit of the doubt."

I studied his expression, looking for lies, but his face was as guileless as a baby's. Still, I didn't believe him, and I told him so.

"I'm not lying. I have no reason to. Your previous life is immaterial right now. Your daughter is with your mother, who will never let you near her after what happened the other night, unless you're willing to take her by force, which I suspect you are not. You are a woman wanted for questioning, although you haven't been charged with anything yet. And you're a vampire who has some serious explaining to do to me. If I'm not satisfied, you're going to be much deader that you already are, and none of your other worries will matter anymore."

We stared each other down for a few moments. He didn't move at all. His eyes didn't flinch, and there wasn't even a hint of a friendly expression anywhere on his face.

"Fine. What is this place?" I asked, walking on into what had once been the yard. Whatever it was, it hadn't been used in years. The vines of the forest were snaking through trees as big as my lower leg. I guessed it had been abandoned for at least three decades. Maybe four.

"I think it's an old Boy Scout camp. Or maybe a CCC camp. I can't detect any human scent outside the buildings. Inside, I can pick up a few old ones, but it's been a couple years since this place was visited—let alone occupied."

I pushed my way through the vinery and into one of the barracks. A pine tree had erupted straight through the floor and out the roof. Two sets of rotting bunk beds lined the walls. Mice droppings littered the moldy plank floor as well as pine needles that had dropped from the tree disappearing through the ceiling. The rock fireplace, the trademark of the CCC, stood tall and erect in the corner, the only structure in the barrack unmarked by time.

The CCC, or Civilian Conversation Corps, had built many places like this across the country during the Great Depression. Arkansas, being desperately poor, had been blessed by its fair share, but a few had been abandoned by the state from lack of funds.

Twelve buildings were left standing here. At least two more had collapsed entirely. The majority of those still standing were barracks like the first one I'd walked into. Another was a mess hall with a wood-burning potbellied stove still standing in one far corner. Picnic style log tables, now hosting only dust and cobwebs, stood in the center of the room, and an outdated kitchen ran the length of the wall behind them.

Levi led the way to the last building hovering on the very edge of the camp, where another mountain was beginning to rise toward the sky. It was a two-story, rock and wood home, small and compact with a screened in porch built partially into the face of the mountain—probably the overseer's cabin from the looks of it. If it had been in better shape, it would have been called rustic, but now it was just called done for. Still it was beautiful in its own way.

"This is where we're staying," Levi said. The door was partially ajar. Too much wind and rain had bowed the wood of the floor and the door stuck as we walked through. Levi pushed it gently until the wood slowly relaxed and let us pass. "No reason to destroy it," he said, indicating the door. "It has a certain beauty. Don't you think?" I did think so, but I didn't say anything.

The interior looked similar to the barracks but in better shape.

The wood had held up more in the face of the elements, and other than around the door, the flooring was overall intact. Another of the rock fireplaces dominated one wall of the room, the firebox cradling the rotting remains of a bird's nest between the andirons. The kitchen was small with only an antique stove and fire pit.

Levi motioned to a stairwell leading up the stairs. "The upstairs isn't light tight." I nodded in understanding. "Those stairs lead to the basement, which is where we'll stay. It's light tight and dry. Pretty comfortable, really."

So his idea of comfort and mine weren't the same, and I told him so. He rolled his eyes. "This is a new life, Annalice. You need to get over some things. Right now, if you're not roasting in the sun, then you're pretty comfortable."

He was right. I was logical enough to know that, but if someone had told me I'd be grateful to sleep in a cold, abandoned basement a mere three weeks ago, I'd have told them they were nuts. But in this new reality, I was being considered for attempted murder, my daughter was gone, I drank blood, and I couldn't go out in the sun. Yeah, things had changed.

"Kind of hard to see it that way," I said as I followed the stairs down into the dank remains of the basement. Light tight was an understatement, and even with my vampire eyesight, I could only see outlines and shapes. Levi could no doubt see much more, but I was hungry again and not at full strength. I wasn't even sure I knew what my full strength really was. I flinched as Levi lit a match.

Levi was right, I realized, as I looked grudgingly around the room. The floor plan was open; the dirt floor brushed smooth from the many shoes that had once shuffled across it. In the far right corner, the comforter from my bed was folded up on a set of wooden bunkbeds. The basement was dry; the wood in good shape as well. In another corner, a leftover chair had been placed with another blanket and some pillows from my house. A handful of candles had been positioned around the room. Levi lit them as I watched. "I can see perfectly in the dark," he said. "Still, I have always enjoyed a little light, and of course, there is no electricity here."

"A lot of effort for a girl you may decide to hang in the sun," I said. I picked up one of my pillows and inhaled the comforting smell of home. I missed it badly.

He finished lighting the candles before he answered. "You're right, but don't let that fool you. I'll strip you and hang you facing east if I decide it's the right thing to do. Until then, there is no reason we can't be comfortable. Consider it similar to a last meal or last rites."

We stared each other down for a minute, he conveying that he was serious, and me attempting to convey that I didn't care. It was a lie on my part, but Levi was pretty convincing. Eventually, I looked away, knowing I'd lost the contest.

"So tonight then?" I asked. My voice was steady. I don't know how I managed that given that I might be burning in the sun in a few hours if I couldn't convince him that I'd put a legitimate end to Asa.

Levi nodded his head, his eyes never leaving mine. "But first things first, you need blood."

My fangs grazed my tongue at the mention of drinking. Levi spread a blanket on the ground and motioned for me to sit. Knowing what was coming after the blood, I hesitated but finally lowered myself down. There was no getting around this.

He held his arm out, wrist up, as I moved closer and bowed my head over his arm, pushing my long hair to my back. I was so hungry. Or thirsty. Or maybe both. I found it hard to describe. I bit through his upper arm where the vessels are deeper but bigger. The wrist veins are shallower, but they're also smaller. They collapse easily if the pressure is too high, just ask any nurse.

The blood came quickly, cool but calming. Just like the previous night, he didn't stop me, and I drank, oblivious until I felt his other hand in my hair. Finally, he pulled me roughly away. I was still thirsty when he did but not burning with hunger like I had been.

His hand was still wrapped in my hair, his eyes closed and he was breathing heavy. I hadn't seen him like this before. Or Asa either for that matter.

"What's wrong with you? Am I hurting you or something?" I asked.

"No. Just give me a minute. Don't move," he said. Other than his breathing, he was still and quiet.

I tried to disengage his hand from my hair. He jerked me hard again. "Do not move!" It was a harsh command but laced with some pleading as well. I froze, having no idea what was happening or what I'd done wrong.

"This is dangerous for us both," he whispered under his breath as he moved his upper body toward mine. He sounded both so resigned and so excited that I instinctively pulled back. The strength in his arm increased as he pulled me closer again. I lost the game of tug of war as he drew me across the space between us. His hand in my hair pushed my head backwards, and I felt his fangs graze my neck. It wasn't a bite, just a nick, and immediately my skin began to tingle around the small puncture wound. I felt his jaw open for a true bite and then a hesitation before he snapped his mouth shut, his teeth grinding against each other. Like statues, he held us in that position for a few moments before he lightly brushed his full lips across my skin. Then he was gone. The air brushed my cheek as he left, and when I opened my eyes again, he was standing on the far side of the room, bent at the waist, his hands on his thighs like he needed the support.

I waited for him to say something. He didn't, and I started to get to my feet. My motion jerked his head up. "What do you *not* understand about the words 'don't move'?" He looked half-crazed. His pupils were large; the blue of his iris reduced to a tiny sapphire ring surrounding deep black space. His hands were clenched hard on his legs, making the muscles of his forearms stand out in hard cords.

Even when he'd threatened to hang me in the sun, he hadn't been this scary. I dropped back down and watched him warily. I'm not a coward, but I'm not stupid. This vampire had years on me, and I wouldn't get five feet before he brought me down as easily as a lion takes a gazelle.

Nearly twenty minutes passed before he finally straightened up to his full height. He paced a few steps around the perimeter of the room, careful to keep his eyes off of me. With his every step, I could feel the tension draining from his muscles until finally he resembled the man I'd met a few days back.

"Let's talk about Asa," he said as he set down in front of me. His eyes were no longer the black pits from a few minutes before. He was calm and collected for the most part. His breathing was still a little rapid, and he kept dropping his eyes to my mouth.

"Let's talk about what the hell just happened to you," I said back. "Can I move now by the way? You know, scratch my nose or something?"

"Vampires do not have itches. At least not the kind you're talking about," he answered. "Back to Asa. How did you meet him?"

"I'm going to need more of an explanation than that, Levi."

"Trust me. I'm going to give you all the explanation you need when we get done with the topic of killing one's maker. If I deem you worthy of living that is. So, again, how did you meet Asa?"

It was inevitable. I couldn't avoid talking about him forever. *Be careful and watch your words*, I mentally warned myself.

"You'll do better if you just tell the truth," Levi said, reading my expression. "You don't have much of a poker face."

"I thought you said vampires were good liars," I answered back.

"One of the reasons I took a couple of days to study you. I know you a little better now. Watched your facial expressions, your body language. I know what I'm looking for. How did you meet Asa?"

I smiled sarcastically. "Like most human women met Asa. Flat on my back at the tip of his fangs."

Levi raised his eyebrows in suspicion. "And yet like most humans who met Asa in this fashion, you didn't end the night dead at the tip of his fangs. Why not?"

"He had other plans and decided to make me a proposition."

"Asa made you a deal." It wasn't a question. I guess he wasn't that surprised. "What was it?"

"He said he needed a human to reacquaint him with the twentieth century." It sounded stupid saying it out loud.

Again he spoke with the raised eyebrows, but this time he pursed his lips. "And you did that? You reacquainted him with the twentieth century?"

"No."

"And why not?"

"Because all he wanted was blood and sex."

He shrugged his shoulders and looked at me hard. "So you taught him nothing?"

"You can lead a vampire to water, but you can't make him drink," I said.

Levi narrowed his eyes. "Don't be a smartass."

"Get a sense of humor," I said. Again with the steely eyes.

I sighed heavily. "Fine. He only asked a few questions about cellphones, but other than that, he didn't want to know about anything."

"And in exchange for this deal, Asa promised you what?"

"I told you the first time we met, Levi. He promised that my mother and daughter would go free. That he'd kill me but leave them alone."

"So you knew you were going to die?"

"Yeah, he made that pretty clear."

"So what happened to the agreement? Why are you still alive?"

"Are you serious?" I asked. "I'm alive because I outsmarted him. He was going to kill me."

"Yes, Annalice. He was. He made that perfectly clear, and you agreed to his terms."

I couldn't believe what I was hearing. "Yeah, he promised me certain death for the life of my family or just my death. So my choice was death or death. The deal wasn't fair."

"Of course, the deal wasn't fair. He was a vampire, but you accepted what was offered. A deal doesn't have to be fair to be accepted."

"I gave my word to cooperate with him, and I did. I did everything he said to do. I answered every question he asked of me. I offered up my body and my blood at his every command. I agreed to cooperate for the full week, and I did. I *never* agreed to not fight at the end. I never agreed that I wouldn't try to kill him in the last moments."

"And how did you manage to ram a stake through his heart exactly? You were a weak, dying human. Was he in his day sleep?" Levi's voice had gotten deadlier with each passing word.

I spoke quickly, fearing hesitation would bring his immediate wrath. "I couldn't go out into the sun, Levi. My skin was on fire. I faced him as almost a full-fledged vampire."

"So he was changing you?"

"Not intentionally."

"And you didn't tell him?"

"Of course not. And why should I? That was my only edge. Asa was alone and bitter all the way up to the moment I rammed that stake into his heart. Otherwise, he would have known I was changing right in front of his eyes."

This wasn't going well. Levi's expression had gone from an open book to a locked diary with a missing key. "And how did you know to stake him?" he asked.

I laughed out loud. "Are you fricking kidding me? Have you not seen any vampire movies? Everyone knows to kill a vampire you have to stake him. Besides, he told me all the ways to kill him."

The atmosphere changed in the room, and even the soft glow of the candles couldn't infuse any warmth into his expression. "Only one reason exists to reveal your Achilles heel to another, and that is because you trust them. He trusted you, and you betrayed him." The candle wavered in the wind as Levi rose up from the floor.

"I never betrayed him. He didn't trust anyone. You can't betray someone who doesn't trust you," I said, knowing my words were doing no good. I stayed put on the dirt floor, not wanting to incense him further.

"You're going to burn in the sun. You will pay for what you did to him."

I was terrified. The kind of terrified that makes you move like molasses. A long entrenched response that your body adopts when the time is not quite right for fight or flight. I inched my legs out from under me and slowly lifted myself to a sprinting position. "I didn't do anything wrong!" I insisted again.

"You were supposed to be his companion, and you betrayed him. That is the only explanation for his revealing our secrets to you. I don't believe you could have bested him in a fair fight. He trusted you, and you betrayed him."

My fingernails dug into the dirt. Levi stalked a circle around me like a mercenary. I spun slowly on the balls of my feet keeping him in front of me. When my back was to the stairwell, I stood up quickly. He spun towards the sudden movement and stopped.

"And I would have been his companion if he'd let me live. I was planning to leave with him if he turned me. He offered me a second deal a few days later. If I agreed to spend the night with him as a true vampire, he'd answer my every question except where his daytime sleeping spot was. I never knew that little tidbit until he was dead. I went with him that last night, and he killed a human in the woods. He made me watch, and when it was over, despite my having done everything he requested, he told me he was going to kill me anyhow, and that he wasn't going to turn me. I didn't stake him when he wasn't looking, Levi. I fought him in a fair fight, and I won. He was simply too blind to see that I'd changed."

Levi watched me blandly, his mind already made up. "You never raise a hand against your maker," he answered.

When he reached for me, I was gone. I heard the last of his answer as I exploded out the top of the staircase and through the front door of the sagging cabin. I was partially fed and faster than I remembered. The forest should have been a blur as I sped through it, but amazingly, my view was crystal clear as I raced away from camp and back towards town. What also had amazing clarity was the sound of the rock Levi threw whistling through the air. I looked over my shoulder just before it barreled into my back and cracked my spinal canal wide open. My legs went out from under me with no precision whatsoever, and I fell face first into the grunge of the forest floor, my face skidding ungracefully across it.

Everyone admires Anne Boleyn for facing her beheading so calmly, and I'd like to say I looked that brave, serenely waiting for the end. In reality, I was spitting dirt out of my mouth, my tongue lacerated and bleeding, desperately clawing the dirt, and dragging myself on bloodied elbows across the ground as Levi walked towards me. There wasn't a hint of pity on his face.

"I sentence you to death. You will be hanged in the first light," Levi said, flipping me over. He was silent as he grabbed hold of my ankles and dragged me back to camp. I was cussing like the proverbial sailor.

Chapter 20

I'd quit screaming by the time he dumped me in the middle of camp. My head was on fire from bumping on the rocks, as was the part of my spine that was still intact. Below that, I was numb and motionless, my legs dead weight.

"You could at least have the decency to quit grubbing in the dirt and face your sentence like a vampire," Levi said as he began to strip my jeans down my legs. I was clawing at his hands and trying to rip his hair out.

"Like a vampire? As far as I can tell, there's nothing at all honorable about any of you. And you want me to face death bravely? Screw you!"

He jerked my boots off, one after another, followed by one of my socks. My toes were starting to burn. Already I was healing. "I am a very honorable man."

"You're not a man. You're a vampire, and a piece of shit at that." I gripped my sweater with both hands, but he jerked it roughly, and I lost my grip. My bra followed.

Leaning over me, Levi gripped my chin so harshly my mandibular joints ground together in my ears. "So says the girl, the vampire, who killed her own maker. Don't talk to me about honor. You don't know the first thing about it."

"And you think Asa did? You know he never mentioned you. Know why? Because he didn't give a shit about you or your *precious* maker. You wanna know what he said about him?"

He didn't want to know; I could tell as he looked away. But finally, he looked back because he couldn't stand the not knowing.

"Asa said he hoped your maker was in hell. He hoped he was burning." I was smiling when I said it. I wanted the words to hurt. I wanted him to hurt.

He looked away again into the distance of the forest, his strong hand holding my ankles. The light Arkansas breeze lifted his hair, and I could smell his anger. "But Asa didn't put him there, did he?" Levi finally answered. His voice was calm, too precise. "But you did. And that's why you're going to burn," he said, pulling off the other sock.

I searched desperately for a response but couldn't come up with one, so I resumed my fighting and managed to get one blow in to the side of his head. He cursed under his breath and got to his feet. I couldn't have hurt him that badly, I thought to myself as he walked a few feet away. The rattle of chains told me I'd been right. Levi wasn't hurt.

I'd tried to hold on to some semblance of calm, but when he came back carrying two chains with links as big as his thumbs, I completely lost it. I hit him with doubled fists, slapped, spit and bucked as much as my broken back would allow. He didn't retaliate at all, except to pin my flailing arms with his knees and avoid my blows as best he could, until I managed to get my teeth into his thigh. His blood spurted into my mouth, and I sucked it down in mouthfuls until he managed to jerk his body away from mine. By that time, I was shackled, and he jerked the two chains, each connected to a limb at both ends, and doubled me up into the letter c.

"My blood is sacred," he hissed. "And you are undeserving."

"Little high on yourself, aren't you?" I answered back, but my struggling had stopped. Putting up a good fight is hard to do when the back of your head is nearly touching your feet.

He dragged me to a large oak tree in the center of camp. Old enough to have been here when the camp was in use, the tree towered over the remains of the small barracks. Two or three of the branches would have been perfect for tire swings. The highest one must have also been perfect for hangings, and it was to this one that Levi dragged me, still bent in half.

I cried out when he cinched my arms up above my head and laced the chains over the tree branch. He re-connected them to the chains on my legs. All the weight was on my arms, and if I'd been human, the force would have dislocated my shoulders. As it was, the pressure just hurt like hell.

"So what about your witnesses?" I asked through gritted teeth.

"Decided I didn't want to wait. I'm witness enough. But no worries. Everyone will hear your screams two counties over."

"I hope I disappoint you," I said, my teeth grinding harshly. One of my back molars splintered with the pressure.

Behind me, he cinched the chains tighter. My hips grated in pain, and I sucked the air in harshly. "I really doubt you'll disappoint me in *that* regard. Pain tolerance doesn't seem to be one of your strengths. Besides, you've already disappointed me enough for several lifetimes."

Grabbing hold of my feet, he twisted my lower body so that the chains crossed each other in an x pattern. My right shoulder couldn't take the pressure any longer and dislocated. I bit my tongue to keep from screaming. Blood ran through my teeth and down my lips. I swallowed it down as best I could.

"What was that?" Levi asked. "Did you try to say something?" He let go of my legs and my body swung around again, jarring the dislocated joint. Blood ran from my eyes. He was right. I'd put on quite a show at first light.

He walked in a half circle to face me, one finger tracing the contours of my waist and the swell of my hipbones. "Such a shame that you must be put to death," he said, placing the flat of his palm over my lower belly. "We could have had lifetimes to enjoy each other." The fine hairs on my lower abdomen rose against his breath while he stroked one of my inner thighs.

"Don't you mean Asa and I could have had lifetimes together?" I lifted my upper body to see him better. And there his logic faltered. I saw the realization on his face when he recognized his own mental non-sequitur. "Because if I hadn't staked Asa, I'd still be with him, right?"

Levi said nothing, just swallowed a little harder than he

needed to.

"Be careful or you'll choke on your pride," I said. He pushed me away from him, and I swung painfully in the chains as I struggled to talk. "You know in your heart that Asa would have never made anyone. But you can't accept the fact that he didn't want me because then you'd have to accept that he didn't want you either."

It hit me then like a bolt of lightning. "And that's what bothers you, isn't it?"

I could see the indecisive tilt of his head as he considered looking at me. "You're jealous because I spent more time with Asa than anyone else, including you. You keep wondering what he saw in this woman that made him even consider turning her. You wanted to be close to him, but he wouldn't let you in. Was it a brother thing? Did you have a brother once and your maker killed him? Were you thinking Asa was going to take his place? You just can't get past the idea that he considered choosing me over you. So now I burn for it!"

He ignored me completely, but I could hear him gritting his teeth. Obviously, I'd hit a nerve, but would it be enough to elicit the response I was looking for.

The next couple of hours slid by like ketchup from a glass bottle. I kept up a steady stream of insults, interrupted with as many logical reasons I could think of that I didn't deserve what he was doing to me. And by the set of his shoulders, I could tell I was getting exactly nowhere. Jealousy is a tough façade to chip. The only reply to all my insults and testimony was "two hours until you won't be so chatty."

I kept going. "And exactly how do you have a maker that doesn't realize he is *making* you? I wasn't even fully formed when I staked him. I still had a heartbeat when Asa died because I hadn't been *made*. As far as Asa was concerned, I was completely human. He had no idea he'd changed me. To *make* is a verb that requires intentional action. Like being a decent man. That also requires intentional action. Something inherently missing from male vampires it seems. Asa couldn't take any more credit for me than Alexander Fleming and his forgotten Petri dish."

But no matter what I said, Levi was committed to ignoring me and another hour passed in complete silence. He'd relocated a tombstone-sized rock up against a tree, leaned back, and studied the sky as my remaining ball and socket joints dislocated. I'd screamed in pain as the tendons pulled apart, but it was actually a relief once the pressure was gone and I was able to get quiet and think about what was happening. There was nothing left to say. No new insults left to gouge him with. I had no more arguments that I could throw at him, and if he wanted me to beg, well, then he could go to hell. And speaking of that, I said a prayer for my daughter and mother and asked God to spare me passing from this fire to another.

I was deep in morose thoughts when Levi spoke. I was so convinced of my doom at first I thought I'd hallucinated. "Did you compare yourself to penicillin?" he asked.

I lifted my head up when he repeated the question. "What does it matter? You don't have the good sense to understand my metaphor." I gave the chains a hard jerk as if it put more power into my anger. The pain was searing. Not the best one of my ideas so far.

"I would expect you to be intelligent enough to know those chains are a circuit. Pressure exerted on any limb will exert an equal and opposite force on another. That's Newton's law. If you don't understand that, I seriously doubt you're going to revolutionize modern medicine in the way penicillin did," he said.

But he was speaking again, and I took that as a good sign. I could feel his eyes on my back as the arguments I'd made bantered back and forth in his head against his own. Two lawyers both with good points. I knew it immediately when my council won out. He still had a few human vestiges, and the breath that he'd been holding blew out in relief. Maybe this had been harder on him than I thought.

Grasping my shoulders, he swung me around to face him. More hot bloody tears tracked down my cheeks from the pain. He pulled my face towards his, his stare determined and hard. I knew he wasn't going to hang me in the sun now but that didn't guarantee my survival. There had been two decisions to make.

To sentence me to burn, which he'd decided against, and whether he should put an end to Asa's mistake. He could still kill me if for no other reason than to make the world a better place. I glared back, unflinching into his face while he decided if I was going to exist or not. The second decision appeared to be made when he narrowed his eyes, his gaze slipping downward to my mouth and then to my naked body. Being owned is not a good feeling. My breasts hardened in humiliation. I didn't look away though. I couldn't stand to appear weak.

He smiled at my bravery. "You would have made a good lawyer. A bit snarky, but you *do* have a valid point. I agree that he did not knowingly make you, the sacred relationship wasn't there, and so you owed him nothing. But we remain with a problem. You are still alive, without a maker. Therefore, I assume the rights and duties of your creator. In my possession and through my blood, you will be made whole. You will never raise a hand to me, and I will never desert you. I bear full responsibility for you now."

Levi unhooked the chains that shackled my forearms to my ankles and my right shoulder slid back into place as he lowered me to the ground. I groaned in pain as I hit the dirt. My spine still hadn't healed and my back was on fire. I was naked, dirty and utterly humiliated. Levi held out his arm as a peace offering.

"Screw you," I said, turning my face away. "And I'd be *whole* if you hadn't done this to me so you can shut up with the crazy talk." The overdone poeticism was pissing me off.

"Refusing my blood won't get back at me. You're the only one who suffers."

"Easy for you to say since you're the one who did this to me," I answered.

"Would it help if I apologized?"

"What do you think?" I asked.

"Then I won't. Asa was a vampire. He deserved a trial for his death."

"Always thinking of Asa," I said, ripping into his arm, his gasp of surprise and pain bringing me some measure of happiness.

Chapter 21

Within the hour, my spine had healed and I was standing on my own two feet. The clothes Levi had so graciously dropped on my belly were a relief to pull back on. He'd let me drink until I'd stopped on my own and then he'd slid down the length of a tree looking dejected. No longer starving, and my anger slightly appeased, I was willing to talk civilly again. "I don't know why you care so much about Asa. He certainly didn't care anything about you."

"You don't have to be cruel," Levi answered. A stick of wood made its way into his hand and he scribbled in the dirt like any four-year-old wanting to avoid eye contact.

"Don't I? You were about to burn me alive over a worthless waste of skin."

He ignored my question, carving deeper into the earth. "He wasn't worthless."

I looked at him incredulously, my anger full blown again. "I don't think you knew him very well, Levi. Maybe you're not the best judge."

"I need to know how it happened."

"Why? You barely knew him?"

His hand paused in his writing. "I think your generation calls it closure."

I was hesitant to give him any details, not knowing what would put him on the killing spree again, but for once, Levi's emotions were blatant in his expression. He'd loved, in some way, this brother he knew nothing about.

"I'm not going to hurt you," he said.

I hoped to God he wasn't lying. "Fine. What do you want to know?"

"How did it happen?"

"I've told you already. I staked him."

"I know that. But after ... the stake ... that. How long did he last? Did he give you no advice? Point you in my direction? He had to have said something."

"He really wasn't in the mood for giving advice, Levi."

"Tell me something!" The stick he'd been writing in the dirt with splintered in his hand. I waited while he took a deep breath. "Anything that will help me to know him."

"There was no *knowing* him. What do you not get about that? Asa was broken."

"There had to be something. Some kind of indication that he had ..."

He stopped there. I think he didn't know what to say, but I knew what he wanted. "You want some kind of indication that he had something good left in him, Levi. But what if there wasn't anything?"

"Please just tell me what happened."

"And if I say the wrong thing and you lose it? When it comes to him, you don't think clearly."

"I give you my word that when it comes to Asa, you have nothing left to fear from me."

So he might kill me for something else. Great. Well, here goes nothing, I thought. I took a steadying breath and let it all pour out. "I've already told you how it happened. He had no idea I was turning. I don't think he realized it could be a slow process. The only experience he had at all was his own turning, which was a quick, fast-forwarded approach. He didn't see it coming, and I had no specific plan. I figured I'd know when the time was right. And I did. But after that, I didn't know what to do or what to expect. He didn't die quickly, and I had time to take the blood I needed to complete the conversion from him. He still wasn't gone by that time, and I pulled the stake out. And I would have left him like that and let him live probably if he hadn't laughed and said he hadn't meant any of his threats. He said he'd have let me go if I'd simply escaped. I staked him again when he told me I was a killer and said he wished he could be there when I killed my daughter. He offered me no advice. He didn't ask anything of me. Not once in that entire time did he ask a thing of me. He didn't mention his maker, and he didn't mention you."

Levi sat quietly absorbing what I'd just said. I knew he was trying to find something to hope for when it came to Asa, but there was nothing there. "So no resolution with himself or anyone else when the end came," Levi whispered. He was still drawing in the dirt, small strokes that mirrored his agitation.

Levi looked so pitiful that I almost felt bad for him. Almost.

"I think your maker is fully to blame. He made Asa, killed his family and then cast him out. You should take it up with that worthless piece of skin," I said as I picked up my own stick. I carved my name deeply into the ground like thousands of humans before me.

"My creator is a good man," Levi answered.

"Whatever. Tell that to the thousands of Asa's victims."

"I'll take you to meet him someday. You'll see for yourself," Levi answered. He spoke with conviction.

I'll hang him in the sun, I thought but kept the sentiment to myself. "I doubt that," I said instead.

"I'd hoped Asa would find peace with himself, with our father. I'd always hoped for a reunion. Now there's no chance of that. You ended any possibility. I don't mean that it was your fault, but you must understand how I feel."

"Not really. It's like hoping for redemption for the devil," I answered.

"Is there no redemption for a sinner?" The stick snapped in his fingers. He cast the pieces aside again and picked up another.

"For the principal sinner?" I questioned.

"Why not?" Levi looked at me wistfully. "Why not even for the biggest sinner of all? Surely there is a god who can forgive even the principal sinner. Isn't that the point of a god? What good are they otherwise?"

"You have to at least want to be redeemed, I think."

He tossed his writing stick aside and got to his feet with the speed of a tired human. The bounce and cockiness was gone from his step. "Then I suppose there really was no hope for him. In this life or the next," Levi said.

More and more sympathy was creeping into me. I couldn't seem to stop it. "Look, he did have this one moment at the very end that was surprising." Levi turned towards me, hope scrawled across his face. "Right before he died, he said 'Thank you'. I think those were the most genuine words he ever said to me. He must have hated himself and wished for death every day, and I think he was glad to finally see it come. So maybe in his last moment he did find some peace. Some form of it anyways."

Levi faced the forest. His shoulders were back, his body rigid. "Did you leave him for the sun?" It was as though he couldn't look at me if my answer was the wrong one.

"I buried him."

Visibly relieved, he exhaled sharply. "He deserved no such quarter. Especially from you."

"I didn't do it for him."

"Then who?" Levi half turned in my direction but didn't look at me.

"His mother."

"Why?"

"I called him a son of a bitch. It was the only time he showed any emotion. True emotion, anyways. He defended her memory." I drew more furiously in the dirt, carving out a picture of my own mother, her short hair brushed to the side. "He thought I was insulting her."

"Semantics have changed," Levi added.

"Yes, I know. Asa explained that. But the point is that he loved her."

Levi nodded and left without another word. I guess he needed time to grieve for the brother that he never had. I didn't bother to follow him. When it came to Asa, I had no grief to spare.

Chapter 22

*T*he next four nights were hell on earth. Before Levi's entrance, I'd been able to visit my own house, pretend I was human. I'd been surrounded by my things, my pictures, and mementos of my family. Human things that Levi said gave me a false sense of who I was. Now I was living in a basement in a forgotten camp. But it accomplished what Levi wanted. It clarified my self-image. I was an outcast.

I wanted my family, to hold my daughter in my arms and do simple things like bake cookies and pick out tomorrow's school clothes for her. It was all I thought about. And I missed being a doctor and the human interactions that came with saving lives, or just simply being there when someone needed you the most.

But Levi had warned me in no uncertain terms that I was not to attempt to return to my house or to Ellie even though the local television studios had never featured my photo on the nightly news. My name wasn't being broadcast on APB's or run into the dirt on the local radio stations. Despite my missing from the news stories, the apartment complex where Ellie lived with Mom was being monitored twenty-four seven, and Detective Rumsfield remained in critical condition. The authorities were interested in me but not enough to make it public.

And their silence was the biggest mystery to me; I worried over it and fretted each evening when Levi brought back copies of the state's two largest newspapers. I studied them in detail, along with Facebook stalking a few of my former colleagues via Levi's account. I could find nothing about myself at all except a few questions as to why I wasn't working any more. No one mentioned me being a fugitive, no one saying, "I knew there was something off about that woman."

Was the lack of media exposure a trap to lure me out? I didn't know, and Levi didn't care at all about the reasoning behind the silence. The only thing he was interested in was putting as much distance between us and Detective Michael Rumsfield as possible. Actually, he recommended killing him in his hospital bed, but I'd refused. I begged him not to kill him either, which made him shake his head in disgust and stomp away. Why should I care to save him? He asked. Honestly, I didn't know either except that killing is wrong. I'd been trained on every level not to just think that but to believe it. Besides, I wouldn't leave Ellie, and murdering Rumsfield wouldn't help that cause. And so the sentence laid down by Levi for my stubbornness was solitary confinement at the CCC camp. It was utterly miserable.

He'd left the evening of my so-called trial and had come back only long enough to feed and check on me. And issue commands about not leaving or venturing away. It had been awkward at first. I hadn't fully gotten over his willingness to hang me in the sun, and his affection towards the animal that had ruined my life rubbed me the wrong way. Levi's sentiment toward Asa was beyond my comprehension, and maybe it always would be. But his interest in my care appeared genuine, and he was willing to let me stay in the same county as my daughter, so I was content to agree to disagree. In the end, Asa was still dead, and I was here living some variation on life with the possibility of returning to my family. If Levi wanted to love Asa from the beyond, well then let him.

Our conversation that first evening was uncomfortable and luckily didn't last long. He'd returned, nearly brimming with blood it seemed, fed me quickly through a self-inflicted bite, and then left. The second night he fed me again through another self-inflicted injury, but he'd hung around longer. We'd managed some small talk that by the end of the hour had trailed into more meaningful conversation. By the third night, we were able to move on to deeper subjects such as why Asa had chosen me, the details of how I'd managed to outwit him, and a brief outline of my three decades on this earth.

Levi was much older than me but not quite as old as Asa, and where Asa had dropped into the absolute anonymity of a serial killer, Levi had embraced the world and became its student. There were few places on the globe he hadn't been to and nothing much he hadn't been willing to try. At least, anything that could be accomplished in the dark of night. The result was an interesting man and a great conversationalist. He enjoyed listening as much as he enjoyed talking, and despite my original anger at how he'd treated me, I couldn't keep myself from opening up to him. He had everything Asa had lacked. Empathy, compassion and a sense of humor. He was a man who was sure of himself, and if he'd been human, he'd have been the boy next door that you fell in love with at first sight. I couldn't have stayed angry with him if I'd tried.

Whatever demons Levi had about Asa, he'd apparently laid them to rest when he returned the fifth night. Dawn was still an hour away, and I'd found some moldy, but mostly readable, newspaper clippings under one of the rusting bed frames. The mattress was the old spring type, musty, but not wet, and I'd carried it back to the cabin the night before last. Sleeping on most anything beats a wooden bunk I'd discovered.

It turned out that Levi was right; the camp was a remnant of the CCC and from the date fading away on the newspaper, the camp had probably shut down around 1940. For a few years, the Boy Scouts had used it, but the last time a human had legally slept in one of the bunks, it was probably about 1965. Since then, it had hunkered down against time and the elements and was simply wasting away.

I heard Levi enter the remains of the clearing and listened as he headed in the direction of the main house. He stopped midway and turned towards the first barrack I'd entered in my snooping. I knocked lightly on one wall and went back to my newspapers so he didn't waste time sniffing out my trail from each barrack to the next. He was with me in seconds.

"What are you reading about?" he asked as he stretched out

on one of the bunks across from me. It sagged dangerously under his weight.

"You were right. This was a CCC camp," I said, pointing towards one of the yellowed clippings lying beside me on the uneven plank floor.

"Yeah, I figured. I saw a few of them being built back in the day." He plucked the newspaper off the floor and flipped over on his back. The bunk bounced but somehow held together.

I looked up at him curiously. "When were you turned exactly?" He'd never told me the year.

"1898. Long before President Roosevelt formed the CCC. Mainly, I saw the buildings through their construction stages. I, of course, was dead to the world while the men worked. I snuck into them at night."

"Into the men or the camp?" I asked.

He slanted an eyebrow in my direction.

"Good hunting place, I guess," I said. "Group of men working by themselves in the middle of nowhere."

"Actually, I preferred the taste of women. Still do. Something Asa and I had in common."

I glared at him and he laughed under the anger in my expression. "I'm just teasing. Loosen up."

"Easy for you to say. You're not the one who ended up undead at Asa's hands."

"You're right. That was callous. But in his defense, I would have likely done the same thing if I'd come across you. At least when I was first changed."

More glaring from me. "So is that normal vampire behavior? Take humans hostage, toy with them for a week, and then kill them."

Levi shrugged and picked up another of the newspapers. "It happens. We get bored or lonely. More likely both. We're not a large population, so it's hard to find a vampire that you connect with on a personal level. We seek out human companionship even if we have to force it. If we're strong enough, and they are too, sometimes we turn them."

"If you're strong enough?" I questioned. I laid the newspaper

I was reading aside and picked up another. Out of habit, I turned towards the candle.

Levi handed me the newspaper he was holding and gestured for another. "Most of the time, we end up killing the human in question. Not killing them takes commitment; the restraint is enormous, and humans aren't that durable. All good magic takes time."

I changed my voice to match that of the average street corner fortuneteller. "The sacred bond between maker and child. Magic." I pretended to rub a crystal ball. "You don't seriously believe that? I thought you were more educated."

"Education can't teach you what to believe."

"Well, this is certainly not magic," I said, sweeping my hand between the two of us.

"Cheating death and living forever, eternally young. This is not magic? What is it then?"

"I can't know for sure. I'm a doctor, not a molecular biologist. But I'm pretty sure it's a virus and probably a retrovirus," I said. "But it's certainly not mumbo-jumbo. You tricked me with the penicillin comment. Maybe you have more in common with Asa than I thought."

"I know you're insulting me if you're comparing me to Asa."

"Well, if the fang fits." I picked up another newspaper clipping, one corner disintegrating in my hands.

"Humans live on one plane, we on another. They need science, but you and I don't. We subsist on a magic that transcends the human laws of mortality. Our blood is sacred. It is beyond science."

My eye roll was involuntary. "We subsist on the retrovirus's ability to remodel DNA into what it needs. It is not sacred. There is no other plane of existence for us."

Levi turned over onto his stomach and placed his hand in the candle flame. His skin seared and popped in the heat. The sizzling sound was like fingernails on a chalkboard. I shoved his hand away; burning flesh never had a nice smell. He held the palm of his hand up to me. "This wound will be healed within an hour because I converted someone's life force into my own."

172

I shook my head and moved the candle out of his easy reach. "It will heal because the virus has the ability to repair tissue at amazing rates. It uses the proteins and amino acids in the human bloodstream to do so."

"And there is no magic in that?" he asked.

"No more magic than is in a mosquito or a bat."

"Mosquitoes and bats die every day," he answered.

"Ours is a very effective virus."

"Why do we die and regain life with the setting and rising of the sun? Why can a stake through the heart not be repaired while everything else can?"

He waited for answers that I didn't have. I turned back to my newspapers.

"Because it's magic. There are no answers." He held his hand up again. The subcutaneous layer was already repairing itself.

"Haven't you ever been told that all magic is just misunderstood science?" I asked.

"Don't fool yourself, Annalice. That's just human talk."

Levi followed me out of the barracks and into the first floor of the cottage. He hesitated there while I walked the steps down to the basement. I could hear him pacing as I lay down on the bed. Some of the springs were sharp, but I reached down under the blanket and bent them down, pulling the blankets back into place. At least I felt more human sleeping in a bed. Albeit, an old, outdated one that didn't even belong to me.

Levi kept pacing, and I kept getting more nervous. Was he reconsidering his decision to not kill me? Maybe getting past Asa's final death was just too much to ask and I'd been lulled into a false sense of security during our easy conversations over the previous evenings. First light would be here soon. He was usually gone to wherever he'd been hiding out by this time. Clearly, he was planning on staying, but for what, and why the change?

"I'm afraid you're going to wear the floor out above my head!" I yelled up at him. He stopped, and I listened for his next moves.

If I had a beating heart, it would have been pounding out of my chest as the steps creaked with his weight. I sat up in the bed preparing to bolt. I might not get far, but I'd sure try. I worked to calm my breathing as he walked to the bed, but I couldn't find the mental resolve and his expression did nothing to calm my fears. I'd seen the same determined look on his face the night he considered killing me. As his hand slid across the foot of the bed, I surged around the other side.

His arm caught me at the waist like a clothesline, and I was pinned against the windowless wall, the cold dirt pressing into my back. "I thought you'd decided to let me go." My voice was shaking a little.

His ice blue eyes stared back at me. "I decided not to kill you. I *never* agreed to let you go."

"What does that mean exactly?"

"I assumed the duties of your creator, and there are many things you need to learn."

I'd heard that from a few men across the years. Granted, it was without the creator part. But usually they thought they were qualified to teach the lessons. "And I guess *you're* the man to teach me?" I sneered.

"Are you challenging my right?" he asked. I didn't say anything and just stared past him at the wall. Some people think silence is submission. I consider it a good cover-up for plotting. "Lesson one. You asked the night we met why I couldn't stay in the same room with you after you fed from me. Tonight, I am going to give you the answer."

He leaned in close, stretching my arms up across the dirt wall of the basement. The movement itself was sensual as he pressed his body hard against mine, and I gasped as he nipped the sensitive area beneath my ear. I started to struggle, but he was so much stronger than me that I didn't stand a chance. His mouth grazed my neck again before his fangs slipped through my skin. He stole only a few mouthfuls, but what followed as he licked his lips and stepped away felt like cocaine had been injected straight into my bloodstream. The puncture site began to tingle, and from that spot, the sensation traced through every connecting blood vessel until my entire body burned with what felt like electricity. And then I began to feel the all too familiar hunger that Asa's saliva had caused.

What I'd felt as a human had been strong, but this hunger was unlike anything I'd ever experienced. It was like taking the lump sum of all human cravings and adding it to the sensation of being starved. My pelvis ached, and I reached for him, but he nimbly sidestepped and grabbing my arm swung me around so that my arms were twisted behind my back. He pulled me backwards until I felt the backs of my legs touch the bed and was pulled onto the mattress.

By the time Levi had stretched me out beside him, I was writhing with the fire of lust and want. His saliva was so powerful that I felt like I was on fire. Hanging in the sun might have been the easier of these two tortures. That would have just hurt, but along with this pain came an intense desire and want for the vampire behind me. In that moment, I would have done anything for him. I would have let him drain me willingly if it meant I could have his lips on me again. I would have killed for him. I would have died for him. I struggled to get to him; I begged for his touch, for his body. But he was immovable. He kept me firmly turned away from him, my face buried into the pillow.

"Listen to me, Annie. I know it's hard, but try. Try to reason with yourself. The sun's coming up in moments, so you'll ache for only a short time before the deep sleep takes you. You need to understand the hunger, the pain, and why letting your own kind drink from you can be a liability, one of the reasons making another vampire is so extraordinarily dangerous to the maker. Their desire strips you of reasonable thought. It makes you irrational and careless. Never let another vampire bare fangs on you unless you trust him or her explicitly. I'm taking a risk every time I let you drink from me. As your creator, I willingly accept the danger, and you can trust me equally."

Speech eluded me at that point. I lay there wrapped in the shackles of his arms while his saliva and his desires tore ribbons of fire through my arms and legs. It was all the more painful that he lay behind me, his chest pressed into my back, the hard muscles of his arms and legs wrapped around me, and for once, I was grateful to feel the sun crest the horizon and extinguish my internal flames.

Chapter 23

I came to myself, my hand clutching my throat, dried blood fragmenting underneath my fingernails as I pulled my hand away. I remembered the burn ripping through me when the death sleep came. I'd managed to pull one hand free from Levi's grasp and was clawing at my neck in my last moments. My fingernails had brought blood to the skin, but it had been as though I had no control over my hand. I couldn't stop clawing at the fire in my throat. Thankfully, the sensations were gone now. My skin felt its typically cool temperature, and I no longer burned. Levi wasn't beside me when I rolled over although the blanket still held the impression of his body.

"Why do you wake up before me?" I asked as I came up the stairs. He was standing beside the remains of the fireplace, his arms crossed, as he stared out the empty panes of the broken windows. The wooden cross of the antique window frame clung steadfastly in place, refusing to acknowledge it no longer served a purpose.

"You're just a babe," he answered. "And babies need their sleep."

I rolled my eyes and went to the other window. Also broken, the cool night air poured through the openings and ruffled the fragments of newspapers I'd left lying on the floor. "Do you get to see the sun? How much extra time do you get?"

He shrugged his shoulders as if he didn't want to tell me. "By my age, about an hour. But don't be in any hurry. I was over fifty before I even had an extra fifteen minutes. And no, I cannot see the sun. I can look outside and see what the rays touch, but that's about the extent of it. And even that can be painful."

That long? My daughter would be well past middle-aged and my mother gone. Half a century to wait to see dusk. "What did you see this evening then?" I asked. Jealousy pulled my voice into a thin, stringy sound. My desire wasn't to see the sun, the thought made my skin crawl. But to see the world bathed in the light of day again, now that was something I craved.

He joined me in front of the broken window, tracing the cross of the decaying glass strut. "The trees had long shadows when I woke. So it must have been a cloudless day, but the light was muted like you would expect in late winter. A pack of coyotes passed through. They were after a rabbit that has a den a few hundred yards from here. I watched him chew on some grass before he took off to his hole. I read a couple more of those old newspaper pages." He turned towards me. "But I spent most of my time looking at you."

I tensed up like lightning had coursed through me. "Looking at me? That sounds really dull."

"Yeah, it was a colossal waste of time," he answered smoothly.

"You know, you're welcome to leave whenever you get the urge," I answered back. "I didn't ask you to come here."

He shrugged as if he didn't care one iota what I requested or didn't. "I came because of my brother. I'm staying because of his mistake. So I won't be leaving any time soon. His mistake keeps mushrooming, and you've got a lot to learn."

I backed up immediately, remembering the fire in my veins from last night's events. "Yeah, you've said that once already, and I don't want any more of *your* education."

Levi reached my side, his hand wrapping possessively around my rib cage before I got very far away. He was smiling, his blue eyes lit up with a little too much knowing. "Oh, but I bet you will."

Chapter 24

lood was dripping down her arm, forming a small stream of red that soaked into the hem of her black dress. The woman was unconscious at the moment, and as such, she didn't take any notice of the fresh blood tracking down her skin; Levi didn't seem to either. She'd been awake, talking and flirting heavily minutes before and, no doubt, she expected to be doing more of the same when she'd walked towards the back of the bar, arm in arm, body linked with Levi.

Of course, she had no idea she'd been armed-up with a vampire, and as I watched Levi in action, I was mightily impressed. He'd led her off, the oblivious lamb to the slaughter, shackled to him by a lust she couldn't process. Their mouths touched, briefly, a few times as she followed him, and I could imagine how her lips were tingling—a burn she swallowed down into the pit of her belly and spread from there to all her limbs. I could smell the desire as it reached her pelvis, the pheromones a thick haze around her. I hung back, not wanting to cast my violent, hungry gaze on her back until I heard him lean her back against the wall in a darkened, forgotten corner of the bar.

She'd given herself over in increments, and the hunt had truly been beautiful to watch. It had started, a girl sitting alone, at least mentally. A collection of her friends were gathered around her, but she wasn't with them in spirit. They'd laughed with exaggerated movements, consumed plenty of wine, made toasts, ate with abandon while they talked about dieting, and she'd made the correct responses each time.

From across the room, I could hear the trite words and clichés that whispered from her lips but she wasn't thinking of her friends. She wasn't thinking of the wine or the jokes. She was in her own world, where something or someone had caused her pain enough that she prayed for a diversion to drive it from her mind for a while. Maybe it was a loss. Or a betrayal. Maybe she'd given up the most important someone in her life, or perhaps she'd just lost her path. I couldn't be sure.

Either way, when Levi had made eye contact from two tables down, she didn't mind being the hunted. The slant of his hungry eyes had the opposite effect of mine; his gaze led her shyly, but willingly, across the floor to sit down at his table. He'd bought her a drink, which she'd poured back quickly for courage lost in his eyes and voice. He'd given her his undivided attention, listened with keen interest to her every word, and stroked the back of her hand when she'd divulged the real reasons as to why she was there. Not that those reasons mattered in the slightest to the master that sat across from her.

And master Levi was, I recognized, as I watched him weave a thick magic across her shoulders that cocooned her like a shawl, the free edges of which he used to pull her closer to him so that in this crowded room even I couldn't hear them as they talked. He drew her farther and tighter to him until they'd gotten up, a couple in one fluid motion, and disappeared to the back.

A bathroom break, I'd heard her say as they'd passed me sitting quiet and alone at my table. Levi had jerked his head only slightly at me, and I'd looked away as they neared me so as not to frighten her with my thirst. That was the only point of my being allowed to come. I was *learning* to sit in a crowded room and not terrify anyone while hungry, the hunger being the most important qualifier, and I was starving. If I accomplished that small feat, Levi said, it would be a miracle. He'd said I looked wild and felt even wilder, but I was certain I could pull it off. After all, I'd spent nearly an hour in a bar in Fort Smith. He ended the conversation by reminding me a man had died, so my track record wasn't convincing.

Tonight, I'd managed to go unnoticed for the most part. I'd

turned a few heads and then turned them back again when I smiled. Desperation drives men away, I'd decided, even more than fear. But no one was running out screaming, so I counted it a success.

I let Levi and his chosen lady get several feet past me before I turned my head back in their direction. The woman followed him with full confidence into a poorly lit corner of a hallway that led to the restrooms, and he'd melted himself against her. A couple, reuniting as they emerged from the bathroom doors, smiled at each other as they passed them, their steps light but fast as they sped past the oblivious couple in the hall.

I'd gotten up from my chair without meaning to and was walking towards them when Levi pulled his head up from her neck long enough to cast an icy look towards me. The look alone was enough to stop me, but the quiet growl was the icing on the cake. I stopped several feet shy of them and sat down at an empty table, resuming my observation status only.

The rise of the woman's chest had slowed. Her hands twitched a couple of times before he pulled back again, his fangs pressing into his lower lip. He slipped her gently down the wall to rest, head on her knees, her black hair hanging across one leg. She looked as if she'd just sat down to take a rest. *Maybe she's had too much alcohol,* a passerby might think. *Or overheated on the tiny dance floor.*

Her friends were still drinking heavily at the table. Earlier, I'd sent over another three bottles of wine and a round of pink panty droppers—from an anonymous admirer, of course. The women had cast giggly looks around the room looking for who could have sent it before collapsing again into another spasm of laughter. One or two of the group wandered away to talk to a small collection of men. Not one of them had come looking for the woman at Levi's feet. Their rational thoughts sifted by the alcohol, her friends would make poor witnesses when they finally noticed she was missing.

Levi pulled me to my feet as he casually walked by the table that I'd sat down at moments earlier. My throat was cracked; the pit of my abdomen burned like the smoldering coals at the bottom of a campfire. As he led me towards the door, I started to protest. Why was he taking me away? This was where the blood was?

I wrenched my hand from his and turned towards a table of men watching a game on the TV. Basketball? Football? I can't tell you. The only thing that mattered to me was that they were breathing. Their body heat reached me from several feet away, the heat hot against my skin. I was ready. I just needed to prove it to Levi.

I snarled as Levi's hand landed on the back of my neck and pulled me into a crushing embrace. I wanted to fight him and every instinct urged me to do it. My newfound confidence took its own glancing blow when he pushed my head down against his chest and pulled one of my arms behind my back. "We're leaving!" he hissed into my ear.

"I want blood!" I demanded. I tried to twist away from him again but he entrapped me against his body, his right arm holding my right arm crossways against my back and my left arm twisted under his own.

"I will feed you," Levi answered. "The girl's still alive. They'll call 911 soon, and no one will remember much about us. If we leave now, that is."

Unimpressed with his warnings, I tried wrenching against his hold again. "I want it fresh."

"This will have to do," he said, pulling me on towards the door, his body still wrapped around mine. He was much stronger. On any given day, he had the advantage. He was a hardened fighter and had lived for over a century. Fully fed as he was, I didn't stand a chance against him.

Outside the bar, Levi stepped off into the shadows. He pulled me with him, and I quit protesting as the fresh air blew the smell of blood out of my nostrils. Freeing my arms as we cleared the parking lot, he kept a hand on my wrist and dragged me farther from the bar.

Fayetteville sits nestled in a hollow of the Arkansas Mountains, a beautiful crown of lights that trails down into the valleys like the shrinking tails of kites as the city fades away into the rural landscape. And there, in the lower valleys, the forests turn dark and secretive at night, with hiding places deep enough to cover every sin, but in the rising light of day, reveal a world of old hardwoods, streams that tumble over and through moss-covered stones and disappear into fern enshrouded rock crevices to mingle with underground caverns.

It was towards these unknown parts of the forests that Levi pulled me. He sprinted away through the quiet of the alley onto a blackened street, and within the span of three minutes, we'd left the city and reached the trails that would lead us into more distant mountains. I tried to pull away again and turn in the direction of a different bar; I didn't want to leave the city with its bright lights and buildings full of hungry people, but he was insistent and pushed me forward, shoving me roughly ahead of him. He challenged me with his eyes and voice. Soon his insistence caught me in its energy, and I raced Levi headlong down the mountain.

It wasn't much of a contest. His speed was twice that of mine, but when I thought to pull up and return to the city he'd pull me forward at times with his insults and goad me from behind at others with threats before disappearing into the forest only to reappear behind me. All in all, he was good-natured, and his mood was infectious. Soon, I found myself enjoying the game, and I chased him with every ounce of strength I had.

The race ended in a valley strung narrowly along a creek whose shallow banks climbed gently out of the water and then stretched short eager arms towards cliffs that shot starkly up to join with the night sky. Heavily dewed ferns made a thick carpet on the ground, and the first of spring's flower offering had tucked their heads in for the night. The creek, swollen with late winter rains, was running hard and fast before boiling over and cascading down triplet falls into a rock-lined grotto.

Levi had stretched himself across a piece of driftwood. Stripped of its bark and bleached from time and the sun, the log looked like the dead white arm of a fallen monster, its roots reaching gnarled fingers towards the cliffs.

"Come and drink," he said, motioning me towards him.

"I want to drink from the living," I answered. But I walked towards him. I was thirsty.

"You're not ready for the living yet."

"And why not?"

"Because I said so. And until I say otherwise, you drink from me."

"I wanted one of those men."

"You'll not be having any man."

"I'll be having whatever I want," I sneered. And I felt that way. Like I could have whatever I wanted. If I were human, it would have been adrenaline racing through my veins. I wasn't sure what the substances flowing through me tonight would be called. Addictive, dangerous, provocative were good adjectives. I was on edge. Every nerve ending turned outwards to the world around me. From the birds settled in for the evening in the treetops and the mice bedded deep under the tree roots to Levi waiting for me. He sat up as I approached, settling back into the limbs of the fallen tree which held him like a throne. Come to think of it, he did look like a god. A ravenous, raven-haired god with eyes so deeply blue they might cure my craving to see the summer sky.

But these were not the calm blue skies that ushered in a dry, dusty July day. These were the temperamental skies of late May that kept you looking over your shoulder for the coming storm, afraid to get too far from shelter, that I was staring into now. Darker clouds gathered and stormed his expression as I knelt down and pushed between his knees, accepting the offered forearm he extended.

"Tonight, I guess you'll have to do," I said.

I was hungry, thirsty. But there was something else, and we could both sense the difference. The earlier hunt had produced an excitement that lingered within me, and the race through the woods had brought all my senses to the surface. The energy bounced along my nerve endings until I thought I'd explode with the power. And I *was* powerful but equally unsettled, which was so different from the human I'd been. Tonight, I was as unpredictable as summer lightning, and Levi was the only rod that could contain me.

His muscles were taut as I pulled his arm towards me. "Do you trust me?" I asked, remembering what he'd told me of makers and their children. His back was rigid; his belly taut as he spun me suddenly around to face away from him. I landed hard against his chest, one arm slung around for me to drink from, the other held me pinned against him. His hand gathered in the thick layers of my hair. Leverage, I knew—the better to pull me away.

"Trust you?" He laughed quietly. "Not in the slightest."

Cradling his arm in my hands, I felt his body go still as I sliced down through to the artery, and I felt more than heard the sharp intake of his breath as I drank from his body. I drank without thought, taking more than I'd ever taken from anyone besides Asa, and I might have continued drinking without care if the plunge of Levi's fangs into the tender skin below the angle of my jaw hadn't taken me by surprise.

Wrapping his arms tightly around me, he pulled me up into his lap. His hand dug hard into my head as he forced my neck back. If I was unprepared for his bite, I was even more unprepared for the effect of his pheromones. The previous night's taste of his teeth had been small, short-lived, compared to what jetted through my neck now. I could nearly feel the heat of the chemical reaction as it split into a larger vessel of my neck, coursed farther down into the deeper veins of my chest before dumping into my abdomen and pelvis. The sensation was nothing short of an electric charge being plugged into each and every nerve ending. Even my toes curled as the waves translated down my legs. I've never shot heroin or cocaine, but I'm pretty sure I could have described the experience in vivid detail.

His legs cupped mine as his chest conformed to my back, the hand in my hair migrating down the back of my neck and around my shoulders to cup one breast. In the small of my back, I could feel the pressure of his other hunger, and I pressed back, grinding against him. He drank briefly before offering his other arm to me.

"Drink," he urged, and I cut through unbroken skin again, feeling the layers of skin and taut muscle give way as my fangs slipped through. He caught his breath when I hit his bloodstream. I made five more bites along the length of his arm, laughing against his skin at the sharp intake of air each time I did. He shook in my hands, and the power was intoxicating. And I wanted more. I wanted everything these new sensations had to offer.

Twisting in his arms, I went for his throat. The downed tree rocked as I turned, forcing Levi back into the hammock the branches had created. I bit him multiple times, drinking deeply, and then shallow nips that trailed my poison along his internal carotid artery. With my every bite, he grew wilder and more insistent until the cradle made from the tree couldn't hold us any longer and we crashed to the ground, breaking the hold of his arms.

I slipped from his grasp as he reached for me and dove headfirst into the grotto of the falls, flinging the remainders of my clothes away as I did so. The Febuary water hit me, icy and knife-like, but I dove farther down until my hands glided across the smooth rocks of the river bottom. I waited there for the cold to put out my fires, to take away the burn of his teeth, but even the falls couldn't extinguish my flames, and I shot back up, my head breaching the surface of the water and spraying the mist into the air.

Levi stood above me on the heights of the falls, the water cascading around him, a silver cloak rippling black in the midnight air. I had him at a disadvantage; his blood was little more than a stream of my pheromones, where as I had taken most of what he'd drunk tonight, and he'd done little more than give me a taste of his hungers. Still, he remained in control. He looked every part the beautiful monster that could command an army of women if he wanted to, but he didn't command me to come to him. He waited while I decided. He was my maker. Apparently, he owned me, but unlike Asa, he wouldn't make me come to him. I realized as I watched him, my own personal river god, that I wanted to be completely lost in him tonight. I craved the lack of reason and the rush of desire that only he could give me.

He met me by the shore as I walked from the river, water streaming from my black hair and across my breasts. I offered up my wrists to him, and he took them in his hands as he pressed his lips onto the smooth skin of my inner wrists softly before he broke the skin. His mouth was warm, his lips full and insistent as he traced the arteries up my arm. I was burning alive before he offered his neck to me again.

The thirst had subsided since Levi had allowed me to take so much, and this time, without the rush and the urgency, I tasted so much more than the mere lust I'd recognized earlier. His emotions had a complexity I hadn't appreciated before tonight. There was more to him than just blood. I could truly taste him, all of him.

He was like a fine red wine made from grapes that had absorbed the yellow sunrays of summer, bathed in the blue-green of spring rains, and matured among the reds and yellows of fall. There was fire in his blood and excitement. I would swear I could taste the snow of the Rockies and the snowcapped peaks of France in his blood and everywhere else he'd traveled. He was rich with time and decadence, and I could taste his lust for everything of this world, including me. I knew he wanted me in more than a maker-made kind of way as I straddled him. And I wanted him too. At this point, I wanted everything. And more than anything, I wanted the wanting to never end.

We spent the rest of the night in each other's arms on the shores of the river. I lost track of how many times we melted into each other so completely that I couldn't have given my name if asked. I lost my sense of self, blending so thoroughly into him that I wasn't sure which were my thoughts and which were his. I couldn't have cared less about the future or about my family. In those moments, there was only Levi. Nothing else existed.

Chapter 25

Somehow, we made it back to the cabin and its forgotten basement before dawn. I remember nothing of the trip back except the times that I forced Levi back to the ground and resumed our lovemaking, begging him to make me not care again. If not for his self-control, I wouldn't have made it to safety from the sun. I'd have been like the vampires he mentioned that were caught unawares at the first light.

The fires that had burned in me during the night were only embers as I awoke wrapped in a blanket on the floor of the basement. Levi and I had made it into the shelter just as the sun was cresting the mountains to the east, and I'd lost myself to the dawn. My last sight had been the ceiling of the cabin as I fell backwards into the room. Levi must have gotten us to the basement during the extra time afforded him by his age.

I lay on the cool floor, my hands caressing the smooth dirt, remembering the night before. Parts of it were still little more than a drug haze, and I sifted through these memories trying to make heads or tails of the pieces coming back to me. Rational thinking had replaced the wild longings from last night, and thankfully, I could think clearly again. And for the first time, I began to understand why the week with Asa had been so tumultuous. It was more than just a home invasion, more than a mere kidnapping. I'd been drugged, in all respects, by his saliva. He was the drug, and I was the addict. Not intentionally. But each time he'd bitten me, I was been injected with something I couldn't fight. It had clouded my thinking and impaired my judgment. I'd done things I would never have thought possible.

Last night, I'd been deeply intoxicated with Levi. It'd been a repeat of those nights with Asa. Except Levi wasn't a psychopath, and maybe that made him even more dangerous. Losing myself in him would be incredibly easy, and loving him was a risk I couldn't take. I could look into the future and see Ellie becoming less and less of a priority. I could see me becoming more vampire than human in my mind. At least after last night, I understood the power of our blood, and I wouldn't underestimate it again.

I found Levi outside, lying on his back under the branches of a moss-covered oak tree. He was paler than usual this evening. I guess I'd ended up with most of the blood, which made it even more amazing that he'd managed to get us safely back to the cabin. Clearly, I had a lot to learn about control.

I dreaded the confrontation that I knew had to happen, but my newfound knowledge of what our blood could do had left me with an open can of worms that I couldn't ignore. I had to know.

I knelt down beside him on the grass that was beginning to shoot up; I'd almost forgotten it was coming spring. I broke a blade off, twisting it around my finger. "What happened last night, that's what you meant when you said it would be a shame to destroy me, wasn't it? It's an addiction. You're a drug addict, and I'm the drug."

Levi was tracing the constellations with one finger. He finished Orion before looking at me. "We're all drug addicts to some extent. Humans, vampires. We each crave something. It's just that vampire cravings are a thousand-fold stronger. And once you've had that drug, you just keep wanting it."

I searched his face for secrets that I hoped he didn't have. He stared at me levelly.

"Is that the true reason you didn't put me to the sun?" I asked. I wasn't guilty of any betrayal towards Asa, and it mattered to me that he believed me. I *needed* to know that I was truly safe—even if he got tired of me.

Levi's eyes narrowed as he lifted up onto his elbows. "Is that what you think I am? A glutton incapable of controlling myself?"

The blade of grass broke when I flexed my hand, staining my

skin with the color of spring. "You must understand why I'm asking."

"I can handle your bite, woman, and walk away without looking back, but I could *never* betray my bloodline. If you were guilty, I'd have burned you into oblivion."

His angry gaze was heated, but I refused to look away. "You can't blame me for asking. I can see how this could be a problem for some."

Finally, he nodded, his expression turning softer. "For some, the pull is too strong."

"What does that mean?"

"It's pretty self-explanatory."

I rolled my eyes. "Self-explanatory? Nothing about being a vampire is self-explanatory."

"It makes some crazy. They lose the natural vampire tendency. Blood becomes less important than the fix, which they can't go without for more than an hour or so. It makes them insane. They lose rational thought. But you can't get the fix without the blood, so they spill a lot of it. Those kind of vampires don't last long."

I walked back into the cabin, picking up cast-off clothes from the floor. I hadn't worn any back last night I'd been so intoxicated, I'm ashamed to say. Luckily, I had enough to assemble something decent to wear. Levi followed me in. I wasn't sure if he'd made it back dressed or not, but tonight he was wearing only a pair of blue jeans. I brushed the leaves off his back. "By a fix, I assume you mean a bite. When you say they don't last long, what happens to them? I thought we were immortal?"

"Was Asa immortal?" he asked.

I slid a pair of jeans halfway up, slipping on my boots as I went. "I guess you have a point there. But surely they aren't staking themselves. So what happens?"

"Every vampire reacts differently. Each bite is an injection. For a few, this causes some type of insanity. I'd say it's similar to schizophrenia in a human. But for most, it's simply an intoxication, and they get addicted like any human meth head.

And like all addicts, they can get so stoned they don't know where they are or what they're doing. They can get intoxicated to the point they forget to seek protection from the sun, things like that. But generally, it's the vampire hunters that get them. They create such a bloodbath wherever they go that they lead the hunters straight to them. Or we kill them ourselves."

I jerked hard on my bootlaces. "You kill them yourselves? Because there's a code of conduct or something?"

Now it was Levi that rolled his eyes. "Quit looking for the good in us. We don't need the attention, and that's why we kill those vampires. No other reason."

"But for those who aren't addicts ..."

He finished the sentence for me. "For those who don't become addicts, the relationship between two vampires is as close to physical paradise as you can get on this earth."

I was beginning to see why he was willing to put the time into me. "And you've never created a vampire for this reason?"

He wasn't in a hurry to answer.

"No, but I'm in the minority."

I'd been holding my breath without meaning to. Relieved at his answer, I shook my tensed muscles out and slipped my shirt on.

"Is that jealousy I'm sensing?"

What? Does he think I'm ten? "Whatever. Just curious."

"There are usually enough females willing to swap spit with me," he said, cutting his blue eyes my way. "So I've never felt the need to create my own. I couldn't tell you an exact number, of course. I've lost track over time." He picked up his shirt and smiled at me.

I forced my expression to go blank. *But seriously, how many women does it take to lose count?*

"I'm surprised that Asa never did though. He had to have known. It was him who explained the effects of his bite to me. I couldn't understand why I was responding to him the way I did after everything he'd done to me. But I just couldn't seem to help myself."

Levi shrugged into his T-shirt. "He probably never realized the effect went both ways. Asa was a loner. He avoided the rest of us no matter what it cost him."

"Thank God for small favors," I whispered. "But why was he such a loner? No. Wait, that's the wrong question. Why did your maker abandon him?"

Levi looked at me sharply. "Don't judge him. You don't know my maker at all, and everything you've heard about him is nothing but hearsay."

"Well, the hearsay says he's a major asshole. How many humans have died because of him? Because he abandoned the monster that *he* made."

"Let him that is innocent cast the first stone."

I shoved a finger in his direction. "That's not the same thing."

"Really? Because I thought 'Thou shalt not murder' didn't specify a number. Like killing one human is okay but a thousand isn't. And if you want to get technical about it, any vampire hearing about you would think you were the lowest of the low, killing your maker and all. So I wouldn't be too quick to judge a man you've never met based on second-hand information."

Throwing my hands up in the air, I stalked towards him. "Asa was not second-hand. He was the one who died at that animal's hands."

"And Detective Rumsfield nearly died at your hands. How would someone listening to his story judge you? Would it be fair or a little one-sided?"

The anger bled out quickly at the sound of his name. I'd all but forgotten the detective over the last few days, and whatever guilt I should have struggled with over his near death I'd brushed aside like a bad dream. Who was the psychopath now?

"I have to go and check on him."

I had a head start on him, not to mention that most of the blood he'd drank at the bar was in me. Levi couldn't catch me, and I was walking into the hospital before I felt him at my back.

Chapter 26

*H*e looks awful, I thought to myself when I first peeked into the hospital room at Detective Rumsfield, who was arguing with some very good points, I might add, that I was a sociopath. But then upon closer inspection, I'd decided that, in fact, Rumsfield looked pretty good with a two-day-old beard. Instead of making him look scruffy, the five o'clock shadow chiseled his jaw and framed his full lips, which he was, right now, using to bad-mouth me. But even that fact didn't detract from the beauty of those lips.

Irritated that I'd noticed, I reminded myself that he did look pale. Very pale. *Because he's a busybody and a sneak*, I said internally. I didn't want to think any good thoughts about Rumsfield at all. He'd practically ruined my post-human life. *But he does pull off pale well.* In truth, there was just something about the man, and my mind wouldn't allow me to feel complete disdain for him.

Beside me, looking both lethal and beautiful while leaned up against the nurse's station, was yet another man badmouthing me. Levi was giving me the what for under his breath. "I still don't understand why we're here. This *human* is of no concern to us." He said "human" as if his throat might constrict on the word it was so harrowing to utter.

"Sshh. They're going to hear you," I whispered to Levi. Behind me, I could feel a bevy of eyes on my back. I looked over my shoulder to check the status of the nurses. I knew them well and wasn't the least surprised when I heard two of them whispering to each other about the god-like creature beside me.

"Must be the money," I heard one of them say. "'Cause she sure ain't that pretty."

Catty, that one. Always catty, I thought.

"These nurses have impeccable taste," Levi laughed beside me. I narrowed my eyes at the lot of them and went back to studying Rumsfield through the thin rectangular window in the door.

"Of course he's important," I said, nodding towards Rumsfield. "I figured they'd believe him in a heartbeat. But I guess they can't make his crazy story stick. So I might be able to go home after all." My mood had improved, and the future was looking up with every word I heard through the door of Rumsfield's hospital room.

Levi looked none too happy. "Don't get your hopes up," he answered.

In the room, one of the officers spoke up again. "Mike, there was no blood except yours at the scene. I'm not sure who you shot, or what you shot at, for that matter. But it wasn't Dr. Annalice Creed. We have her blood type on file. She's a doctor for mercy's sake; she's got a fingerprint and blood trail a mile long, so we've got plenty of prints and DNA to compare to. Her blood was not there."

Detective Rumsfield, struggling to cast his web of truth, spread his arms wider as he argued with the three men gathered around his bed. Another stood by, listening but not participating. "I'm telling you, I'm not crazy. I shot her multiple times. She attacked me. Bit me even. She's nuts, and I loaded her full of lead. So something is wrong with *your* forensics."

"It's not our forensics. It's the state's team, man," another of the officers said.

The three men, each of them cops, stood awkwardly around the hospital bed. *"Forensics don't lie."* I could read the message clear in their body language. Their hands shoved deep in pockets or crossed stoically across their chests, they shifted their feet and eyes, looking anywhere except at Mike. I knew two of them. One was the young cop that had irritated me the night Mom and I had eaten at the diner, the night after I'd died as a human. He was tall and skinny and not man enough yet to grow a five o'clock shadow. The guy opposite the kid was the officer who had come with Rumsfield when he'd searched my property when I was still human. I think his name was Terry. The third guy I didn't recognize at all, but his jacket said "Madison County Sheriff." His name badge read "Langford." The fourth was the sheriff of Sebastian County, John Taylor. I wasn't sure why he was here, as it wasn't his jurisdiction. Just moral support, I suspected. He was standing over towards the window.

"Maybe we could start back at the beginning," Langford suggested. "Why were you at Dr. Creed's in the first place?"

"Because she's a murderer." Rumsfield looked around, making eye contact with each man in the room. "Langford, there's two people dead in Madison County within two miles of her house. And there's that man found up near Brasshears." He looked towards the window. "Taylor, you've got a dead man in Sebastian County who was talking to her when he died. Are you guys too dense to see this pattern?"

Langford, taking some offense to being referred to as "dense," stood up taller and squared his shoulders. "Mike, were there any warrants for her?" the sheriff asked. He looked at each man in turn to illustrate his point.

An ominous silence filled the room. No one said a word. Rumsfield pursed his lips, clasping his hands roughly together. He probably lost a layer of skin cells before he broke eye contact with the sheriff. Having his answer, Langford continued, "Then you had no right to be out in her field. You didn't have a search warrant. She wasn't a suspect. So I ask again, why were you out there?"

The tension in the room swelled until I thought the door would bow outwards with the force. One man scratched his head and turned away from the bed. Through the window, I could see him pretending to check his phone. He was faking. He had his eyes closed. Taylor just shook his head. Rumsfield eyed them each suspiciously again, applying his own mental litmus test. Would they believe him? he was wondering. I leaned forward, knowing what he was about to say and mentally tried to force his mouth shut. Levi laid a hand on my arm. I'd forgotten he was there.

Rumsfield swallowed hard and took a deep breath, his eyes partially closing while he did. Then they opened wide, and I knew he'd forged his resolve. His voice was steady when he spoke. "I found evidence that Dr. Creed was involved in those murders the night we found that hunter's body in the woods."

He had Langford's attention now. "And why is this the first we're hearing about it?"

Rumsfield sighed heavily and ran his fingers through his hair. His IV got caught on the corner of the bed, and he gave it a little jerk then winced at his own stupidity. "Because I didn't think you'd believe me. It's crazy stuff. You know, really messed up shit."

Langford was losing his patience. "Like what?" It wasn't so much of a question as a demand.

Another deep breath from Rumsfield. "Guess it doesn't matter now since I don't have much to lose, so here goes. About two weeks ago, that elderly woman got killed. She lived out close to Dr. Creed. There's very few houses out that way, and I went to each one of them asking about suspicious activity. The night before we found Ms. McElhaney, we got a call that a woman was being roughed up out at the Oak Grove Country store. Any guesses as to who the tags belonged to?"

He didn't wait for them to answer. "Dr. Creed. What a coincidence, right? I knew she lived out there, so going to her place was killing two birds with one stone. But when I got to her house, something wasn't right. I couldn't tell you what exactly except that she was nervous. Real nervous and pale. She looked like death warmed over and quiet as a church mouse. She wouldn't even let me in the house, man. Then I show her the pictures of Ms. McElhaney. Whoever killed her had really messed that old lady up. And despite the fact that there were pictures of Dr. Creed and her daughter all over that old lady's house, she gave me almost no emotion. She might've been a tad upset at first, but then calmed down just like a pro. Got hateful. Actually, she got a little smart-ass with me. Still wouldn't let me in the house. So I left, but I told her I'd be back. I scoured the town for info, and I mentioned Dr. Creed to this one waitress down at the Screamin' Eagle. Turned out she'd been in with some strange man, and Creed wasn't acting quite right to her either. So I went back with a search warrant."

Langford broke in, one arm folded across his chest, the other nearly pulling his short beard out by the roots. "You called in a favor with the judge is what you did. That warrant was bullshit and wouldn't have stood up in court even if you'd found something. It had no merit."

Rumsfield nodded. "I thought I was doing the right thing. I'm telling you. There's more to her than meets the eye."

"But you didn't find jack-crap. More importantly, you didn't have jack-shit to get a warrant," Langford said.

"I found plenty," Rumsfield said. He was sitting straight up in the bed now, which is no easy feat in a hospital bed. Plenty of ab muscles needed to manage that. Your butt sinks down. It's just the way hospital beds are built. But he was shaking slightly. A mild tremor. Weak from blood loss. Probably a little muscle mass atrophy as well from being on the vent. The average person loses one percent of their muscle mass per day. He wouldn't be able to hold that pose for long, and I felt slightly guilty.

"But it was stuff that y'all wouldn't pay attention to, and no court would care about. The house was a disaster. The kitchen looked like a raving mad starving person had been turned loose. The floor was littered with boxes and trash. There was rotting food on the counter. Nothing had been cleaned up. But the living room? Well, it had been cleaned up like nothing flat. The floor mopped. The curio cabinet was practically empty, yet it was dusty and I could see the imprints of where things had been sitting but were now gone. I stepped on some broken glass she'd missed when she tried to clean it up."

"I'm still not hearing anything that speaks to murder," Langford said. I could almost hear his teeth grinding, and I could certainly see the muscles twisting in his jaw.

Worn out, Rumsfield dropped back down into the bed. He was

breathing harshly. He needed some blood, but with the new transfusion guidelines, the doc was probably holding off. "I found something else, Langford. Something really strange."

"Mike, we crossed the strange bridge a long time back," Langford answered.

"You don't get it, man. A lot stranger than anything else I've told you." Rumsfield paused here. He wasn't looking at any man in the room for support. If he went here, he was going it alone, and he knew it. "I found a wooden ... I don't know what you'd call it. A sharpened wooden ... projectile of some sort. And some clothes—a shirt with a hole in the chest."

Again dead silence. Anyone could have heard a pin drop. Every man in the room was looking at him with that oddly confused expression that says, *I've nearly got it, but I'm just not quite there yet.*

"Come again?" Sheriff Taylor finally spoke.

"It looked like what you might spear a fish with. You know what I'm talking about, John," he said towards the man at the window again. "You probably whittled a hundred as a kid."

Taylor was rubbing his chin thoughtfully. I was about to herniate my brainstem from holding my breath. Levi was looking darker and darker, and Rumsfield was beginning to have that deer in the headlights stare.

"I'm assuming you tested these clothes and this ... this wooden fish spear for blood and tissue?" Langford asked.

"Of course. But they were clean."

"Fingerprints?" Langford continued.

"Dr. Creed's fingerprints were on the spear." For a moment, Rumsfield looked vindicated. He was looking at each of them like he'd just shared the secret to the universe.

"But nothing on the clothes?"

"No. But it has to prove something," Rumsfield answered.

Langford was trying to put it all together. His mind was working hard to process a lot of things that in the end pointed to nothing. I could see that on his face. The big fat nothing that he, as a sheriff, knew they had and yet Rumsfield had acted on. Of course, Rumsfield was right. His internal manometer had picked up on what everyone else around him had missed.

John Taylor was looking more and more confused. "Where was the hole in the chest? On the clothes, I mean."

Rumsfield looked more disgruntled, if that was possible. "Over the heart."

Langford finally had it. "Wait a minute. You mean to tell me that you found a stake and some clothes with a hole over the heart in the woods, with no blood or body tissue of any kind and a few fingerprints, and that finding alone made you stalk that poor woman and then shoot something, or nothing for all we know, in her pasture?"

"Well, how do you explain it?" Rumsfield asked.

"My thinking pattern would have taken me to an old forgotten Halloween prank. Not that Dr. Creed was a damn vampire. That is what you're trying to get at, right? You've finally lost your ever-loving mind and gone off the deep end!" Langford said. In his mind, he was wondering how he'd explain that to the press.

If Langford was angry, Rumsfield was pissed. "I should have just kept my mouth shut. I'm not crazy. Why don't you call the hospital and ask them where the hell Dr. Creed is? Why isn't she at work? Why not go talk to her momma? She knows there's something wrong because she took her kid and moved to town."

Langford listened, shaking his head the whole time. "I'm not saying the woman ain't up to something, Mike. I'm saying that none of it adds to murder, and none of that nonsense is going to stand up in court."

"I shot her, and she didn't die!" Rumsfield said before Langford could get anything else in. "I'm not crazy, and I'm NOT saying she's a vampire. But I did shoot her, emptied my clip like I said, and she just got back up. And she *did* bite me. Maybe it was drugs. That happens to docs every now and again. Bath salts? That can cause biting behavior. I don't know." Rumsfield stopped, rubbed his hands through his hair and took another deep breath. "But it happened."

Langford was having a good laugh now at Rumsfield's expense. "Yeah. Well, show me the fang marks, and I'll go arrest her now. Where are they? Come on, show me."

All the men were waiting, staring at Mike like they half-expected him to produce fang marks. "You know I can't do that."

"Well, why the hell not?" Langford asked.

Uncomfortable, Rumsfield looked away for a brief second. Lost in thought, he rubbed a hand across the side of his neck. "Because they're gone," he answered.

"Yeah. Like your damn mind," Langford replied.

Terry had taken a step forward and was trying to placate him. "Mike, man, listen. I don't know what happened. But you're a good cop and an even better detective. We've worked together a long time, and I know you shot at something. There were shell casings all over the ground. Gunpowder residue on your hands. But I'm telling you the only blood that was found was yours. Is it possible that you got a little confused? That the long hours got to you a bit?"

"I think you were hallucinating," Langford interrupted. "There was no blood at the scene except yours. There were no bite marks on your neck, or anywhere else for that matter. I think we all *know* what happened." His tone insinuated something that I didn't catch. *What does he mean?* Whatever it was, the insinuation sent Rumsfield over the edge.

Mike jerked himself upright, curse words spewing from his mouth, and tried to get out of the bed, cussing under his breath more violently as his arms got caught in the IV tubing. Then an ankle got caught in the bed railing, and he yelped with pain.

"Mike, you've got to calm down. Your heart rate is sky high," Sheriff Taylor said. He reached a supportive hand towards Rumsfield's forearm.

Rumsfield jerked his arm out from under the offending hand. "Quit patronizing me, John. You don't believe me any more than my own partners do," Rumsfield said. "Tell me something, Sheriff. If I didn't shoot her, then where are the damn bullets? You found the casings, but what about the bullets? Did I hallucinate them too?" Rumsfield asked, a wolfish grin on his face as he waited for an answer. He looked back to Langford. "I guess your little lapdogs forgot to answer that one for you. You know,

I always thought you were too much of a dumbshit for this job, and now I'm convinced. I'll tell you where the bullets are. They're buried inside that bitch! Wherever the hell she is."

That was my cue, and I didn't wait for Langford, who was boiling for a chance to explode.

"I'm not sure, Detective, but the bullets are certainly not in me," I said, walking into the room. Like thousands of times before, I went straight to the bedside and grasped his wrist, unwinding the plastic tubing from off his arm. "You're going to pull out this IV if you're not careful. And you'll probably whine like a baby if the nurse has to re-site it."

Rumsfield looked like he'd seen a ghost. No, make that a mass-murdering ghost. His eyes widened and his breathing picked up. I think he'd been in some degree of denial. Maybe he'd thought that my body just hadn't been found. Maybe he'd even questioned his own sanity.

"I hear you've been stirring up quite a scene, telling everyone you shot me and all. So I came up to visit so that you'd know that I'm safe and you didn't shoot anyone. At least, not me." I used my best clinical but caring voice. I'd almost got his IV unwound before he pulled his arm roughly from my grasp.

"Get out of here!" he said, inching towards the head of the bed. "Get the hell out of my room! You've done nothing but ruin my life from the moment I first laid eyes on you!"

He was yelling now. Out in the hall, I could hear them calling for hospital security. Didn't they realize the room was full of cops? Levi was out in the hall, leaned against the nurse's station, looking for all intents and purposes like a wall cloud right before the tornado drops out of it. He wasn't happy that I'd come here. He thought Rumsfield could easily be and should be disposed of. His only question was why we hadn't done it already.

"Mike," I said, trying to calm him down. "You need to settle down. They'll sedate you." I'd seen the doctor's name on the door, and I knew that particular physician thought Haldol was its own food group.

"The hell I will! It's hard to calm down when there's a psychopath standing in my room!"

The skinny kid-cop had joined in the calming talks. "Mike, if you shot her fifteen times, do you think she'd be standing here? Look at her. She's fine."

Rumsfield was looking back and forth between me and the young cop in rapid fire movements. A glimmer of self-doubt softened his features momentarily before hardening into a mask of confidence, and his gaze froze on me. "Don't call me 'Mike.' We're not friends," he said to me.

I shrugged at the other men gathered around his bed. "Well, Detective Rumsfield, it was you who told me we were. Remember? On the night you followed me to the bar in Fort Smith."

"I didn't follow you. I heard your name come across the scanner, and so I knew someone was dead," Rumsfield answered. Still working on maneuvering his IV around the railing of the bed, he continued his tirade. "You may have them fooled, but I'm not that stupid, Dr. Creed. I know …" he started.

"You know what?" I taunted him. I hoped he'd say it because there was no way anyone in this room wouldn't think he was a flipping lunatic. I turned towards Sheriff Langford. "I assure you, Sheriff, I have not been shot multiple times. Luckily for me, I wasn't home the night he supposedly shot me. Thankfully, or I suspect I'd be dead."

"You were there!" Rumsfield started. Langford held up a hand and cut him off.

Not wanting to lose ground, I jerked my shirt up to my bra line. My belly was flat and smooth and not a single flaw marked my skin. I was lying of course. The bullets had slipped out of my abdomen while in the death sleep the day after he shot me. Guilt should have been my new best friend, but all I could think was how I was going to get to go home. Mom and I could work things out if I could keep Rumsfield away from her. Not once did a shred of remorse at what I was doing to him cross my mind. Hadn't I come here to check on him? But Rumsfield always brought out the bad stuff in me.

"Dr. Creed, with all due respect, I do have a couple of questions," Langford said, his hand still in the air like a personal stop sign for Rumsfield. "And I can see that you've not been shot," he said, motioning to my abdomen.

"Is this an investigation? Do I need a lawyer?" I asked, lowering my shirt.

"No. There's no investigation. And you don't have to answer. It's completely voluntary."

Avoiding the police would only lead to suspicion, and it certainly hadn't worked with Rumsfield. What did I have to lose at this point? "Go ahead," I said. "Ask away."

Langford smiled and nodded towards Mike, giving him a look that said, "I've always been the better cop." Internally, I bristled. *He's a good cop. Smarter than the rest of you dumbasses*, I thought. I caught myself mid-thought. *What are you doing? You hate this man.* But that wasn't quite true. I didn't hate him. Rumsfield was a good cop. His instincts were right on. Still, I was going to have to lie to protect myself. He'd get a couple weeks off and a psych eval, but in the end, everything would be normal again for Detective Rumsfield. He'd live, and I'd be a mom again. I'd eventually be able to return to work. Everything was going to be fine.

Langford was still glowering smugly when he turned towards me. "Have your Mom and daughter moved out of your house and into town?"

I covered my eyes as if I was holding back tears. I added a deep breath and a pause for effect. "Yeah, they have. I've developed a skin disorder, Sheriff. It's pretty rare and makes living and working in the daylight hours nearly impossible. My mom came to help with my daughter while I began treatment. Take her to school, run errands, buy groceries. Unfortunately, what was already a difficult and painful situation has been made far worse by your detective, who has now convinced my mom that a man I had two dates with killed Ms. McElhaney, and I then wouldn't provide information about his whereabouts. Of course, he has not a shred of real evidence to speak of. I would never have hurt her. She was my neighbor and my friend."

"And what about the clothes and this sharpened spear he found?" Langford asked, looking even smugger.

"I don't have a clue. He showed up at my house waving that spear around in the air. It looked like an old broom handle that I'd thrown out months ago to me. The clothes could have belonged to anyone. They were non-descript. Detective Rumsfield said they matched the description of the clothes a man I had dinner with was wearing. I'm not sure because I don't remember what my date was wearing. And even if the clothes did match, there is nothing to tie the man I had dinner with a couple times to Ms. McElhaney's murder."

Rumsfield was about to come unglued now. "You said you staked the clothes symbolically!" he nearly shouted across the room. "You said that! And you were out in the woods when I showed you that spear!"

I blew out my breath and looked at him as if he were an idiot. "I was joking, Mike, because you were standing in my yard accusing me of killing a man in the woods. It was so absurd I just said the first thing that came to my mind. And no, we were standing in my yard." Levi was right. Lying came so much easier now that I was one of the undead. "We were in my yard because that's where you spend most of your time. Hanging around my house and harassing me and my family. I can't get any rest. I even moved out because you won't leave me alone. I'm afraid to stay at my own home anymore because I never know when this lunatic is going to show up, Sheriff," I said, turning back towards Langford. "And I'm asking you to make this stop. I'd like to return home and know that I won't be targeted for something I haven't done."

The sheriff was gloating; I could see it in his expression. "Dr. Creed, I assure you that this matter will be handled. You can go home any time, and Detective Rumsfield won't bother you further."

The smile on Langford's face seemed genuine. I couldn't smell any fear or sweat to indicate he was lying, but still, I was nervous. Something didn't seem quite right. Everything was just way too easy. The other three men in the room were on edge; the air was laced with anxiety, and in one corner of the room, even a little sorrow. Heart rates and respirations were up, and for once, I wasn't the cause. So what was? I wondered as I looked around the room.

Rumsfield was glaring at me like I was the white elephant in the room that no one else could see, and he seemed oblivious to the tension hanging like storm clouds over the other men. Except Sheriff Langford, who was very collected in comparison to the edginess in everyone else. His scent was *sticky,* if I were forced to find a word to describe it. Sweet and sickly smelling, like desire gone too far. Something was going on that I hadn't picked up on. I guess I'd been so concerned about my own personal drama that I hadn't noticed. *Why are these men here with Rumsfield?* I questioned for the first time. It certainly didn't feel like a social visit. Besides, it was late. Well after typical office hours. I got the feeling they were here because they didn't want to wait any longer. They had put this conversation off as long as they could.

"So, we're good here then? No more moonlight visits from the detective? No more meritless search warrants? Everything can go back to normal at my house?" I asked.

"Yes, ma'am. You have any problems with Mr. Rumsfield and you just contact me personally. Here's my cell number," he said, handing me his business card.

The thick, sweet smell brushed against me as I reached towards him. I could feel the imprint of the letters of his name as the thick paper of the business card slipped between my fingers. I hesitated momentarily, rubbing my thumb across the indentations of his title, as I tried to decide why I felt like Judas Iscariot.

"Listen, I realize Detective Rumsfield was just trying to do his job. I get that. So maybe we can all just put this behind us. He'll probably realize soon enough that all of this was a mistake. My guess is he just needs to get back to work and move on."

The same sweet smell washed over me again. I couldn't help it; I wrinkled my nose it was so strong. It reeked of a mid-seventies outdated powder on an old woman. Or the sickly sweet pea-green drainage of a Pseudomonal infection. Pea green with envy suddenly had an entirely new meaning to me. Langford was jealous of Rumsfield, and he certainly didn't mind making the detective look stupid. "Thanks for stopping in, Dr. Creed. If you don't mind, we'll let you step out. We've got some business with Mr. Rumsfield to attend to. But rest assured, he won't trouble you any further," Langford said.

I let him usher me towards the door, careful to stay in front of him. I glanced back at Rumsfield. His glare hit me like a ton of bricks. I'd say if looks could kill, I would have been dead. Since I already was, I tried not to think about Mike Rumsfield at all. Shifting my gaze back to the sheriff, I slid his business card into my pocket in case I needed it.

"Thanks," I said, crossing the threshold to the corridor. Behind me, I could hear Rumsfield's sheets slide off into the floor. I didn't look back.

"Do you know what this means?" I asked as we rounded the corner outside of Rumsfield's room. "Levi, I get to go home. It's all over." I had him by the shoulders and was near to swinging him around I was so excited.

"Nothing's changed, Annalice. This means nothing," he said, knocking my hands away.

I looked at him incredulously. I could feel my smile caving in on itself. "How can you say that? The man that has ruined my life has just been told to cease and desist. I'm a free woman. He can't do anything to me now."

"Are you really that naïve? He's not the reason that you can't go back to your old life. You're a vampire. That's the reason. This man—Rumsfield—is an excuse. You're trying to make everything revolve around this pitiful human. And honestly, I don't see the attraction."

"Of course it all revolves around him. He's the prime reason that I can't go home. He's hunted me every night. Not to mention that he's turned my mom against me. So yeah, it's pretty much about him."

"Maybe you *want* it to be about him," Levi said. He was standing with his back leaned against the wall. Behind him through the plaster walls, I could heard Sheriff Langford's voice rise. Rumsfield's rose to meet the older man's. He wasn't backing down, it appeared. I listened in between mine and Levi's conversation.

"I know what you're trying to imply, but there's nothing between Rumsfield and me. I can't stand the man. You're wrong, but even if you weren't, what do you care?"

He reached for my arm. "Caring is for humans. So no, I don't care. You can long for your *detective* all you want. But don't forget who you belong to is all I'm saying."

I jerked my arm from his grip. "I don't belong to anyone." I'd had enough of that crap with Asa to last a lifetime. Or many lifetimes for that matter.

His right hand grazed my cheek then slipped down to wrap lightly around my neck. Not in a violent way, but his point wasn't lost on me. "In my possession and through my blood, you are made whole. I wasn't joking when I said it," he answered.

"You don't own me," I said. "And what does that even *mean*?"

"You accepted my ownership the night I said the bonding words to you. You sealed the deal by drinking from me."

"I've had enough owner ..." I cut my angry speech off as the raised voices in Rumsfield's room drifted through the walls.

"Don't worry. I'm easy to belong to," Levi said. "We can come up with some arrangement regarding Rumsfield."

I waved him off. "We'll get to that later. Something wasn't right in there," I whispered to change the subject. "I'm not sure what. I can't seem to put my finger on it." I went back to listening, turning my head so I could press my ear firmly to the wall.

Unfazed and looking bored, Levi started flipping through his cellphone. Thank God they still made Blackberries—the cellphone of choice for vampires everywhere. "Something wasn't right about which part?" he asked. "The part where you cared enough about this Mr. Rumsfield to come up here and check on him? Or the part where you lied through your teeth about your meetings with him? Or that we gave up what could have been a fabulous tryst in the woods to come here and check on him. It's hard to tell, you know, because there's so many wrongs on so many levels."

"Mr. Rumsfield ..." I started to say but then corrected us both. "Not *Mr.* Rumsfield. It's *Detective* Rumsfield." That's when it hit me. "Shit," I said aloud this time.

Levi shoved his phone in his pocket and turned towards me. "What?" he demanded.

"Shhh'" I waved him off again. "Listen."

In Rumsfield's room, Sheriff Langford was preaching about responsibility and legitimacy. "Credibility is all a police officer has," he said. "And you've lost it, Rumsfield. You've become a liability to our force. I need you to surrender your badge and your gun."

Besides the thumping hearts of the men and the soft hum of the electronics, Rumsfield's room had taken on the eerie quiet that can only precede coming disaster. The quiet moment right before a car wreck or the sickly green sky of a tornado-pregnant storm cloud. Even I felt the storm coming, all the way through the wall.

"On what grounds?" Rumsfield finally asked, his voice a razor blade.

Langford cleared his throat. I couldn't hear it, but his very full pause gave his nerves away. I guess he'd heard the cutting edge of Rumsfield's tone himself. "Your drug screen was positive for methamphetamine, opiates, and PCP. Bring your things by the station as soon as you get discharged from the hospital."

"This is bullshit, Langford!" Rumsfield said. His voice had only gotten sharper.

Langford hurried this time, barely letting Rumsfield finish his sentence. Nervousness made his voice a little too high. "Your office will be packed up and waiting. You know I could arrest you for it—you being a cop and all. But I'm not going to. Just do the right thing and bring your badge in."

Langford turned on his heel, his cowboy boots squealing against the linoleum of the floor, and left the room. The others turned and followed him, one by one.

Sheriff Taylor stopped at the door and turned back towards Rumsfield. "I asked them to repeat the screen twice, Mike. The station owed that to you, but they were all three positive. I'm real sorry."

The door shut behind them, and Rumsfield was alone. He took

a deep breath, letting the air slide out of him staccato style. He was holding back tears, I realized from the punctuations in his breathing. "A real piece of work," I heard him say. Then his IV hit the floor, the plastic tubing slapping against the bed rail as it fell. The bed alarm screamed as he pulled himself out of it. His heart rate shot up with the exertion and he faltered, the bed rail rattling with the grasp of his hand. He was leaving, I knew, signing out against medical advice.

I'd had my predictions of what my saliva could do, but I hadn't thought far enough ahead to give exact names to the compounds or to consider that they'd show up in drug screens. Whatever the hormones were, they were the chemical equivalent of the most addictive drugs in production, and I'd just destroyed his career.

I let my forehead rest against the coolness of the wall and tried to not think about the life I'd ruined. I focused on the positive. I was going to get to go home. My daughter would be coming back, and Rumsfield was still alive. *I haven't done anything that bad*, I told myself. He'd find a new career.

As if he'd read my thoughts, Levi ran a hand through my hair and squeezed my shoulder. I turned towards him, ready to argue that I really was worse than he was giving me credit for and that he was wrong, I should feel bad. I was needing an "everything is going to be okay" speech.

I would have sworn he could read my mind, he was looking at me so intently. I waited for the words of encouragement. He slid his Blackberry into his jacket pocket as he moved towards the exit. "It might have been easier on him if you'd just killed him in the first place," he said.

I was still standing in the hospital corridor when Rumsfield's door opened. Levi had left, and I hadn't bothered to follow him. I was too angry. His last words to me had been hateful. Spiteful, actually, and none of this was my fault.

Rumsfield was arguing with the nurses and pushing their hands away when they tried to cajole him back into his room. The charge nurse told him she was going to call security, but it was just a bluff. Rumsfield might be an ass, I knew, but he was mentally competent. No one could hold him here. I considered going to him and explaining why he needed to stay. He'd lost a lot of blood and had a flail chest along with aspiration pneumonia. He needed more antibiotics. I thought about it, but logic told me I'd done enough and to leave well enough alone. I left before he could see me.

I took the stairs, flying down them in a handful of seconds, there was no one to see. But I did remember to slow down before I burst from the stairwell into the ground floor plaza of the hospital. The glass wall of the plaza stretched several stories above my head. The coffee station had opened up in the far corner for that last coffee call that so many night docs and nurses relied on, and there were several employees gathered around it, their badges pulled out to pay. But Levi was nowhere to be seen. He wasn't waiting for me outside either.

Chapter 27

I found Levi back at our makeshift home or base camp. Whatever you called it, I was looking forward to not ever seeing the place again. I couldn't wait to go home. First, I'd stop at the grocery store and stock up on all the normal things that normal people eat, especially foods that little girls like to eat. Then I'd drop by the knick-knack store and refurbish the living room. A couple new pairs of jeans wouldn't hurt and maybe a new pair of boots. Ellie and I could go shopping together. I'd take Mom and Ellie out to dinner. How I was going to convince Mom to go, of course, I hadn't yet figured out, but optimism was oozing from my pores. I'd dropped the guilt about Rumsfield quick enough and was already planning out the next year.

Levi was building a fire in the remains of the hearth when I walked in. The bird's nest had been cleaned out, the bird having long since flown the coop, and he was breaking up kindling. He'd dragged a couple dead, dried up trees to the edge of the porch. I'd seen them lying out front when I'd walked in.

"I'm certain you're not cold," I said as I sat down on the left side of the hearth. Behind me, winter's last gasps were rattling the broken window frame.

"Doesn't mean I don't like a nice fire," he answered, not looking at me.

"Why'd you leave me back there?" I asked. I reached for a long, gnarled limb and started breaking it into kindling. "I would have thought you'd be happy that I get to go home."

Snorting lightly under his breath, he paused momentarily

before he thrust another piece of wood into the fireplace. Sparks erupted under his hands from the parched leaves still clinging to the branches. "You can't ever go home, Annalice. You can't go back. No matter how much you want to."

"I can, and I will. My house is waiting. My *daughter* is waiting." He was wrong. Was this *jealousy?* I wondered. I tossed a couple sticks of kindling into the fire, watching as a flurry of sparks erupted and danced like a sparkler before ascending up the chimney. Toying with one last piece of wood, I peeled the kindling, pulling strips of wood off in long fibers that resembled locks of silver hair. My dad had made a doll this way once.

The fire was crackling now, and inside the fireplace, I could hear the sizzling of decades old cobwebs. Some roosting creature, its wings scraping the rock walls of the chimney, flew out the top of the flue, which still functioned after all these years. Talk about craftsmanship.

"I'm not talking about the house or your daughter, Anna. It's not about them. *You* can't go home. You've changed. I mean, you can *go*, of course. But it's never going to be the same. You need to move on. Let your family go."

I snorted in disgust. "You don't understand because you've forgotten what it's like to have family."

Sparks showered from the firebox and landed on my clothes and bare skin. I slapped at them and slid away, but the embers had burned deeply into my skin, leaving smooth, round holes.

Levi had picked up another log. "I should run you through with this one."

My mouth opened to deliver harsh words, but luckily, I realized how uncaring I'd sounded. Levi had his own story, and I'd not taken the time to read it. "I didn't mean for it to sound like that," I started.

"You didn't mean to sound like a selfish bitch? You think I could have possibly forgotten the smell of my wife's rotting body? Or how light my son's corpse was when I laid him on my wife's chest in a shallow, unmarked grave?"

I tried to find any other place to look than at him. "Of course not," I answered.

There was another flurry of embers as he slung the wood in the fireplace. "Don't you look away from me, you little coward."

Swallowing hard, I met his gaze again. I couldn't help but be relieved that, at the moment, he didn't have any more sticks of wood.

"They didn't even get a decent funeral. The only commemoration my family had was the sea of bloody tears I cried over their bones. And you dare to say I have forgotten?"

I stammered, looking for words, ashamed of what I'd said. "Look, that was insensitive, and I'm sorry, but how, after losing your own family, can you just tell me to leave mine?"

"Because *all* you have to do is leave them. I'm not asking for anything more. I'm not asking you to watch them die," Levi answered.

My answer came easily, without thought. "You know I can't do that."

His shoulders slumped forward as he sighed heavily and he nodded his head. "I know you can't, and that's why I should free you of your human attachments. I should do that for you," Levi answered. He'd quit looking at me and was staring out the front door instead. It framed him against the darkness. "A good creator does this for his newly made. I should rid you of those who have that hold over you. It's the duty of the maker, and it falls to me now."

I still had a piece of kindling in my hand. The small stick of wood wasn't long, but it was long enough to reach the heart and it was strong enough to do it. Levi's back was a very broad target, and wasn't he bringing it on himself? The difficulty would be slipping the wooden dagger through the ribs of the thorax from behind. If I missed, I was dead. Truly dead. And if I succeeded, could I live with what I'd done? A coward's attack from behind. At least when I'd staked Asa, I'd had the decency to do it to his face.

"*Never raise hand against your maker,*" Levi had said. I thought of every reason I shouldn't do this. Freely, he'd offered his blood to me, and I'd taken it. He'd offered protection, and I'd accepted. *But what choice do I have?* I questioned myself. I never asked for any of this. Levi was to blame for talking about my family this way. I shifted the wood in my hand, arranged it for a down to up blow. My thrust would have more strength that way. My fingers curled around the width of the wood.

Levi was still looking out the door, oblivious to my murderous thoughts. His stance was relaxed, one hand on his hip, the other resting on the doorframe. Only his hair moved in the wind. *Why is he making this so easy?*

"Never raise hand against your maker." His words echoed in my mind. I thought of our earlier lovemaking. I could still feel the high of his blood in my veins. I thought of his hands on me. And his teeth. And I felt like a traitor. I'd been many things in my life, but a coward hadn't been one of them. I flipped the stick up, balanced it in the palm of my hand for a moment and then flung it into the fire. My dreams of freedom evaporated up the chimney with a shower of sparks. There was only one thing more important to being with my family, and that was being someone who deserved to be.

"Through my possession, Annalice, and through my blood, you *will* be made whole," Levi said, turning towards me. Maybe he'd known I was poised to end him and maybe he hadn't. I couldn't be sure.

"I have no clue what that means," I said.

"Neither do I," he said. "Except that I have to find a way to make you functional. And I'd like to find a way that doesn't make you hate me."

"Then threatening to kill my family is definitely a poor way to make me whole. And I'd do far more than just hate you," I said.

"I know that. So their blood won't be on my hands. I give you my word."

Relief made me smile. I reached for him and started to answer, but he held up a hand.

"Do not underestimate the words of the bond. Through my possession, you will be made whole. You are mine, Annalice. Every last piece of you, and you'll do what I say. And I say that we're leaving here. I'll give you a day to say your good-byes and wrap stuff up, but then we're gone."

My back stiffened without thinking about it. Nothing made my hackles rise like being told I had to do something. "And if I don't agree?" I asked.

Levi leaned towards me. "Then I'll stake you myself. You see, the rule is never raise hand against your maker. Not the other way around, and I will not leave you here alone and ungoverned."

"I don't need a governor," I hissed.

"No, you need a teacher, and they are one and the same."

I studied his eyes. They were harsh, I thought at first, but finally decided that determined was the more accurate description. He'd made up his mind. "All I want is a life with my family. It doesn't seem that I'm asking for the world," I said.

"And all I'm asking is that you put a little distance between you and them for now. I'm not saying I'm not willing to work through this, or that I'm swearing them off forever. But this is uncharted territory for me, a departure from everything I've been taught. You can never have the life you had before Asa."

I looked away before he saw the red tears that I couldn't contain. "None of this is my fault," I said again.

"You sound like a broken record. When are you going to realize that some of this *is* your fault?"

The tears evaporated in a cloud of rage. "My fault? How the hell do you figure that?"

"You should have never tried to stay around. You talk about loving your daughter and saving your family, but all I see is selfishness. You put them at great risk hanging around here after you turned. You were a wreck when I found you, and you're lucky you hadn't killed half the county, including your daughter."

"I could never hurt her," I answered back.

"That is called arrogance," he said. "The only thing that saved your daughter was your mother and her very large dollop of common sense. You had *nothing* to do with it. And there's more than one way to hurt someone. Like Rumsfield, by the way. You certainly ruined him."

"It's not fair." The words came out hopeless and nearly mute.

Only once in this entire deal had I bemoaned my fate. Asa had once asked me what I was thinking, and I'd told him that knowing he was going to live while I died made me sick. He'd elegantly told me, "It is what it is, Annalice," and he'd been right.

Some things just *are* and there is no equality or fairness to it at all. None of those truths changed the fact that it was happening. Like the eighteen-year-old with breast cancer that I'd cared for several years back. One in a million chance of it happening, and yet it had still happened. She hadn't lived enough to have a serious boyfriend or choose a career. She never saw her first day of college or had her own place. She didn't deserve it, but that didn't stop her from dying, a cancer-starved girl hugging a teddy bear in a hospital bed. Not one ounce of her suffering had been fair.

She hadn't even been angry. I remember that about her. She had begged a god that didn't listen for more time, and when the time didn't materialize, she'd accepted the fact, chalking it up to some sort of greater good or a plan she couldn't understand but was certain it was for the best. That's called faith, and I was flat busted of it. The exact opposite of my patient, actually, because I was more than faithless. I was pissed.

"I never asked to be anything more than I already was. I never asked for immortality," I stated.

"And neither does the human ask to be born," he answered.

"That's not the same thing. Life is a host of opportunities when you're human. And when you die, your life is gone. Just gone. You don't have to watch it go on from the sidelines. I lost everything to Asa. My child, my mom. My soul, maybe, I don't know. Maybe I've lost that too."

Levi reached for me. "Why would you say that? No one is ever doomed."

"Asa said we were doomed to hell because of what we were."

Levi laughed darkly. "What did Asa know of religion?"

"Maybe more than I give him credit for. But I'm facing hell right now, right here. It just doesn't have red flames." I said.

Levi sat down beside me on the hearth. "Doesn't make it burn any less," he said. "Or any less real."

"Are we doomed, Levi? I told Asa that God wouldn't hold him

accountable for something he didn't control. Because Asa honestly didn't choose this. He said I didn't know God. Maybe he was right."

He folded one hand, warmed by the fire, over mine. The sensation was almost human. "You feel doomed, don't you? Because you did choose this. You could have let Asa kill you, and you didn't."

I nodded. "I didn't feel like I had much of a choice at the time. Death didn't seem a fair deal, but now neither does living like this. Maybe I'd have been better off dead like Mom said. I don't want to second-guess myself or to spend multiple lifetimes asking what if. But what have I gained? I'm supposed to be strong, and I've been strong, but right now, I'm angry. At everyone really. Asa, my mother, Rumsfield, myself. Every life lesson I've ever been taught tells me to stay strong and fight back. But maybe there's a time when fighting is the wrong thing to do and choosing death is the right choice."

He wrapped an arm around me for support. I guess I looked like someone who needed a shoulder to cry on. "And you're angry at God. You don't want to say it, but I can hear it in between the lines."

He had me there. "Humans have so many more options. I *had* so many more options, and as long as you're human, you can turn back. Now I feel like I'm on a road of inevitability, and it's not fair."

"Do they?" he asked. "If, before you were born, you could have been given the option of life or nothingness. What would you have chosen?"

I turned toward him. "Are you serious?"

"Answer the question."

"Life obviously."

"Without a doubt?" he asked.

"Of course."

"Because with life comes the reckoning at the end. Paradise requires a price of faith, devotion, and love. I know of no religion that lets you in scot-free. So once you make that decision of life, there is no guarantee. Still ready to take the gamble?"

217

I shrugged confidently. "Why wouldn't I? Except of course that I might run into an Asa. But assuming that wouldn't happen, why wouldn't I accept the challenge?"

"And now let me also warn you that you're going to be born with a host of weaknesses. Maybe you're born with an addiction problem or perhaps, even worse, a doubting personality. Maybe genetically, you're the kind of person that simply can't believe. Maybe you question everything, and it's just who you are. You spend your entire life questioning God's existence and in the end can't muster the belief. So you're doomed to hell because of a character flaw that God gave you. How fair is that? Would you still want to be born, knowing you're a doubter? Would you still take the gamble?"

I wasn't so confident anymore. I opened my mouth to argue, then closed it again.

"So you see, humans don't have any choice either. We are all born, at least the first time, without consent into circumstances that are out of our control. At least this birth you accepted of your own free will. Make the most of it. Don't spend the entirety of your second life looking back."

The tears had begun at the mention of looking back. They streamed cool and red down my face. Looking back is all I'd been doing. I turned away, embarrassed at their color. "How do I not?"

He reached for me, running a hand through my hair. "You learn through the years how to look back and touch only those fragments of memories you hold the most valuable. You bury them under layers of time. The barbs aren't as sharp that way, and the hurt is a little less when you prick yourself on them. The memories of the ones you have lost lose their focus, and when you look back, they are more golden and you can enjoy them again."

"Everything hurts now. Everything brings a memory. Every place another recollection of my former life that's still there. Of my family that's still there. And I keep thinking that it's all in my grasp, but the more I reach for it, the more everything slips through my fingers."

"It all fades. Everything that hurts you now will fade. Not

today or even in a year, but a human lifetime from now, and you'll start to understand."

Considering a lifetime of pain seemed pointless. I couldn't even see how I'd get past next week. But Levi was right. I'd been holding so tight to the idea of my daughter that I'd forgotten to consider my actual daughter. She needed stability, and right now, the combination of Levi and me were the antithesis of that. She needed a mother. Just a mother. I could see that now.

I wiped my tears away, resolute that they'd be the last for a while. "Give me a couple days to get things wrapped up. I've got some things to do. Sign my accounts and property over to Mom. Try to come up with a way to say good-bye to Ellie. Assuming there is any way Mom will let me near her. God, I have no idea how that's going to go."

"You have twenty-four hours from the coming sunset. We'll leave this camp then and head north. Don't make me look for you, Annalice. I'm resolute about my decision, that this is the right thing for you. For the both of us. And don't think your tears have softened me."

Chapter 28

*I*nside the hearth, the fire was cracking and popping. As a human, I'd loved fire. As a vampire, it was divine. At least to look at. Oranges and reds intertwined with blues and greens and colors that I'd never seen glowed on the water-stained walls of the cabin. Those same colors glinted in the residual tears on my cheeks and reflected back into my own eyes so that everything was cast in burnt orange and deep reds.

Just as the addition of people can rejuvenate an old house back into a home, fire had transformed this ramshackle cabin into some shade of its former self. The walls lost their chill, and the smell of a thousand long-past fires filled the air with their homey scents. Levi had pushed the door as far shut as it would go, warming the interior by at least ten degrees. Cold didn't bother me, but Levi was right. The fire was nice and the warmer air made me feel, I guess for lack of a better word, more human.

"Let me take the pain away. At least for a while." Levi moved towards me, his pale skin cast golden by the fire.

I shook my head. I knew what he wanted. And it wasn't that I didn't want the same thing. Being wrapped in his arms with his pheromones twisting through my bloodstream was intoxicating and for an hour or so, I'd have no pain.

"I can't spare the blood and neither can you."

"I know how to keep you fed, Annie. I promised you protection."

Flames lit in my belly like a match had been struck. *I was* hungry. But wasn't I always? And why should I resist? He'd spread a couple of blankets on the hardwood floor in front of the fireplace, and they looked very inviting. As did Levi's full red lips. He must have drunk again on the way home from the hospital and so had plenty to give me. How had I not noticed the change in his skin when now it was all I could think about?

I crossed the short floor space between us, encircling his chest with my arms, my legs clasping around his waist. There was no hesitation as I bit deep into his neck and found the wellspring of still-warm blood. It spurted thick and salty into my mouth.

Levi moaned hard, his hands kneading my back as I drank deeply. He didn't seem to care how much I took, just stood, his erection hard against my belly while I took so much from him.

Finally, I pulled back and kissed him full on the mouth, my lips staining his even redder than before. "I want your bite," I said. "I want to feel what you're wanting."

My legs still locked around his waist, he let go of my back to pull my head to one side and brushed my hair away with the other. It is risky to expose your jugular like that, and for a vampire it was like saying, "I'm open. You own me. Do with me what you want." It was dangerous. Levi had warned me about it.

But I held the submissive position, feeling next to naked, until I felt the sharp hot pain of his teeth. I closed my eyes as his poison spread through my body. He left a line of small bites down the side of my neck and onto my shoulder. He wasn't drinking, just fanning the fountains of lust that had welled up in the pit of my belly with his touch.

Pulling away, Levi smiled, his lips parting to show pared fangs, and I caught my breath. God, he was beautiful. And I mean really beautiful. Like in an "I would gladly join your harem and screw you senseless" kind of beautiful.

"I'm going to make you realize tonight how much I own you," he whispered. The meaning in his words sent a cold chill down my spine, and I shivered in anticipation. "Take your clothes off. I don't trust myself to not rip them off."

I unzipped my boots, tossing them into the corner, and continued until I was standing naked in front of him. Behind me the fire roared, a hollow buzzing sound that reminded me of all the times as a human I'd been put on the spot and could hear the blood pumping through my ears, and I felt that way now as Levi's eyes swept across me. I was close enough to the fire that the flames were nearly painful on my backside, my skin lit up golden red in the firelight.

"Be careful, Annalice. Vampires burn you know," Levi said, pulling me towards him.

I'm pretty sure it was double speak. Either way, I didn't need him to tell me vampires could burn. My insides were a hot mess. His pheromones were raging through me, but his desires tonight weren't the urgent ones of earlier in the evening. This was more of a slow, persistent burn, and at the edges I caught the undertones of ownership and jealousy. This was the kind of lust that begins after the first tensions have been released; the frustration has died away and what's rekindled has been smoldering longer. He wanted me in a way I hadn't realized before. This wasn't just about my family or what was best for me; it wasn't sadistic either, like Asa. There was some loneliness here and a need to find something to make the everyday mean something again. And possession. I could taste that clearly.

We joined on the makeshift bed in front of the fire many times. Our skin hot from the flames; our personal desires cascading through the other until I could no longer determine which ones had been mine or which ones his. By the time we'd finished, he'd consumed and fed me many times, and I'd belonged to him in every imaginable way.

Except the one that mattered.

No one was going to own me. I wasn't chattel. And although I couldn't kill Levi, that much was certain, and for a multitude of reasons, it didn't mean I was going to stand by my vampire. Or this vampire; he didn't belong to me. The belonging seemed to go one way, and the handle of the leash wasn't in my hands. But I couldn't end him. For starters, he wasn't trying to hurt me or, more importantly, my family. He'd helped me, protected me, and I wasn't a traitor. Although we had only spent a few days together, it had forged a bond of sorts, and I knew that deep down, I'd developed more than an infatuation for him but less than a love. Not enough to give up a family for.

I'd also apparently agreed to some bond, a contract of sorts, which named him my creator, and so Levi was protected from me. Now I'm an honest person, for the most part. Although I do taste the grapes in the grocery store before I buy them. Which is technically stealing I suppose, but I do it anyways. That's about the extent of my thievery over the years. But contracts are a different thing. Doctors sign contracts every year where we promise our loyalty to one hospital or another. More often than not, somebody changes the terms and the agreement is null and void. Usually the hospital. *"But all contracts,"* one administrator had told me, *"are made to be broken."*

And the verbal contract I'd made with Levi was about to fall by the wayside. The terms had changed. No way in hell was I leaving my daughter. I was going to leave *with* my daughter but *without* him. I knew that before I fed from him in front of the fireplace. And for that, I felt guilty although I tried to look at it like a severance package. My "going away and get a new position" blood until I was safely moved. I'd realized the combination of Levi and me was detrimental to my daughter. What I wasn't convinced of was that *I* was bad for Ellie. There was a chance, and I was going to take it, that Ellie and I alone would be fine.

If I felt guilty about anything else, it was that I'd let him wrap around me in the bed in the basement before first light. He was nuzzling my head with his chin when the blackness claimed me.

Chapter 29

I was awake now, the day having come and gone, and burning with a plan. It had built itself in my mind while Levi and I had made love, like a rose unfurling from the clenched bud, until I could see plainly the algorithm. The plan had given me hope, and I'd wrapped my legs tighter around Levi and pulled him farther into me on the makeshift bed. I wondered what the emotion had tasted like on Levi's tongue. Did he know I was up to something? Could he sense it? What does hope taste like?

He wasn't beside me now, and I stretched out my hand to where he'd rested the night before. The bed was cool, even the indentions gone from where he'd lain. He had a good forty-five minutes on me and most likely had gone to hunt. That's what he called what we did. There's a certain perverseness in that, as if it was some kind of sport, but an accurate description. But he didn't kill. He'd said eternity was too long to carry unnecessary acts around with you. There was no need for continued violence.

I caressed the space with my hand but got up quickly. I couldn't waste time on nostalgia; I wouldn't allow myself to miss him.

My plan was simple. I'd stop by the house and grab the important papers: passports, SS cards, the cash I kept in the safe, and birth certificates. I'd pack a small bag of clothes so we wouldn't have to stop anywhere except a hotel room. Then I'd get Ellie, one way or another. Which meant I'd go to the front door of Mom's apartment first. I'd ask nicely, but either way, Ellie and I were leaving. Mom could come if she wanted to, and I hoped she did.

Come sunrise, we'd be two states away and safely tucked into a nameless hotel paid for by cash. No cellphone to trace me by. No real names to be used. Levi might question Mom, if she chose to stay behind, but he wouldn't hurt her. And she wouldn't know anything of value, except that I was gone. Another state or two over, and Ellie and I would find an apartment. I'd home school at night and hire a babysitter for the day. I'd start looking for a job. Not a physician position, of course, since all state medical boards list the physicians licensed in their respective state, a perfect avenue for Levi to find me, but I could do consulting or chart review. I had enough money in my account to take care of us, if we lived frugally, until I found something. What mattered was that Ellie and I would be together.

I had nothing to pack. The only thing in the cabin besides myself was the comforters that Levi had retrieved from my house that first night he'd brought me out here. I didn't even have a change of clothes. I walked up the stairs, crossing the blankets we'd made love on, and out the door without looking back.

Chapter 30

My house rose up forlorn and quiet out of an eerie fog that had settled across the low-lying pastures. Until the night I died, I never thought of the place as lonely. Mom had hated it on sight, whereas I'd loved it. I'd adored the quiet, fertile valleys ringed by the blue hazy-green mountains that rose up like a crown in the distance and the cool, dark forest had been a mysterious den for my daughter's imagination. Tonight, the place was dismal, and even though I was one of the undead, I shuddered at the sight.

No dog barked to welcome me home. The horses had been rescued; the remaining cows, the ones I hadn't killed, were gone as well. The other one had been buried by Rumsfield, at least that's what my mom had said. The normal welcoming porch lights were dead without electricity, and a forgotten police streamer fluttered soundlessly in the breeze. The interior was a darker hole in the dark night. Like a black hole, the house pulled the starlight right out of the air. The place looked dead.

I fought the urge to be sentimental as I studied my home. So much had happened here, and tonight, I'd be leaving the place, probably for good. Ellie and I had made many memories, mostly good ones, here. In this pasture, I'd taught her to ride a horse and fly a kite. She'd taken her first weaving bicycle ride down this driveway, and in this yard raised her very own strawberries. Just a handful but still, they'd been hers.

But with so much good can come just as much bad. I'd met Asa here, hated him with an intensity that I didn't know I possessed, and just as passionately as I'd hated him, I'd pitied him. Then I'd killed him. In this same pasture, I'd ruined another man's career, nearly killed him, and met my second vampire.

I felt bound to this house. Here, I'd lived, died and been reborn. How could I not feel connected to this land, and maybe that explained the old legend of pouring dirt from their homeland into a vampire's casket. Maybe that was the only way they could keep a piece of their home, a part of themselves that wouldn't change no matter how much the world around them did. They could take their home with them when it forced them out. Kneeling down, I cupped a handful of dirt in my hands and squeezed it into a ball. It smelled like spring and ground ready for planting.

A new life was waiting for me. I just had to cross this pasture to get to it, and I needed to hurry. I wasn't a vampire forced from my home. I was taking the initiative. The dirt sifted between my fingers and into the wind as I crossed the fog-shrouded pasture.

Levi knew I was here, under the pretense that I was getting papers together, and Rumsfield had been completely discredited. He wasn't anything more than just a concerned citizen now, and I had every right to be in my own home. Still, I felt a sense of trepidation as I reached the door. Something didn't feel right. Could it be this easy?

The house was just like I had left it. Levi's hand-written message was still visible on the deck. The back door was ajar, the electricity remained off, and what food was left in the refrigerator was rotting. The smell was rank. Rumsfield's business card was lying on the kitchen bar from his first visit, a thin layer of dust barely visible to my eyes settled across the gloss print. I flipped it onto the floor for good measure as I passed.

I grabbed a paper bag from a cabinet as I went down the stairs to the basement. The safe had been a recent addition to the house when I'd bought the place, and I'd never quite understood why the previous owners had put it down here. There was no telling how many men it had taken to move it down the stairs. It was amazing that the old wooden slats had ever held.

I made a quick job of filling the bag up. All of the important documents were in one place, and I grabbed them along with what little cash I had in there. Just enough for a few nights' hotel stays and some fast food on the run. Folding the bag up as I climbed the stairs three at a time, I stopped into my office and grabbed my medical diploma and license. My stethoscope was looped up across my white coat, and I bagged that too out of a sense of nostalgia. I certainly didn't need it. I hadn't seen a patient in nearly a month, and even if I did, I could hear more by laying my ear to their chest. Of course, that would be a little awkward. But, I hadn't passed a month of the last decade without it hanging around my neck, so it didn't seem right to just leave it behind.

In my bedroom, I packed a couple changes of clothes and some extra shoes as well as the small amount of jewelry my ex-husband had given me. That wasn't nostalgia, just something to pawn if I needed cash. In the living room, I grabbed two photo albums in which I'd meticulously journaled Ellie's childhood in film and a few of her clothes Mom had left. We'd buy more once we got to where we were going.

I stood in the living room, the small suitcase, into which I had stuffed everything I deemed important, clutched in my hand. It was time to go, but I stood rooted to the spot. Walking out this door would make it all painfully official. I wasn't human. I wasn't going to live a normal life. Up until this moment, I'd kept the memory of my old life in a bubble. Walking out the door would shatter it for good. I could never come home again.

I thought of one more thing to grab from the basement safe, and I was coming up the stairs when I heard a harsh knock on the door. I froze at the sound, cursing the soundproof quality of the basement, my arms askew, held from my body as if I was falling. And I *felt* like I was falling into some sort of trap. Because what else could it be? No one dropped by this far out in the country. The only routine visitor Ellie and I had ever had the pleasure to receive was Ms. McElhaney. Until Detective Rumsfield who had become a fixture around the place, who wasn't so much of a random visitor as a dangerous one. No pizza boys got the wrong house this far out. No Girl Scouts ventured into my yard. Not even the Jehovah's Witnesses came to save souls out on this dark and winding road.

I half-expected it to be Levi at first but decided Levi wouldn't have knocked. He'd have just walked in or blasted the doors down if he thought I was trying to hide something, all the while preaching a sermon on how broken I was but how he'd fix me.

More likely, it was the detective. *Former detective,* I corrected myself. I focused and heard two heartbeats. One standing by the door and another a couple hundred yards or so away. My heart sunk. It was almost certainly Michael Rumsfield with some poor counterpart he'd talked into believing his crazy talk. But I couldn't take any crap from them tonight. My schedule was tight, and I had a lot of distance to put between Levi and myself. I stalked heavily up the stairs to the door and threw it open wide, my mouth already open to wage war on Rumsfield.

"Didn't they take your bad … ?" The words ground to a halt on my tongue. Sheriff Langford was standing quietly on my front porch. He raised his eyebrows and smiled. "Badge," I finished. "Sorry, I … um, I thought you were Rumsfield."

He patted his chest, the gold metal humming under his fingers. "No, I still have mine. But I've been using Rumsfield's as an ashtray."

I didn't say anything, just forced a half-smile and waited for whatever he'd come here to say. He laughed and shrugged. "Just a little police joke."

I nodded and looked over his shoulder for whoever was hiding farther out. The other heartbeat was out there. It hadn't moved. "Smoking's bad for your health. You should consider stopping," I said.

He shook his head no. "Too old to change," Langford answered. He leaned against a porch column and reached into his jacket pocket. "Do you mind if I smoke out here?" He pulled a pack of cigarettes out, the cellophane crinkling loudly.

"Knock yourself out, but if you're going to get comfortable, you might as well have your sidekick join us," I said, motioning to the thickly clustered trees bordering the driveway. Whoever was out there was far enough back that I couldn't see them, and they were dressed to blend in.

Langford looked over his shoulder and then turned back towards me before lighting his cigarette. "I didn't bring any backup." He took a couple drags and tossed the remains in the mulched flowerbed. Too moist to burn for long, I knew. Apparently, he was more of a quick hit type of guy.

"I thought bringing backup was normal police procedure," I said, pretending that I'd guessed about the second person. Whoever was in the woods was holding steady, not moving.

Langford smiled. "I'm not your *normal* police. I didn't think I'd need backup to talk to a good law-abiding citizen. I didn't even bring my patrol car." He smiled again. "I don't, do I? Need help, that is."

I smiled back and shut the door behind me as I stepped out onto the porch. "Of course not, Sheriff. How can I help you?" I asked. My gaze kept shifting to the finger of forest that touched my driveway. Langford was lying. He didn't realized I knew, and I couldn't hold it against him. I'd probably be playing my cards close to my chest as well. Which made me realize I should keep my eyes on him and not on his colleague in the woods. "I do have an appointment though, Sheriff, so I don't have much time."

"You seen Rumsfield?" Langford asked, ignoring my comment about time.

I shook my head. "Not since the hospital with you."

Langford reached into his pocket and pulled out a pocket watch. The links of gold chain clinked in his hand as he pulled it from his coat. Flipping it open, he studied the clock face. "You say you're pressed for time?" He held out the watch, motioning that I should take it.

I reached for it even as I wondered what his game was. "I don't understand," I said as he dropped it in my hand. The watch was old; I could tell that as soon as it landed in my palm. The engraving had once been intricate and still was except where the opening mechanism sat. Here it was worn as smooth as a river stone by the passage of fingertips across the surface. But it was the weight that gave its age away. The mechanism was real, not the recreated fluff of today's digital timepieces.

"Rumsfield brought it to me when he dropped off his badge," Langford said. The mention of Rumsfield's name brought that sickly sweet smell from his skin again. "Look familiar?"

I wrinkled my nose. I couldn't help it. The jealous smell was so thick it enveloped me like a fog. Using the watch as an excuse, I took a few steps away from him towards the light, as if I needed it, and studied the etchings of the metal.

I shook my head and handed it back. "No. Just looks like an old watch to me. The real deal though. Probably get a pretty penny for it at an antique shop." But I was lying. I had seen it before in the root cellar with the rest of the jewelry Asa had stolen.

"Don't you want to know why I brought this out here?" Langford asked.

Not really, but I have my suspicions. "I figured you were going to tell me," I answered.

"This watch was reported missing when a local man died out at Brasshears couple weeks back. His family looked for it among his effects. A family heirloom, you see, but they couldn't find it. It was the only missing link that made anybody consider that it wasn't death by natural causes. He was killed out by his chicken coop," Langford said. His voice didn't hold any sorrow or even accusation. I guess he'd added the chicken coop tidbit for effect. No one should have to die lying in chicken crap, and everybody loves the bizarre.

"And?" I asked, hoping he'd get to the punchline.

"Rumsfield found it in a root cellar on your property. Along with several pieces of jewelry, including one of Ms. McElhaney's necklaces. He also thought you, or somebody at least, had been living in the cellar. You, part of the time, since he found some of your clothes in there too. He brought it all to me. Pretty tough guy. I'll give him that. He walked out of the hospital and straight to your place."

I didn't say anything at first. What could I say? The evidence pointed to me or, if not to me as the killer, that I knew who was. I couldn't see any way around it.

"Evidence obtained with a legal search warrant?" I asked.

Langford smiled and pulled out another cigarette. "You don't think any of those minor details actually matter, do you? I can slip that into the evidence bag from his first search and no one will ever notice, or even care by the way."

I stared hard at him. Was he bluffing? Probably not, I figured. It was a little pond and Langford was the patrolling shark. "I didn't kill that man in Brasshears," I finally said.

"Oh, I never thought you killed them, but I think you know who did," Langford replied, handing the watch back to me. The metal was warm where he'd been holding it in his hand. "But obstruction of justice," he added, "is a serious charge. Not nearly as serious as accomplice to murder, but still a problem."

"Look, maybe my boyfriend did it. I don't know, but I don't know where he is. Rumsfield kept asking, and I honestly don't know. He never confessed to me, except about Ms. McElhaney. I'd have come to the police, but I knew the man was dangerous, and he threatened my family. Threatened to kill all of us, so I buried his clothes out in the forest. So Rumsfield was more right about some things than I let on. He's a good detective. As much as I hate to admit it."

At this point, I was trying to salvage whatever part of my innocence I could. If Langford thought I was only obstructing justice that had to be better than being consider an accomplice to murder. I just needed to get him off my front porch with the promise that I'd come down to the station tomorrow. Tomorrow wouldn't come because I'd be long gone with Ellie.

Langford nodded his head, the movement fanning the sickly sweet smell of jealousy towards me. "I wouldn't waste my breath saying too many nice things about Rumsfield. He thinks you're a real freak. And he's not *that* smart, is he?"

What's he getting at? Something about Rumsfield brought out the protective side of me. And this sheriff truly brought out the irritable side of me also. "With all due respect, Sheriff, he figured out something wasn't quite right about my story before any of you. You should really give him his position back."

Langford held his hand up like the Pope giving a decree. "Actually, I've always thought of it as luck. Luckier than most, I'd say, but this time not lucky enough that he'll ever get his job back. And as far as smarts go, he couldn't be that bright bringing all this evidence straight to me," Langford said.

"Okaaay. Shouldn't he bring all the evidence to you?" I asked, my fingertips rubbing the engraving on the pocket watch as I mentally searched for his angle. "What are you trying to say?"

"I'm saying that I'll give all this evidence back to you. Except that ridiculous stake. I told Rumsfield to keep that because that's just hogwash, and any jury would laugh him under the table. Look, I'm sure you have a lot of money, you being a doctor and all. Accomplice to murder and obstruction of justice showing up in the paper would be very inconvenient for you, Dr. Creed. Very inconvenient for your daughter too and your mother. Now you need to understand that Rumsfield's more concerned about justice. Me, on the other hand … I'm willing to overlook some minor infractions."

I rolled my eyes at the rich doctor comment—a common problem for me whether I was buying a new car or hiring a plumber. "I don't have any money for you, Sheriff. Just enough for my daughter and I to live on. Especially now that I've developed this medical problem."

"And that problem is not *my* problem, Dr. Creed. This can end one of two ways tonight. You'll either be sitting handcuffed in the back of a patrol car charged with accessory to first-degree murder. Or the more pleasant option, I'll stay with you tonight, to make sure you don't skip town or anything, and tomorrow morning, I'll follow you to the bank. And once you hand over a hundred grand, I'll hand you back all the evidence Rumsfield gave me. And we can forget any of this ever happened."

I was staring at him, dumbfounded. How had I lived in this world this long and never noticed the corruption I was seeing tonight. I didn't even resist when Langford reached over and pulled the watch out of my grasp.

"What about Rumsfield?" I asked. "Isn't he going to talk?"

Langford pulled out another cigarette. The second one was still smoldering beside the first one in the flowerbed. "You mean the drug addict?" He laughed, smoke erupting from his lungs in staccato fashion. "Who's going to listen?" He took another drag and grinned back at me.

"And you might want to think a little more about your girl, Dr. Creed. With you gone, it'd be a real shame if your mother wasn't allowed custody of her. A judge might find your mom too old or absentminded to care for her. It's funny the excuses judges can come up with when someone make's a few suggestions. Who knows, she might even end up in a group home."

"You would do that to an innocent child?" I asked aloud, but it was more of a statement of fact to myself.

"Don't force my hand, Dr. Creed. It doesn't have to be that way."

"And what if I tell everyone in the department about you blackmailing me?" I asked.

He opened his hands in front of him like any good politician spreading the bullshit. "They'll call you a liar and figure you went wild for a man. They'll think you were a desperate, lonely woman and swallow everything I'm telling them. But no one has to know. No one knows I'm out here, and nobody ever has to find out. Rumsfield's lost all credibility, only he's too stupid to realize it. Else he wouldn't have brought all those juicy pieces of evidence to me. He would've been standing here himself."

"I don't think he was willing to believe that you could stoop to this level," I answered.

He laughed at my comment. "But everyone *is* willing to believe the worst about a woman, Dr. Creed. You should know that. Just look at Rumsfield."

For once, I wished I was still hallucinating and Asa was there telling me to kill him. I'm pretty sure I'd have listened. "But *you're* not willing to believe the worst about me, Sheriff?" I asked. Obviously, he wasn't or he wouldn't be out here.

I suppose he thought his smile was disarming because he cast another broad one at me now. "Of course not, Dr. Creed. I'm willing to give you the benefit of the doubt."

"Your mistake," I said as I reached out and smacked his head against the porch post.

He landed at my feet, his body crumpling to the porch floor

like an accordion as his joints gave way. His knees hit first and then he fell forward at the waist, his head smacking the concrete with a sickening thud. I listened for his breathing and was only slightly relieved that his respiratory drive continued on at a steady rate. Not that I was likely to have started CPR if it hadn't, but I was glad he was alive. Tomorrow morning, he'd have an unparalleled headache and hopefully some short-term memory loss to boot.

I talked to him as I dug through his pockets, pulling out the other two watches and the handful of jewelry Rumsfield had given him. A quick inventory showed it was all there—everything that Asa had taken from his most recent victims—the direct link to me of any specific crime.

"Sorry about this, Sheriff. Although, I guess you weren't that good of a cop, and I really shouldn't be wasting any sympathy on you. As annoying as Rumsfield was, at least he was on the up and up. You know, he was trying to protect me when all of this started. I was in danger then. The mortal type. And he honestly tried to save me. Now I'm in danger of losing my family and everything else I hold dear. Not life or death necessarily, but still, important stuff to me. I can't stay here with you all night, nor can I go to the station with you in the morning because Rumsfield was right. I *am* a vampire, and you shouldn't have threatened my daughter."

I stood, leaning back against the front door as I slid the stolen jewelry into the pockets of my jacket and blue jeans. I was debating about grabbing my clothes out of the sheriff's car when the first arrow slid through my belly, pinning me to the oak door at my back. The second one caught me in the sternoclavicular notch, the v shaped space at the bottom of the neck. And just as I realized what I'd been shot with, the third pierced my right lung. All three burned with an unexpected fire as they cut through me.

I'd have screamed if I could have pulled air into my lungs, but the second arrow had sliced nearly through my trachea. All that came out was one prolonged syllable as what air I had remaining in my lungs whistled across the remains of my vocal cords. Even though I didn't need to breathe, I reached for the arrow in my neck first. The sensation of my own blood pouring down my throat was fear-provoking to say the least.

I'd gotten so wrapped up in Sheriff Langford that I'd forgotten about the person in the woods. He'd been smart to bring backup, and I'd been stupid to have forgotten. The bad part was I couldn't even drop my chin to see him better. I could hear the slap of pants-legs against the tall grass at the edge of the forest, and I could just see the shadow of a man walking towards me. I couldn't make him out until he was close enough that I could smell his arrogance. What little heart I had left dropped to my feet. Sheriff Langford had been telling the truth after all.

Rumsfield stopped about fifty feet directly in front of me, a crossbow in one hand, the stake I'd used on Asa tucked into his waistband. He was breathing hard and leaning more towards one side, splinting to help himself breathe better. His skin was white ash, and the scruff he'd been wearing in the hospital was now a full-on beard. If he'd slept, I couldn't tell it. Sheer adrenaline must have been keeping him upright, but just barely. I gave him a handful of steps before he collapsed. Why had he wasted his shot?

I didn't look any better. Blood was pouring from my wounds, and it took both of my tremoring hands to haltingly inch the arrow out of my neck. A gush of blood slipped down my throat, and more dripped onto the porch at my feet. In a paroxysm of coughs, I cleared my airway of the blood that was stealing my speech so I could curse him properly, but something was wrong. I couldn't force enough air to produce anything other than a rasp across my vocal cords. I choked out more blood and tried again. Oxygen isn't important, but air is essential for communication.

"That bad of a shot?" I whispered, struggling to make my voice loud enough that Rumsfield could hear me. The wound made a sucking, whistling noise while I talked, a slow ooze of blood dripping down the back of my throat.

Rumsfield took a few unsteady steps towards me as he pulled a final arrow out of the rack on the crossbow. "If I'd wanted you dead right away, rest assured you would be," he answered.

"Feel funny, Annalice? I silver-tipped the arrows. It's a type of poison for vampires. But you probably already knew that."

I attempted to shake my head. "No. I didn't know that," I whispered. The wound wasn't healing. Now I was getting nervous. Looks like he had more time than I thought for that kill shot.

He nodded as he stepped closer, the crossbow held more or less level with my heart. "You're pretty new at this, aren't you? At least, that's what I think. That man that you were with a couple weeks back. He was the real deal, and you're his upstart. You been at this about two weeks the way I figure it."

I nodded my head as much as I could. The muscles of my neck were weakening, and I could barely lift my head up to look at him.

"You're really starting to feel it, huh?" Rumsfield said. It wasn't so much of a question as an observation. He took another couple of nervous steps closer, still splinting for deeper breaths.

I felt funny all right. Each movement was like pulling a tank through quicksand. My lips had cracked from the loss of blood. I was oozing from each hole he'd given me, and the one in my neck wasn't healing at all. At least now I knew why. The arrow I'd pulled from my neck slipped from my hand and dropped at my feet. My vision was dulled from the silver. It was the arrows nailing me to the door that held me up.

"Nice arrow. You make your own?" I asked. The serious bow hunters usually did. Their arrows were more distinctive that way. Rumsfield's carried red and black striped feathers tipped in white.

Rumsfield had made it nearly to the porch by this point. "The silver is a weakening agent, and I didn't want you getting away from me. A little selfish, I know, but I wanted you to have time. Time to answer a few questions and, if I'm being honest, time to know that it was me that was putting an end to all of this." Rumsfield notched the final bolt and loaded the crossbow. He struggled to do it. The poundage on an average crossbow is nearly eighty pounds, and he was on his last legs.

I cleared my throat from the blood again. "So were you working with Langford or was he lying?" I whispered. My hands were scratching at the arrow in my belly. I could barely keep a grip on the shaft at all, I was so weak. It wasn't any use, and I knew it, but I couldn't seem to stop any more than a man couldn't dance on the gallows.

Rumsfield shook his head and inched closer. "No. I was playing him. I've been following him for a couple of days. Langford's always been a little dirty. Never liked me much. And I never liked him at all."

"Is this a revenge killing, Mike, or a mercy killing?" I asked. "A revenge execution doesn't truly befit a cop." I guess I wanted answers, too.

He looked over at Langford's unconscious form. The man's mouth was open, drool and blood mixing on the concrete under his head. "You're forgetting, Annalice. I'm not an officer any more thanks to you. But we both know this killing is for the best, whatever the reason."

I choked at his words, flecks of blood spewing from my mouth and landing at my feet. I watched them drop as they fell in slow motion, riding the breeze on the way down. Hearing your own death talked about so nonchalantly is more than a little disturbing. "Everyone seems to know what's best for me, and no one bothers to ask my opinion."

"I don't think you can be trusted to decide," Rumsfield answered. He lifted the crossbow up, my heart in the crosshairs. "I also wanted to make sure you had time to make your peace. Or whatever your kind does."

"Aren't you the gentleman? But it's probably a little too late for that. The one who made me said my kind go to hell."

The bow was starting to shake as his muscles fatigued. He realized it and tried to still the trembles. "I hate that for you, Annalice, I really do. I never wanted it to end this way. But it did, and I'd be lying if I said it wasn't a little personal. It didn't start out that way though. I want you to know that." He re-leveled the bow. The tip had started to drift downwards.

Bloody tears were beginning to track down my cheeks. I could taste them at the corners of my mouth, a metallic twinge that burned my tongue.

"Don't start that. You're not some helpless damsel in distress.

It won't help. You're not walking away from this."

"I'm not crying for your benefit, Mike. It's the silver. But while there's breath in my body, there's a few things I need you to know. I didn't kill Ms. McElhaney. I knew who did, but I didn't call the cops because you guys wouldn't have believed me. And Asa, the vampire who attacked her, warned me he'd kill anyone I had any contact with, and that included your nosy, busybody self. I couldn't help the dead, but I did keep him from coming after you the night you doubled back to my house. I saved you that night, and a couple other times as well. You just didn't realize it. I didn't kill that man in the woods, but I couldn't protect him either."

"Saved me? You? You *ruined* me!" Rumsfield nearly shouted, pulling the crossbow back up again. "And it was your spit in my blood stream that got me fired. You ruined my life."

"I didn't mean to. I tried to protect you."

He was shaking his head, a man in disbelief. "And that man at the bar? Were you protecting him, too?"

"I'm learning, Mike. To be something I was never meant to be."

The crossbow came up again, the trembling taken away by his anger. "You say you saved me, but it was *you* that almost killed me! You put me in the hospital on a ventilator with a collapsed lung and lacerated spleen. I nearly bled to death in your pasture. The only thing that kept me alive was the lead bullets I put in you. You didn't *save* me. You're dangerous, a menace to our society, and I won't let you live to do it again."

"I'm not dangerous. I'm not like Asa. Nothing like him. I can learn to not hurt people."

He laughed at that. "Wake up, Annie. If you need to learn to not hurt people, then you need to be put down. You can't teach that. You should know better. You were a *doctor* once. Psychopaths can't be fixed."

"I'm not a psychopath."

"No, you're worse. You're a vampire. And you eat people."

"But I don't have to kill them. Can't you see? I just need their blood to live. Not their death."

The wheels were turning in his mind, the crossbow faltered

for a few seconds, the arrow tip falling to my mid-abdomen. "Shit, Annie, seriously," Rumsfield said, taking a few steps back. I could see the mental distance he was putting between us as well. "Humans don't have to eat the whole fricking chocolate cake. But they do. So your expecting me to let you live on the off chance that you can stay on the vampire diet wagon? Listen to yourself. If you have any human left in you at all, think about what you're saying."

He'd called me Annie. That had to be a good sign. I started to argue more points.

"Shut up! No more. Your daughter and mother don't have to know. I won't tell them, but they would thank me if they knew what you really are." He took a step closer, the crossbow lining up with my heart. Resolve turning his face to stone.

It was over, and I knew it. "Just look in on Ellie some. Please. Would you do that?" I asked before he shut me out completely.

He nodded a grudging yes, and I let my hands slip off the arrow I'd been struggling with and fall to my sides, my fingers digging into the brick of the porch for support. Support to keep my hands from reaching towards Rumsfield and begging for mercy. *I will not beg. I will not beg.* The end had finally come. I knew there would be no mercy from Rumsfield.

"You want to say some kind of prayer or something?" he asked. "Last chance."

I wanted to pray for Ellie, but I wanted to ask God for revenge, too. To cut Michael Rumsfield down in a fiery blast. "It's probably wrong to pray for peace and revenge at the same time," I answered.

"Have it your way," he said.

I will not beg. Not God or Rumsfield. I stared into Michael Rumsfield's cool, blue-eyed gaze for the last time with my own resolve. Every last ounce of strength I had left, I used to hold my head up straight. *I will not beg.* "Just get it over with."

I closed my eyes as he pulled the trigger.

Chapter 31

*T*he arrow whipped through the air. I could hear it coming straight and even; the whistle the tip made in the air didn't wobble. The shot had been good—made by someone who knew how to deliver death to an animal. That's what I was to him, an animal. Rumsfield had exhaled with relief when the bowstring was released, and then time slowed. I could feel the milliseconds creeping by. *One-one thousand*, I ticked off internally. *Two-one thousand. It shouldn't take much longer than that and this will all be over.*

I heard the sucking sound of tissue being penetrated just as I felt a rush of wind from my right. My eyes flew open to Levi's broad back standing in front of me. I blinked a few times, not understanding what I was seeing. I'd been so convinced of my own death that it had never occurred to me that help might come. Levi shouldn't have been here. I was supposed to have met him at the camp at just before dawn. We were to leave together the next evening at dusk. How had he known? Was I that transparent?

Then I remembered the silver. "Levi, pull it out. Quick. It's silver tipped!" I could hear the hiss of air from a punctured lung. Maybe there was a chance he could get the arrow out before the silver did what it had done to me. Rumsfield had been holding that bow at full tension long enough that I didn't think he could draw it back again. Not to mention that his crossbow only held four arrows and he'd used them all. Levi had a fighting chance.

Levi looked over his shoulder at me as he shoved Sheriff

Langford's body to the side. I hadn't noticed the sagging form until he did, but now I could see the arrow impaled through the Sheriff's chest and out the back. It had buried up to the feathers in his chest, blood spreading outward from his heart in an oval-shaped stain before dripping onto the concrete of the porch. Like a kid making the mouth of a balloon sing, the remaining air in his lungs leaked out in a high-pitched whine. A low groan escaped the open hollow of his mouth as his body landed heavily on the porch and then not another sound came from him. I stared down at the body, still processing what had happened.

Rumsfield was standing open-mouthed across the yard as his brain struggled to interpret what he'd just seen. What he'd just done, actually. He was a former cop, and I could see the wheels begin to turn when he realized the crap he'd got himself into tonight.

"Nice shooting," Levi said, leaning down to fish the dead man's cellphone out of his jacket. "Bad news is you're out of arrows. And I hate to break it to you, but that stake in your belt is a poor backup plan. Word to the wise, so listen up. When going after a vampire, don't chat them up before you deliver the fatal blow. And we normally run in packs, so you may kill one, but chances are, you're not going to get two. So what was the thought process here, Rumsfield? Did you actually think she was here unprotected?"

Grasping the two remaining arrows that impaled me, Levi jerked them out of the wall behind me. They were hunting tips, the barbs digging in and holding tight. I screamed in pain, mainly air and blood spewing out rather than sound.

"They're silver tipped," I told Levi again. If the arrow heads broke off in me coated in silver, I knew I'd be in serious trouble. He nodded at me, took my neck in his left hand, and then shoved the first arrow clean through me and out the other side. My vision went red, what was left of my voice breaking and cracking in pain. He did the same with the second one, the feathers of the shaft catching momentarily then balling up and dropping at my feet. I pointed to the blood staining his shirt, the arrow that had killed Langford must have nicked him, and started to say something, but he silenced me with a violent look.

Stepping across Sheriff Langford's body, Levi walked towards Rumsfield. The detective had moved farther back towards the trees bordering the forest and sunk to the ground, his head buried in his hands. The crossbow had been dropped a few feet away. His eyes were wide, his breathing rapid. One hand was holding his side and blood was oozing from the flail chest that hadn't healed yet. Dragging a body away was not going to be easy for him.

"This is going to be very hard to explain, Detective," Levi said. He jerked his head towards the sheriff's body. "Lying on the spot can be tricky. Let's see how good you are at it."

Levi sat my feet on the ground and leaned me up against his chest as he lifted the sheriff's iPhone to his mouth. Siri came alive under his cold finger. "Dial 9-1-1," he said. I was too weak to move, and Rumsfield was still too dumbfounded to realize what was going on. He was in a state of complete shock.

"9-1-1. What's the nature of your emergency?" the operator asked.

"This is Sheriff Langford. 2332 Deerwood Drive. Help me!" Levi said into Langford's phone. He wiped it carefully on his jeans, and then tossed it at Rumsfield's feet. Langford's blood was on it, but Levi's prints had been wiped away. "You're going to be wishing these arrow's weren't so distinctive." The two he'd pulled from me were still in his left hand and he took a moment to rub Langford's blood from the arrow tip down the shaft before he tucked them into the waist of his jeans. "Be a real shame if these were to be found."

Rumsfield looked at the cellphone for a few seconds as if he didn't realize what was happening or even less how to respond, the 9-1-1 operator getting more insistent by the second. She'd already dispatched the police when Rumsfield reached out with one shaking hand and hit the end button, silencing her many questions.

"You were wrong about one thing, Rumsfield," Levi said as he pulled me back into his arms. "It *wasn't* personal. Now, it's a vendetta."

My eyes met Rumsfield's as Levi streaked from the property. In the distance, I could hear the sirens. Rumsfield could hear them too, and he had gotten to his feet. He should have been panicked. He should have been scrambling for a getaway plan. He should have been trying to get that arrow out of Langford.

Instead, he was calm. The shock was gone from his face and in its place was the face of a man who had undergone his own transformation. He wouldn't be stopped. He wouldn't be distracted. The vendetta had just begun, I realized, and I couldn't decide who would be the most determined—Rumsfield or Levi.